The Crawfords
Series

MW01127697

NO Ordinary DUKE

SOPHIE BARNES

NO ORDINARY DUKE
The Crawfords Series

Cover Design and Interior Format

ALSO BY SOPHIE BARNES

NOVELS
No Ordinary Duke
The Illegitimate Duke
The Girl Who Stepped Into The Past
The Duke of Her Desire
Christmas at Thorncliff Manor
A Most Unlikely Duke
His Scandalous Kiss
The Earl's Complete Surrender
Lady Sarah's Sinful Desires
The Danger in Tempting an Earl
The Scandal in Kissing an Heir
The Trouble with Being a Duke
The Secret Life of Lady Lucinda
There's Something About Lady Mary
Lady Alexandra's Excellent Adventure
How Miss Rutherford Got Her Groove Back

NOVELLAS
The Duke Who Came To Town
The Earl Who Loved Her
The Governess Who Captured His Heart
Mistletoe Magic (from Five Golden Rings:
A Christmas Collection)

CHAPTER ONE

RAIN STREAKED DOWN THE CARRIAGE windows while Caleb Maxwell Crawford traveled from the London docks to his family home on Grosvenor Square. Dusk had turned to night since he'd stepped off the ship on which he'd sailed from Calais yesterday afternoon. Jaw set, he tightened his grip on the leather satchel beside him on the bench. It held all the evidence he needed to prove how wrong his father had been when they'd parted ways ten years earlier. Filled with letters of praise and articles heralding Caleb's architectural abilities, it would show the old bastard he'd made a success of himself. It would prove that refusing to join the clergy and being cut off financially had not led to his downfall, as his father had claimed it would when he'd railed about Caleb's ungrate-fulness.

Peering out past the heavy rivulets of cas-cading water, Caleb narrowed his gaze on the murky darkness. He couldn't wait to gloat and see the astonished look on his father's face when he showed him the lithographs printed in the Paris Gazette. They illustrated in fine detail the mansion he'd designed for the Duke of Orléons. Building had commenced six years earlier and had just been completed last month. Inhaling deeply, Caleb tightened his hold on his satchel. The carriage drew to a jarring halt moments later, throwing him slightly off balance. Muttering a curse, he opened the door and climbed out into the unpleasant downpour, satchel in hand. The driver helped him retrieve his valise from the boot.

"Here you go sir," the man said while water streamed over the brim of his hat.

"Thank you." Caleb paid him and walked toward the imposing Mayfair mansion that loomed before him. The heavy front door with its massive brass knocker was less than inviting.

Rain gushed down the curved slope of the roof and pelted against the ground. Pulling his hat down over his forehead, Caleb drew the collar of his greatcoat up to protect the back of his neck and climbed the slick stone steps.

He still owned a key and withdrew it now from his pocket to unlock the door. It swung open and gave way to a dim interior. Entering the foyer, Caleb paused to listen. All was silent. Not even the longcase clock ticked away the progression of time.

Shivering, Caleb nudged the door shut behind him. It closed with a resounding thud. Where the devil was everyone?

He sighed and muttered another oath. He didn't like the idea of having to hunt down his family at one of the country estates. But even if they'd left town, there ought to be servants about. His parents had never left a house completely empty.

A soft snick caught his ears, and then the sharp click of approaching footsteps filled the air. The sound accompanied a man whom Caleb instantly recognized, even though his features were far more drawn now than when he'd last seen him.

"Murdoch," he said, addressing the butler. "It has been a while."

The old man drew a sharp breath. The candelabra he carried displaced the darkness. "I thought I heard something, so I came to investigate." Moving closer, he peered up at Caleb. Light from four guttering candles flickered across his face, accentuating the creases there. "Is it really you, my lord?"

Caleb drew his hat from his head and swiped back the wet strands of hair that clung to his forehead. "Yes. I have returned." He set his valise and satchel on the floor and proceeded to take off his gloves. "Where are my parents?"

Murdoch stared at him as if he could still not believe he was actually there. "Your mother is upstairs in her rooms." Breaking eye contact, he proceeded to help Caleb off with his coat.

"And my father, the duke?" When Murdoch failed to reply, Caleb knit his brow. "Is he not at home?"

"No, he is not." The butler busied himself with hanging the coat and setting Caleb's hat and gloves aside. "But your mother will be pleased to see you, I'm sure. Please, follow me." He led the way up the stairs while Caleb followed behind, his curiosity piqued by the servant's unwillingness to supply him with details. Perhaps his parents had quarreled during his absence and were now living apart?

They reached the top of the landing and turned left toward the duchess's apartment. Caleb knew the way well enough, but was glad the butler would be there to announce his arrival. After all, he doubted his mother would be as pleased to see him as Murdoch believed, considering he'd left without saying farewell. But he'd been too angry to do so at the time, and his decision to leave had been made in haste without consideration for anything besides getting away.

Arriving in front of the door leading into his mother's sitting room, Murdoch paused to knock. A maid answered seconds later, her eyes widening when she noticed Caleb.

"Please inform Her Grace that her son, Lord Caleb, is here to see her," Murdoch said.

The maid nodded and the door closed, only to be opened again moments later by the duchess herself. "Thank God you are here!" She stared up at him with shimmering eyes, and then, in the next second, her arms were around him, and she was holding him to her as if he offered necessary support.

Unaccustomed to such a display of affection from his mother, Caleb hesitated briefly before wrapping his arms around her as well. He hadn't expected such a warm welcome and was slightly thrown by the effect it was having on the resentment he'd harbored for the past ten years.

Placing a kiss on his mother's cheek, he listened to her uneasy breaths until she was ready for him to release her.

"Shall I have some tea sent up?" Murdoch asked, reminding Caleb of his presence.

"Please do," his mother said. She opened the door to her sitting room wider and invited Caleb in. Unlike his mother, whose youth had departed during his absence, the space looked unchanged. "Come sit with me, Caleb. There is much for us to discuss."

He wasn't even sure where to begin. This reunion wasn't going at all the way he'd imagined it would. Since leaving Paris five days earlier, he'd pictured himself storming into his father's study and shoving the evidence of his success under the man's haughty nose. Now, inhaling deeply, he approached the sofa and lowered himself to the vacant spot beside his mother. There was so much to say. Too much, in a way.

Perhaps the best place to start was with an apology. "I am sorry," he told her and reached for her hand. "I should have written to you, but the more time passed, the more difficult it became."

"I know."

He looked at her and was swiftly accosted by guilt at the sight of her watery eyes. Christ, he'd been awful to her. She hadn't deserved it, but his pride had been wounded, and he'd only been able to think of himself and of getting away from the life he'd come to despise.

"At least I am not your only son," he murmured. She had three besides his older brother, George, the heir who'd received all their father's affection.

"You haven't been in touch with Griffin or Devlin?" she asked in reference to the brothers who'd been born only minutes after himself. He shook his head. "They left shortly after you, for similar reasons, I suspect. Now, after everything that has happened, I am hoping they will return as well. I've sent out letters, but it will take time for them to reach your brothers." She met his gaze. Her brow puckered ever so slightly. "I'm surprised you are already here since I had no idea of your actual location. I suppose the agent I hired to find you was good at doing his job."

Unease traversed Caleb's spine. He tightened his hold on his mother's hand. "No one came to find me, Mama. I returned of my own accord."

"But then…" She swallowed and closed her eyes. Her lips trembled and it became suddenly clear to Caleb that she was making a stoic effort to maintain her composure. "You do not know." The words were only a whisper.

"Know what?" he asked even though he sensed he had no wish to hear whatever it was she would say in response.

"Your father is dead, Caleb. A fire broke out at the Everly stables last week," she said, referring to one of the dukedom's larger properties. "He and George went to inspect some repairs. They were supposed to be gone only for a few short days but now…" A sob cut off her words, and her free hand rose to smother the sound.

Caleb's heart thudded against his chest. "And George?" he asked, already dreading her answer.

"When your father didn't come out, George went in after him." Tears streamed down her cheeks. "They're both gone, Caleb. I buried them at St. George's this morning."

It was as if time slowed to a halt. A distinct

feeling of disappointment and deep regret trick-led through him, numbing his veins. Slumping back, he tried to make sense of it, to accept what his mother told him as fact, only to find that he couldn't.

The door opened after a quick knock, and Mur-doch returned carrying a tray. He placed it on the table, exchanged a few words with the duchess, and departed once more. Caleb's mother with-drew her hand from Caleb's and dabbed at her eyes. She then busied herself with pouring tea while he watched with a strange sense of detach-ment.

He shook his head. "No. It cannot be true."

She sniffed and took a sip of her tea. "You know what this means," she said, as if he'd not spoken. She waited for him to meet her gaze before say-ing, "You are the Duke of Camberly now."

Caleb stared at her in dismay. "I don't want to be." It was the first thing that came to mind. He liked his uncomplicated life, free from all the responsibilities his father and older brother had faced. He'd never envied either of them. But he had cursed the way his father's sense of duty and obligation had affected his life.

"Unfortunately, that hardly matters. With your father and brother gone, the title falls to you."

He instinctively shuddered and bit back the comment that threatened. To say that he ought to have stayed away would only cause his mother pain. She was happy to have him home and proba-bly quite relieved with the prospect of him taking over the day-to-day running of things. And for her he would do it, or at least he would try.

He drew a deep breath and felt his chest tighten. "Very well. But if I am going to do this, I will need something stronger than tea. Please tell me you still keep a bottle of sherry in that cabinet over there."

Her wobbly smile tilted as if trying to find its balance. "Yes. I dare say I could do with a glass myself."

Raising her hand to his lips, Caleb pressed a tender kiss to her knuckles before going in search of their fortification. He was conscious of his heart beating a dull tattoo, like a drummer marching him off to the gallows. Recalling the satchel he'd left downstairs, he closed his eyes briefly and muttered a curse. Everything he'd worked for these past ten years had been for nothing. His father would never know of his success. How ironic that the son he'd named his greatest disappointment would now be continuing his legacy.

As had become his habit in recent weeks, Caleb arrived at White's shortly after nine in the evening to enjoy a drink and possibly a game of cards with his friend, Robert Moor, Viscount Aldridge. The two had known each other since childhood and had been sent off to Eton together as lads. The moment Caleb's return to London had been announced six months ago, Robert had immediately come to call, and the two had spent an hour washing away the years wedged between them with a few glasses of brandy.

Since then, Robert had offered invaluable advice

and support. He'd invited Caleb out for rides and to Gentleman Jackson's boxing saloon whenever he'd needed to lose himself in something besides accounts, ledgers, investments, and his mother's most recent obsession – his need to think about marriage.

He'd cut her off and walked away the first time she'd made the suggestion and every time since. But when the Season had been well underway and she'd produced a list of potential candidates she considered appropriate for courtship, he'd had no choice but to listen, even though he detested the extra pressure it placed on his shoulders.

"You look more somber than usual," Robert said when Caleb found him. "Trouble with the dukedom?"

Dropping into a vacant chair, Caleb frowned at his friend, who poured a large drink and handed it to him. Caleb took a long sip, enjoying the powerful flavor and the heat it exuded as it slid down his throat. "I cannot stand it any longer." Leaning back, he cradled the glass between his hands and stared at his friend as if he had the power to save him. "It is awful, Robert. I just…" He sighed and scrubbed one hand across his jaw. "I hate being a duke."

Robert had the decency not to argue. Instead, he watched, his eyes increasingly somber until he finally said, "Then don't be."

Startled by the comment, Caleb grinned, the expression so foreign to him now it actually hurt his jaw. "As if it's that simple, but you know as well as I that it is not."

His friend inclined his head, paused for a

moment as if on the verge of divulging some
piece of information, but then set his own glass to
his lips and drank. "Is it not getting any easier?"

Caleb thought back on the endless hours of
work that held him hostage in his study. There
had been little reprieve and no time at all to consider his own wants and needs since his return.
Even now, the satchel holding his architectural
designs remained unopened. He'd had no opportunity to share them with anyone or to dream up
new ones.

"No," he told Robert with unwavering honesty.
"If anything, it is getting worse. The demands on
me are increasing with each passing day. Women
I've never met are showing up at my home, intent
on praising their daughters' charms. Meanwhile,
every business in Town is paying me court, and
every hostess wishes to make me her guest of
honor. And that's not considering repairs I am
asked to fund and approve at my various estates
and the tenants who all have concerns they've
decided to air in a steady stream of letters I receive
daily."

Robert's lips twitched as if struggling to contain
his laughter. He cleared his throat. "I see."

"Do you really?" Caleb wasn't certain. "You
were groomed for this sort of life from the day
you were born, while I was largely ignored until I
was dropped in the middle of it."

"I also have the added benefit of being happily
married to a woman who helps me endure the
burden of the responsibility I carry." Robert considered Caleb for a long moment before saying,
"Maybe your mother has the right of it. Perhaps

marriage is precisely what you need."

Caleb groaned. "Don't be daft. The last thing I need at the moment is another female to coddle." He winced, aware he'd just referred to his mother in rather disparaging terms, but the truth of it was that as much as he loved her, her constant weeping and insistence he fill a mold he didn't quite fit had driven him to the point of madness.

"Then what do you need?" Robert stared him straight in the eye. "Do you even know?"

It took a moment for Caleb to turn the question over in his head and find the right answer. "Yes," he finally said. "I believe getting away for a while would help."

Robert studied him with increased interest. "Where would you go?"

Caleb snorted. "I have no idea. If I head to one of my country estates, all the problems I'm trying to escape will surely follow."

"So you want to go somewhere where you won't be bothered."

"Just long enough for me to find my bearings again." Because he could not believe this was all there would be to his life— now until he drew his last breath. There had to be more to it than sitting in a study, going over numbers. Somehow, he had to rediscover himself, recover from the shock of losing his father and brother, and find the means to stay true to himself while being a duke.

"Is your secretary capable of running things without you during this absence?"

"I believe so," Caleb said with conviction. The man had worked with his father for the past two decades. He knew everything he needed to know to handle things efficiently, which made Caleb warm to the idea of taking a break. Perhaps it would be more possible than he'd dared to believe.

"In that case, I have a proposal I'd like for you to consider." A smirk made Robert's mouth tilt with a hint of mischief. "I have a modest property in Cornwall. Clearview is its name. It's a decent place, but the money I've sent for repairs has, as I understand it, been spent on other things."

Caleb frowned. "If you think your servants are stealing from you, it might be prudent to go and investigate the matter."

"And so I would if I had the time, but with Vivien's pregnancy, I am reluctant to leave her side at the moment, so I thought perhaps…"

Understanding dawned. "You want me to go in your stead?"

Leaning forward, Robert rested his elbows on his knees and pierced Caleb with a direct stare. "I believe a man like you who enjoys working with his hands might take pleasure in seeing to some of the repairs himself."

"You could be right," Caleb said. The prospect of mending a leaking roof or a crumbling wall held a lot of appeal. "I can also hire new servants for you, if you think that might be helpful."

A flicker of amusement brightened Robert's eyes. "There are no servants there, Caleb. Just my sister, her friends, and the orphaned children they offer sanctuary to."

Caleb blinked. "Your sister?" Robert had several, some younger, some older.

"Cassandra, to be exact. She's five years younger than us, so you might not recall her. She debuted after you left England." His expression cooled a fraction as he added, "She made the scandalous choice of bedding her fiancée before they were married. Poor devil died on his way to the church, struck down by an oncoming carriage."

"Jesus!"

Robert nodded. "Cassandra sought my help shortly after. Apparently, that one indiscretion had gotten her pregnant. When she refused to pass her child off as another's, which was what our parents advised, they threatened to turn her out of the house. So I secretly bought a place for her to live. When two other girls encountered similar hardships, Cassandra invited them to come with her. During the last five years, they have taken in several children, who cost more to keep than they can afford with the measly donations they receive from friends and family."

"In other words," Caleb said slowly, "these three spinsters are mismanaging funds in an effort to run a make-shift orphanage?"

"More or less," Robert said with a shrug.

"And you have allowed this to continue for five years?" Caleb could scarcely believe it. It wasn't that he didn't approve of the kindness these women were showing toward the less fortunate, but if they let the house fall into complete dis-repair, the day would come when they wouldn't even have that. And then what?

"She's my sister," Robert said. "I have tried to help her as much as I can while keeping her scan-dalous circumstances at bay. She and her friends have been hidden away and mostly forgotten, but they are constantly in need of assistance, and

I simply don't have the time or the resources to keep ensuring they're well looked after. I have my own family to consider, estates to tend to as well as investments and parliamentary responsibilities. You know how it is."

Wasn't that the truth of it? Caleb flattened his mouth and considered his choices: stay in London, tied to a desk and with endless demands placed before him, or ride off to Cornwall for a breath of fresh air and the physical activity awaiting him there.

He knew which he preferred, but there was still one problem. "It would be unseemly for me to live in a house with three unmarried women."

"Spinsters, Caleb, not debutantes. Makes all the difference, you know. But I actually agree, which is why I suggest you stay in the caretaker's cottage."

"There's a caretaker's cottage?" How big was this place?

"It's nothing to get excited over since it's only one room, but if you want to stop being a duke for a while and pretend you're a…" he waved his hand between them before settling on, "laborer instead, then you're welcome to it."

Uncertainty settled between Caleb's shoulder blades. "How come no one's living in this cottage right now?"

"Because the caretaker I hired to keep things in order had a massive row with my sister's friend, Mary Clemens."

"About?"

Robert sighed. "Using the funds I sent for repairing the roof."

Caleb gaped at his friend. "So this…Miss Clemens, is the real problem I take it?"

"She's part of it," Robert agreed. "She's certainly not afraid of speaking her mind. This is the third caretaker she's frightened off in just over a year."

Raising an eyebrow, Caleb stared at his friend. He was no longer entirely sure he was up to the sort of change he offered. "I will have to think about it." Long and hard and then a few times more to be absolutely certain.

But when he arrived home and found three Society matrons waiting for him with their very eligible daughters, Caleb quickly retreated to his study. He spent the next three hours discussing matters with his secretary and ensuring that the man was indeed capable and willing to handle all his affairs if Caleb chose to remove himself to the countryside for a while.

That settled, he went in search of his mother, who was not the least bit pleased with his decision. He understood her of course and promised he'd soon return, assuring her that when he did, he'd be ready to focus on finding a wife.

CHAPTER TWO

SMILING FONDLY AT THE FIVE children who played nearby, Mary hung another pillowcase on the clothesline. It was a sunny autumn day with a brisk breeze, so the laundry would dry quickly.

Reaching inside the basket beside her, she pulled out a sheet, struggling a little when it billowed and flapped against her hold. Her life was so different now from what it had once been, before she'd fallen in love and allowed herself to dream. But dreams, as she'd learned, were fickle things easily torn apart.

Inhaling deeply she forced the sheet to comply by pinning it with a couple of pegs. She then grabbed the now-empty basket and marched toward the house.

"Come help me prepare the tea," she called to Bridget, Daphne, Penelope, Peter, and Eliot whose scruffiness proved a fondness for the outdoors. Their laughter danced through the air as the kitten they played with toyed with a piece of string. His name was Raphael, and he'd been gifted to them by Mr. Townsend, a gentleman farmer whose interest in Mary had recently increased.

Daphne swept the kitten up into her arms and raced past Mary with the rest of the troop close on her heels.

"Remember to wipe your shoes," Mary called.

The reminder caused quite the ruckus in the narrow doorway, and Mary could hear her friend Cassandra on the opposite side, issuing threats to anyone who dared bring dirt inside the newly swept kitchen.

"Do you ever have any regrets?" Mary asked when she reached Cassandra. She cleaned her own boots with a brush and entered the boisterous interior where cups and saucers clattered together as the girls helped each other prepare two trays. Eliot, the youngest of the boys, reached for the tin filled with biscuits, and Mary charged toward him. "Clean your hands before opening that, or you'll not have a single one."

"Never," Cassandra grinned, answering Mary's question. "This is where happiness lives. I would not trade it for anything else in the world."

Agreeing, Mary filled the kettle with water from a jug and hung it over the fire. Despite the various challenges they'd faced over the years, they'd acquired their freedom in this tiny corner of the world. They could walk about as they pleased and keep the company they chose without causing a stir. Now that she and her friends had been labeled spinsters, nobody seemed to care what they did, which was, to be honest, rather liberating.

Reaching for the tin filled with tea, Mary spooned a little into a strainer and glanced across at where Peter was sitting. The twelve-year-old boy had moved in with them six weeks earlier after his parents had died. He'd kept to himself ever since, his eyes always downcast, his mood always somber.

No matter how hard they all tried, they'd failed to reach him so far, and while Mary knew he would need time to heal, she wished there was some way to help him.

"I've finished cleaning the grates and polishing the brass tools," Emily told Mary and Cassandra as she came to join them. A wallflower whose fondness for sweets had been evident in her figure, Emily had never secured a dance and had eventually given up trying after enduring her third failed season.

It was a pity really, for the active lifestyle she now enjoyed had helped her shed enough weight to reveal a woman many would likely call pretty.

"Well done," Cassandra said. "The weather is unusually pleasant for this time of year. It will likely turn sooner than we expect, and when it does, we'll need to be ready."

"Which means we'll need firewood too," Emily said. She glanced at Mary. "Do you suppose Mr. Townsend might be willing to offer his assistance with that?"

Mary glanced at Cassandra and then back at Emily. "I'm sure he'd be happy to oblige." Especially if she invited him back to the house for tea after church on Sunday. She hesitated on that thought and bit her lip. "I just don't want to take advantage."

"And you wouldn't be, as long as he's happy to oblige," Cassandra told her.

Mary gave her a quelling look. "You know

what I mean." Mr. Townsend was a nice man, but it had also become alarmingly clear that he was in the market for a wife and that he favored Mary for this position. The only problem was she had no intention of ever marrying anyone. Because if her time as a debutant had taught her anything, it was that even the most honorable gentleman was not to be trusted.

"Perhaps we should set our minds to matching him with a lady who'd be more appreciative of his advances," Emily suggested.

"Good heavens," Mary protested. "No man would wish for three spinsters to involve themselves in his search for a bride. Not even a man as charismatic as Mr. Townsend."

A knock at the front door interrupted their conversation. Cassandra frowned. "Who could possibly be calling at this hour?" She made her way toward the front of the house while Mary and Emily trailed behind.

"Perhaps it is Mr. Townsend who's come to call on Mary," Emily suggested. "How convenient would that be, considering we were just discussing the need for his help?"

Not bothering with a response, Mary rolled her eyes and followed Cassandra and Emily out into the front hallway. Another knock sounded and Cassandra opened the door to reveal a tall, broad shouldered man with dark, windswept hair and a shrewd gaze.

"Lady Cassandra?" he inquired. His eyes searched each of their faces, and Mary instinctively retreated a step. "Viscount Aldridge's sister?"

Cassandra raised her chin. "I am she. And you

are...?"

Again his gaze drifted from one to the other, this time with a hint of expectation, as if he waited for them to guess his name. When none of them added anything further, he said, "Mr. Crawford, at your service. Your brother sent me to inspect your home and to make any necessary repairs."

Mary drew a sharp breath, because just as he said that, their eyes locked. Not for too long, but for long enough to unsettle her. Unwittingly, she assessed his age, which had to be close to her own though perhaps slightly older, the perfect shape of his mouth with its broad lower lip, his angular jaw line and aquiline nose. All combined to create the most handsome face she'd ever seen. It also provided a sharp reminder of a similar pair of eyes a few shades lighter. Those eyes had gazed upon her as if she'd been special—as if she'd mattered. Except she hadn't. At least not enough.

"I'll fetch the tea," she said and turned away, deliberately breaking eye contact. "Just in case you decide to invite Mr. Crawford inside."

Returning to the kitchen, Mary took comfort in the peace that had settled over the children because of the biscuits they'd all procured from the tin. They halted in the process of chewing the moment they saw her, their anxious eyes waiting to see if she'd scold them for starting on their snacks before they'd been invited to do so.

"We have a guest," she told them, ignoring the issue as she went to fetch the kettle. The water was already boiling, so she grabbed a dishrag, pulled the kettle off the hook above the flames, and poured the water through the strainer into the teapot. Steam rose in thick swirls, filling the air with hot humidity. Glancing over her shoulder, she narrowed her gaze just enough to remind the children of who was in charge. "I hope there are still a few biscuits left for him."

"There's three," Cassandra's daughter, Penelope, said before wiping her hands on her skirt. "One for you, Emily, and Mama." The little blonde girl stared back at Mary with big round eyes. "We didn't think to save one for a guest."

Mary bowed her head to hide her smile and nodded. "Very well then. No biscuits it is." She picked up the tray and started for the door. "But this will cost you when the tickle monster hears what you've done." And then she swept out into the hallway with a grin while squeals erupted behind her.

She could still feel her lips twitching with mirth when she walked into the parlor. Cassandra and Emily were both seated on the only sofa the room had to offer while Mr. Crawford filled out one of the armchairs. His bright blue gaze latched on to Mary with intense interest, and in spite of her conviction that she'd never respond to any man ever again, her stomach tightened and her hands began to tremble.

A slight dimple puckered the edge of Mr. Crawford's mouth, affording him a humorous expression. Mary's pulse quickened and she hastened forward to set the tray down, eager to be rid of it before she dropped it.

"—so with that in mind," he continued, returning his attention to Cassandra and Emily, "it could take anywhere from a week to a month before the roof is completely intact."

His voice…

Mary placed the tray on the low table between the sofa and the armchair and tried to ignore the rich cadence of it. Swallowing, she sat in the remaining chair before pouring tea for each of them.

"Milk and" —she cleared her throat which had suddenly gone quite squeaky—"sugar?"

Mr. Crawford turned his gaze toward her, and all of her strength seeped out of her limbs as they instantly turned to jelly. Determined not to let it show, she stared back at him and did her best not to blink. But his eyes were like azure blue lakes on a hot summer's day, and for some inexplicable reason, she found herself leaning toward him.

A grin tugged at his lips. "Neither."

Mary took a sharp breath and leaned back. Averting her gaze, she set Mr. Crawford's cup before him and then offered tea to her friends, who both watched her with curious expressions. *No.* She would not let this handsome stranger addle her brain. This was a path she'd been down before, and it had broken her heart and denied her the chance of marriage.

On that sobering thought, she returned the teapot to the tray and took a sip from her own cup. Mr. Crawford was a laborer, a man sent by Cassandra's brother to patch up the roof. She didn't care how handsome he was or how well he looked in those beige colored breeches that hugged his thighs. Sighing, she slumped back in her seat and almost spilled her tea in the process. Of course she'd noticed. She'd have had to be dead not to.

"We cannot offer much in the way of accommodation," Cassandra said. "To stay with us in the house would be inappropriate, and even if it weren't, I'm afraid all the rooms are occupied."

"I understand." The deep timbre of his voice stroked its way along Mary's nerves as he spoke. She shuddered slightly and reminded herself once again to take control of her senses. "But your brother mentioned a caretaker's cottage. Is that still available?"

"It is," Cassandra said. "In fact, it was vacated by the caretaker only a week ago, so it should still be somewhat clean and ready to move into, though I must warn you that it is pretty sparse."

"That's quite all right." He smiled warmly at Cassandra, and Mary felt the oddest pang in her chest. "My needs are few. As long as there's a roof and a bed, I'll be content." He picked up his cup and cradled it carefully between his large hands. Sipping the tea he then asked, "Why did the caretaker leave?"

It was so to the point Mary felt like she'd just been pushed into the path of a charging carriage. "Because he accused us of squandering our money on others instead of seeing to Viscount Aldridge's wishes."

The room fell silent in the wake of her sharp response. Mary took another sip of tea, not daring to look at any of them while heat warmed her cheeks.

"Not a very sympathetic man then, I take it," Mr. Crawford murmured.

Heart pounding, Mary raised her gaze to his and stiffened her spine in an effort to maintain at least some of her composure. "He did not understand why we would feel any responsibility toward children who aren't our own."

"He was a very plain-spoken man," Emily added while Mr. Crawford's gaze remained fixed on Mary. It took a moment for him to turn slowly away in order to face her friend, leaving Mary's insides in a jumble and her head slightly dizzy. "Too plain-spoken, in the end." Emily grinned and jutted her chin in Mary's direction. "Miss Clemens put him in his place. I've never seen a man pack up and leave so quickly."

"I'm sure you haven't," Mr. Crawford said. His voice was soft and his eyes trained on Emily, and yet Mary felt her insides quiver as if he spoke only to her.

Reaching up, she pinched the bridge of her nose and muttered a gentle reminder to herself about not letting any man tempt her.

"You probably want to take a look at the damage and at the cottage where you will be staying," Cassandra said. "Mary can do the honors while Emily and I start on supper. You are welcome to join us for our evening meal if you like, unless of course you prefer the tavern in the village."

"Thank you, but I do believe a hearty home-cooked meal would be just the thing this evening," Mr. Crawford said. He stood and lowered his gaze to Mary. "Shall we proceed with the tour, Miss Clemens?"

She was a lovely woman, Caleb decided as he

followed Miss Clemens out of the parlor and toward the stairs. Feisty too, judging from her impassioned defense of the caretaker's dismissal. He liked that she'd stood her ground and thrown the man out when he threatened her principals. In fact, he had to admit he was slightly surprised by what he'd discovered when he'd knocked on the door and the three young women had bid him welcome.

When they'd asked his name, he'd hesitated just long enough to ensure that none of them knew him. He doubted they would since he could not recall meeting any of them before, not even his best friend's sister, Lady Cassandra.

As soon as he was certain of anonymity, he'd introduced himself as Mr. Crawford, which wasn't so much of a lie since it was his last name. It would allow him, he hoped, to be treated as a normal person while he was here, which was all he really wanted, aside from the task of fixing the roof.

The women were remarkably pretty, which instantly piqued his curiosity. It made no sense that none had married, though he supposed they all had their reasons. So far he only knew of Lady Cassandra's, but when Miss Clemens had walked into the parlor carrying the tea tray, her eyes spar-kling and her lips drawn up in a radiant smile, he'd been transfixed. He wanted to learn her secrets now, and he wanted to know why she'd fled the front entrance with the hasty excuse of fetching refreshments.

"How did you end up here?" he asked, going straight to the point without any finesse.

The tip of her shoe caught the edge of a step

on the staircase. Her body jerked as she stumbled, her hand clutching the banister firmly for support. Caleb was tempted to reach out and steady her, but that would probably be unwise, so he clasped his hands behind his back, hid a chuckle, and allowed himself to savor her discomfort.

"That is a rather personal thing to ask," she grumbled. She'd regained her balance and was now marching up the stairs. "We have only just met."

"That doesn't mean I'm not curious," he told her lightly. She reached the top of the landing and turned to face him, effectively bringing her daringly close to his person when he stepped up onto the landing as well. Her lips parted, either in surprise or to offer a sharp rejoinder, he wasn't quite sure, until the flint in her green eyes eased, and she blinked a few times in rapid succession.

"Curiosity can be a burden, you know." She swirled around and rushed onward as if she hoped to escape his presence.

Caleb followed her easily enough with a few long strides. Reaching a door at the end of the hallway, she undid the latch at the top, yanked it wide open, and hurried up the next flight of steps as if fearing he might accost her.

That gave him pause, and he immediately frowned. He hoped her reasons for being here didn't include falling victim to a dishonorable scoundrel.

Climbing the stairs a bit slower than before, Caleb stepped up into the attic and instantly sucked in a breath the moment she came into view once more. She was peering out a dusty window while sunshine spilled through it and onto her face. Bathed in light and with a few stray strands of golden hair falling across her cheek, she looked like a creature from another world. Her lips were rosy and slightly moist, as if she'd recently licked them, her nose an elegant line that curved with perfection.

Caleb took a moment to gather his thoughts, completely upended by the beauty Miss Clemens portrayed. And although her gown was plain, the way she stood, leaning slightly forward, allowed him to admire her shapely contours with greater ease.

A surge of heat erupted inside him, and he clenched his hands to ward off the sudden desire that assailed him. After all, he hardly knew this woman, and if she feared him, she'd be right to, because the only thing he could think of now was how she might respond if he stepped up behind her. Would she lean into his embrace and sigh with pleasure?

No, he decided with a wry smile. From what little he'd learned of her so far, he rather suspected she'd smack him. And as pleasant as that might be in the end, he could not take the risk of her sending him packing. Because then he'd be forced to go straight back to London, to the desk that awaited him there in his study, and the dull future looming before him.

Sighing, he left Miss Clemens to ponder the view and forced himself to consider the roof. Without looking too closely, he could see the extra light pouring through where tiles had gone missing. Water stains here and there on the floor suggested a series of long-existing leaks. Some had caused the floorboards to rot, which not only made them unsafe to walk on but probably resulted in heavy dripping in the bedrooms below whenever it rained.

"This roof is sorely lacking in attention, Miss Clemens. I'm not surprised the previous caretaker was frustrated by his inability to fix it for you."

"Providing food and clothing was a little more pressing," she told him tartly.

He glanced at her with a raised eyebrow. She'd come away from the window and was making her way toward him, watching her step to avoid the rot. "I'm also sure you'd like to prevent yourself and the children in your care from getting sick, as you are all at risk of doing if you live in a damp and chilly home."

"We have fireplaces." Her voice had grown defensive.

"And heat rises," he told her gently. "If the roof is not secure, all that heat will go straight outside."

She pressed her lips together and drew a deep breath. "You're right," she said, startling him with her concession. "Do you think you can fix it before winter sets in?"

He gave the roof another quick glance and nodded. "Viscount Aldridge gave me the funds to do it, so yes, I believe it will be possible."

The smile she gave him in exchange for his assurance left him feeling slightly unsteady.

"Thank you, Mr. Crawford. I cannot tell you how pleased I am to hear you say that." She placed both hands on her hips. "Now, shall I show you where you will be staying?"

Caleb nodded, his gaze holding hers until her cheeks colored. There was no doubt in his mind that he affected her somehow, which was definitely gratifying since she so clearly affected him. He was also sure that she felt it too, this unmistakable attraction between them, but rather than accept it, she seemed quite determined to fight it and deny it and run from it as fast as she could.

Whatever happened to you, Miss Clemens?

Most women he'd known appreciated a man's attention. Except her. If he had to guess, she'd rather shut herself away in a wardrobe than grant him a second to admire her looks.

Her feet tapped loudly on the steps as she hurried down the stairs like a scampering mouse being chased by a prowling cat. Caleb took his time, enjoying her breathless pauses when she stopped to check if he was still behind her. Hell, she was lucky there were children and two other women in the house, or he might make an effort to catch her. Watching her cheeks flush each time she glanced his way and hearing her gasp when she saw he was close was starting to wear on his urge to pull her back to him and kiss her senseless.

Lust and desire, he told himself bluntly. How long had it been since he'd had a woman? Damn if he could remember. He'd been so absorbed in his building projects in France and later by his return to England and the deaths of his father and brother, he'd not had the time or energy to consider his baser needs. They'd lain dormant until the door to this house had swung open and he'd looked into Miss Clemens's eyes, at which point they'd surged to life with a vengeance.

Christ!

This really would not do.

Raking his fingers through his hair, he muttered an oath and strode out of the house to where Miss Clemens now waited. Except she wasn't waiting. She was walking toward a small stone building about a hundred yards away from the main house. Caleb quickened his stride to catch up with her.

"It's a beautiful property," he said. Squeals sounded from somewhere behind him, and he instinctively glanced back to see two little girls chasing after each other. "There's certainly plenty of space for the children to run about."

She tilted her chin. "Do you like children, Mr. Crawford?"

He blinked and stuck his hands in his pockets. What a strange question. "Doesn't everyone?"

She pressed her lips together. "No."

"Hmm." He wasn't entirely sure what to make of that. "I don't have much experience with them, I confess, but their ability to offer unconditional love to those who care for them is worth all the effort, I suspect."

"It most certainly is," she agreed, and although she didn't look at him and he didn't look at her, he could tell she was smiling from the sound of her voice.

"Do you not wish to have some of your own one day?" He wasn't sure where he'd found the nerve to ask such a forward question, and yet somehow he had.

She didn't answer right away, and he began to think she never would, which was not surprising, but then she said, "I believe the time for that has passed."

The sadness with which she said it tore at his heart. "Why?" They arrived at the door to the cottage, and she busied her hands with finding the key which seemed to be lost in one of her pockets. "You're still young enough to attract a man's attention, Miss Clemens."

Her gaze shot up to lock with his. "I…" She lifted the key to the door between them, paused for a second, and then quickly unlocked the lock. The door creaked open, catching on the floor and sticking. "Sorry. This probably needs to be fixed as well," she muttered before pushing her way through the narrow opening.

Caleb squeezed inside as well and considered the space he'd been offered to live in. It was small but just as clean as Lady Cassandra had promised, and the roof here looked much more solid than the one that covered the main house.

"I'll give you some sheets for the bed," Miss Clemens told him. She cleared her throat and appeared to consider each corner of the room, looking everywhere but at him. "If there's anything else you need…"

She glanced at him at that moment and went completely still.

He wasn't surprised, because he knew he was staring at her while compiling a long list of all the things he needed. Each item more wicked than the last. Her eyes widened and as they did so, he knew it must show on his face. Worst of all, he wasn't sure how to stop it. The presence of a bed wasn't helping.

"I'll get you some fresh towels too," she said.

"And a wash basin and pitcher so you can..." She waved her hand aimlessly before dropping it to her side. "Perhaps a book or two would be nice as well. Do you read, Mr. Crawford? Yes, of course you do since you're quite well-spoken. There is a library that you are welcome to use, though it's not very grand, but it does contain a few novels I think you'd enjoy and—"

"Miss Clemens," he muttered, closing the distance between them in two easy strides.

"Yes?" she squeaked.

He met her gaze boldly before lowering it to the fullness of her lips. Her breath hitched and he knew she thought he might kiss her. The temptation was certainly there, burning through his every restraint. But it would be a mistake.

This knowledge made him look up even as the tips of his fingers tingled with the urge to touch her. He took a deep breath, inhaling her scent: fresh linen and starch with a hint of lavender.

Inspiration struck and he decided to allow himself a moment of pleasure. "Cobwebs," he murmured.

Confusion puckered her brow. "What?"

Her voice was but a soft exhalation spilling over her plump lower lip. Caleb steeled himself and reached up, shamelessly sliding his fingers between a few stray locks of her hair.

He couldn't regret the lie he'd told her. Now that he'd touched her, discovered how silky her hair felt against his skin, he knew he would have been mad not to take the liberty.

"It must have attached itself to you in the attic." His knuckles deliberately grazed her cheek before he withdrew, dropping his hand to his side. "There. All gone."

She stared up at him, and he heard her breath tremble as she inhaled. Her response to his closeness and touch was not only palpable, but thoroughly arousing.

But then she blinked and when she looked at him again, it was with a mixture of surprise and unease. It ruined the moment and made Caleb feel like a cad for taking advantage of this woman's trust. She'd shown him hospitality without a chaperone's protection, and he'd thanked her by making her the subject of his most depraved fantasies.

"Thank you," she told him crisply.

He almost laughed. If she knew his mind, she'd scold him instead.

Keeping that bit of information to himself, he dipped his head and aimed for politeness. "You are welcome, Miss Clemens."

She hesitated briefly before brushing past him. "I must help Cassandra and Emily with supper," she said as she slipped through the door. "We eat at six."

He turned to watch her flee and then thought of something. "I don't suppose there's a lake on the property?"

"Over there behind those trees," she called with a wave of her hand.

Caleb waited until she was out of sight before

leaving the cottage and striding briskly in the direction she'd indicated. Summer was long gone so the water would probably be frigid, which was precisely what he needed in order to cool his ardor.

CHAPTER THREE

MARY ROSE FROM BED LATER than usual the following morning, not because she wasn't awake, but because the idea of encountering Mr. Crawford again unnerved her. When he'd touched her hair the day before, her body had sagged with pleasure and yearned for more. Which was something she could not afford. Not when she'd spent five years telling herself she'd never fall under another man's spell.

To do so would be a sure recipe for heartbreak, so she'd actually been proud of herself when she'd managed to resist Mr. Townsend. But Mr. Crawford... He was entirely different. He'd torn down her barriers within seconds and forced her to face her desires.

"Dear God."

Patting her flushed cheeks, she got out of bed and dressed, deliberately selecting a high-collared dress she usually reserved for winter. Perhaps it would stop him from looking at her like she was a delicious dessert he meant to devour.

Stifling the thrill the memory of his regard evoked, Mary crept downstairs and carefully peeked inside the dining room. She breathed a sigh of relief when she spotted only Cassandra, Emily, and the children at the table. No sign of Mr. Crawford. Yet.

"Good morning," she said as she went to take her seat next to Bridget so she could help the six year old butter her toast.

"You look cheerful," Emily said. She took a sip of tea while eyeing Mary over the rim of her cup.

Mary shrugged and reached for the teapot. "I'm just glad to know the roof will soon be fixed." Selecting a piece of toast she spooned some jam onto it and took a large bite. "It is a relief."

Cassandra studied her. "Mmm...hmm..."

"What?" Mary asked.

"Nothing." Cassandra shook her head and helped her daughter refill her glass with milk. But then she smiled and leaned across the table toward Mary with a conspiratorial gleam in her eyes. "You just never looked quite so pleased when any of the caretakers we've had in the past offered to take care of it."

"Well," Mary said, "they were either inefficient, lacked the necessary skills, or made ridiculous demands."

"And Mr. Crawford is simply perfect," Emily muttered.

"His looks certainly are," Cassandra said with a far too knowing glance directed at Mary.

Mary picked up her toast once more and took another bite to distract herself and the others from the frayed state of her nerves. "Where is he, by the way?" So she could avoid him, of course. Or at least that was the reason she gave herself for asking.

"He rode off about an hour ago," Emily said, "with the intention of buying supplies. Not sure when he'll be back."

Oddly, Mary felt a twinge of disappointment, which was silly since she'd decided to ignore the man completely. Doing so would be infinitely simpler if he were somewhere else, like a mile away in the village.

Finishing breakfast, she helped the children clean their teeth with powder before escorting them back to the dining room for their lessons. She would start them on mathematics while Emily and Cassandra washed the dishes. Later, when Cassandra took over to teach them French, Mary would clean the bedrooms, do some laundering, and iron for a bit.

She placed a sheet of sums in front of each child based on their age and level of experience, guiding each of them in turn when they got stuck and needed help.

"Is something the matter?" she asked when she came to stand beside Peter's chair.

He shrugged. "Not really."

Mary pondered the page she'd given him. It was blank as usual, as if he hadn't even tried. But it couldn't be because he found it too hard for she'd seen him correct one of Eliot's sums once when he hadn't thought she was paying attention.

"Is it too easy for you?"

He tapped his pencil aimlessly on the table. "I just don't see the point."

"But..." He started to rise while Mary tried to think of something useful to say. "The more you know, the better your prospects will be later in life."

He seemed to consider this with a soulful expression far too serious for someone so young. And then he asked, "Will it bring my parents back?"

Mary almost choked on the unexpected rush of emotion that tightened her throat. What could she possibly say when her own heart was breaking.

Peter nodded as if her silence said more than words ever could and quietly left the room.

It took a second for Mary to move, to go after the boy with the instinct to offer him comfort. "Can you please keep an eye on the children?" she asked Cassandra and Emily as she popped into the kitchen. The two friends were already putting the clean dishes away. "I have to check on Peter."

"Everything all right?" Emily asked.

Mary wasn't entirely sure. The haunted look in his eyes concerned her. "I hope so," she said and rushed out into the garden. But Peter wasn't there, which meant he must still be inside. Except he wasn't. She searched every room along with the attic, even though the door to the stairs was locked.

Irrational dread began to set in after almost an hour went by and he still wasn't found. Cassandra helped Mary look while Emily distracted the rest of the children with stories.

"I don't understand," Mary said. She'd gone back outside, hoping to spot him. He had to be here somewhere, surely.

"We should check beyond the garden," Cassandra said.

"But he knows not to leave it. All the children

do." Mary spun around, unsure of which direction to turn. Her heart was racing too fast. She'd sensed something was wrong, and she'd just stood there while he'd walked away. If anything happened to him, she would never forgive herself.

"He's here," Emily's voice calling from the house released the pressure inside Mary's chest. "Mr. Crawford found him on his way back from the village."

Mary laughed with relief as Cassandra embraced her. "Thank God!"

Together they walked back, entering through the kitchen where Peter was sitting with a biscuit in one hand and a glass of milk in the other.

Mary frowned. The worry and dread she'd experienced transformed into anger. She moved forward, intent on demanding an explanation, but Mr. Crawford stepped into her path, blocking the way.

"I would advise against that, Miss Clemens." He acknowledged Cassandra with a nod. "My lady."

Bristling, Mary raised her chin. How dare he interfere? "Please step aside, sir." Her voice was strained with emotion, her body quivering with agitation.

Mr. Crawford remained precisely where he was. Removing his attention from Mary, he addressed Cassandra, which only irked Mary all the more. Did her request not matter? "Perhaps we ought to discuss this outside." He gestured toward the door, and to Mary's dismay, Cassandra urged her toward it. "The lad has had a trying couple of hours," Mr. Crawford added once they were outside and Peter was well out of earshot.

Mary snorted. "*He* has had a trying couple of hours?" Good grief, she'd been beside herself imagining the worst and here he now was, drinking milk and eating biscuits after enjoying a pleasant little walk.

"I don't think railing at him will help at the moment," Mr. Crawford continued. He was still speaking to Cassandra and ignoring Mary completely. Perhaps if she stomped on his foot he'd take notice? "Indeed, I fear it will only push him away even more, which I believe is the opposite of what you hope to achieve."

"Yes," Cassandra said. She sounded pensive. "The most important thing is that he is safe. We can have a word with him later. In an unruffled fashion," she directed a firm look at Mary. "He's more likely to offer an explanation for his behavior if he doesn't feel cornered."

"Cassandra," Mary tried. "Don't you think we should—"

"I know he frightened you," Cassandra said. "I feared for his safety too, but Mr. Crawford is right. Confronting Peter in anger will likely make matters worse. We need to calm ourselves and steady our minds before we speak with him." She turned to Mr. Crawford. "Did you find the supplies you were seeking?"

Stunned by the sudden change in conversation, Mary retreated a step.

"Yes. I'm expecting a delivery of oak planking and slate tiles later today. In the meantime, I'll start preparing the areas I plan to work on this afternoon and…"

His voice faded into the distance as Mary walked

away. She needed to move if she wanted to regain her composure, so she walked across the lawn in the direction of the lake. Her heart had still not fully recovered, its beats vibrating fiercely against her breast.

"Miss Clemens!"

Sighing, Mary thought of quickening her step to prevent the man who called to her from catching up. She really didn't feel like facing him right now, but at the same time, she was too emotionally exhausted to bother with trying to evade him. So she turned, momentarily startled by his piercing blue gaze and resolute stride. Of all the things she needed right now, turning to goo wasn't one of them. She straightened her shoulders and braced herself, determined to keep her attraction to him under control.

"What is it?" she said, more forcefully and more curt than she'd intended.

He drew to a halt before her. The breeze tugged at his hair, disturbing it in a haphazard way that made him look even more charming.

Oh bother!

"I want to apologize for upsetting you." His voice was soft and gentle and oh-so tempting.

"You did not upset me. Peter did."

"But I stopped you from confronting him, and it is obvious you did not like it."

She crossed her arms, protecting her body from the effect he had on her senses. But it was a futile effort. Her pulse was already picking up speed, her skin warming in spite of the chill in the air.

"You're right," she said, latching on to his words and forcing herself to focus. "You arrived here only yesterday, and already you're interfering in matters that do not concern you."

He frowned. "Would you have rather I left the boy on the road?"

"No. Of course not. Don't be stupid."

A smile tugged at his lips. "Miss Clemens, I do believe you just insulted me."

"Yes, but you may take solace in knowing it's not as bad as what Mr. Rivers had to endure."

"Mr. Rivers?"

"The previous caretaker," she explained. "I told him he was an ugly old man with a vicious character."

Mr. Crawford stared at her a moment and then, to her utter stupefaction, he laughed. "Did you really?"

She nodded, and for some absurd reason she could not keep from smiling. "It was the truth," she said, and Mr. Crawford laughed even harder. "I daresay I should not be chastised for being honest."

"Oh dear God," Mr. Crawford choked. "You really are a rare creature, Miss Clemens. Do you know that?"

"Is that a compliment or an insult?"

He drew a deep breath and brought his mirth under some measure of control. "Oh, it is definitely a compliment."

"Then I thank you, Mr. Crawford, even though I'm still very cross with you." It wasn't really true, but she didn't want him to think she could be disarmed with a bit of humor. "Peter gave me a terrible scare. He knows he's not supposed to leave the house or the garden without at least informing someone, but he did so anyway only to act as if he'd done nothing wrong."

His expression sobered. "I understand why this upset you, but can you not take a moment to think back to when you were a child? Were there not times when all you wanted was to be left alone? When you were angry or upset at the world and nothing seemed fair?" He moved a bit closer, and Mary's breath hitched in response to the scent of leather and spice that clung to his person. "Peter lost both his parents a few short weeks ago. Life as he knew it was turned upside down from one moment to the next. He needs time, Miss Clemens, though I do agree that he must learn to show some consideration for you and your friends."

"But he will be more likely to listen if we speak to him calmly," Mary said.

Mr. Crawford nodded. "Connecting with him might help as well."

"I've thought of that too, but I don't know how. He doesn't show any interest in the books I've suggested he read or in the games we play with the other children." She sagged a little beneath the concern she felt for the boy. "Ensuring the comfort and happiness of all the children we've taken in is our primary goal. Knowing how miserable Peter is distresses me to no end, especially since I have no idea what to do in order to help him."

"Would you be willing to let me try?"

Mary stared up at the man she'd only just met the day before and shook her head in wonder. "Do you wish to?"

He held her gaze until her stomach dipped in the middle. "Of course." The smile that followed swept past any lingering defenses and filled her heart with warmth. "I'm ready to assist in any way I can."

"You…" Words failed her and for a second she was tempted to turn away and avoid his gaze. It was intense and searching and it pierced her skin with smoldering heat. "Thank you," she managed.

"You are welcome." He hesitated briefly before stepping back, his eyes sharpening as if with renewed focus. "I should probably get started on the roof."

And then he turned and walked away.

Watching him go, it occurred to Mary that she was a fool. Choosing to wear a high-collared gown made no difference at all. Indeed, she could wrap herself up in heavy wool blankets, and it still wouldn't make her feel fully clothed in Mr. Crawford's company.

Caleb applied himself to his work in the hope that removing broken tiles and cutting away rotted sheathing would rid his mind of Miss Clemens. It did not, though it did offer his body a welcome release in the form of physical exertion.

Christ, she'd been lovely in the midst of her fury, her eyes sparking with indignation when he'd stopped her from talking to Peter. And the prim gown she'd worn, buttoned up all the way to her chin like a piece of armor to protect her in battle. It had stirred his blood until all he could think of was how he might peel the garment away from her body to uncover the skin beneath. He'd do it slowly, taking his time to torture her a little and to heighten the anticipation for them both.

Bloody hell.

He pried additional shingles from the roof and tossed them onto the ground below. He'd been here only one day and already Miss Clemens had put him in a state of need unlike any he'd ever experienced before. It was not only troubling but also invigorating. Especially since he'd discovered her to be a lot more than just another attractive woman.

She was fiercely protective of the children under her care, and she was ready to fight for what she believed in. But she was also willing to listen to reason, and this was something he truly admired. Most people he'd known were too stubborn to do so but not Miss Clemens.

And the fire in her eyes whenever he approached her, stood near her, or looked at her, revealed her to be a passionate woman, even though he was sure she'd deny this if asked. Cutting away another large piece of sheathing, Caleb chastised himself for thinking in such unruly terms. A gentleman did not ask a respectable woman if he stirred a desire within her. But the prospect of doing so and where it might lead was yet another fantasy for him to enjoy later in the privacy of his cottage.

"Mr. Caleb!"

He looked down at the ground to where Miss Emily Howard was standing. "Yes?"

"Luncheon is ready. Would you care to take a break?"

Caleb glanced at the widening hole in the roof

and then back at Miss Howard. "Thank you, but I would like to finish this first so I'm ready when the supplies arrive. I'll grab something later if that is all right."

She nodded and disappeared back inside, leaving Caleb to continue with his work. He would also have to add flashing around one of the chimneys since it looked like the wind must have ripped part of it off. Clambering sideways, he set to work on the next group of broken tiles, pulling them off one at a time until the sheathing beneath was revealed. He tested the wood with his knife and sighed when the tip of the blade sank into the spongy surface. This would have to be cut away and replaced as well. He proceeded to do so while taking care to preserve the good wood.

"Mr. Crawford?"

Caleb stilled in response to Miss Clemens's voice. It was closer than he would have expected, considering his current location. Placing his palm further up on the roof for support, he shifted his weight and turned his head. The top of her face peered over the gutter, and for a second his instinct was to leap toward her and pull her to safety. But he was on a slanted roof and would likely send both of them tumbling to their deaths if he did that.

So he drew a deep breath and steadied his voice. "Why are you standing on the ladder, Miss Clemens?"

"So I could bring you this," she said. Her hand came into view, sending a jolt through Caleb as he realized she wasn't holding on to the ladder as well as she should be. And then she reached out and placed a small parcel close to his feet. "You must eat something, so I thought I would bring you a ham and cheese sandwich."

Caleb glanced at the offering and slid his way slowly toward it. "Thank you, Miss Clemens." He was actually quite hungry.

"How are the repairs coming along?" she asked while he picked up the sandwich and peeled back the cloth she'd used to wrap it.

He took a bite to hide his smile because really, the fact of her standing there with most of her face hidden from view, conversing with him while he sat on the roof above her, was simply too absurd.

"It's a rough bit of work," he admitted. "I won't manage more than a couple of patches today, and that's still assuming the supplies I purchased arrive within the next couple of hours."

"Hmm…" Her eyes, the only part of her face he could see, grew pensive. "You enjoy it though, I think."

"The work?"

"Well, yes. You were humming before I alerted you to my presence. It was a cheerful tune." He chewed his food while he watched her. "Have you always wanted to be a laborer?"

"I do enjoy doing practical jobs that allow me to work with my hands," he told her carefully.

"Did it require a lot of training?"

He took another bite of sandwich, allowing himself to mull that question over for a bit. "I picked up most of my skills as I went along. Sometimes all that's required is a willingness to learn. I applied myself, asked questions. And paid attention."

"Hmm…" She was silent a moment, during which he continued eating. It was strange, her standing like that high off the ground, but stranger still was how much he liked having her there. "You must have some good credentials for Viscount Aldridge to have engaged you."

Caleb finished his food and considered how best to reply to that question. Perhaps a bit of honesty would not be remiss. "He and I have actually known each other since we were children."

Miss Clemens's eyes widened. "How on earth is that possible? I mean, you are…well…" She raised her gaze to the sky as if in contemplation.

He grinned. "Our fathers were acquainted with each other."

"Oh. I see."

And in that second, he saw in her eyes the truth she imagined, of his father in the Earl of Vernon's employ and of him being granted the opportunity to play with Aldridge. The urge to correct her was there, but if he did so, he'd lose his anonymity and the normalcy with which Miss Clemens and her friends treated him. He'd be a duke, one of the most powerful men in England, and not at all the sort of man who ought to be climbing about on roofs.

In fact, they'd probably send him packing with the declaration that he was too good for their modest home. And they'd be appalled and embarrassed by the thought of having put him up in a cottage that was barely more than a shed.

"It pleases me to know you and your father were treated well. The aristocracy can be so horribly snobbish," she told him emphatically.

Caleb swallowed any remaining wish to tell her the truth. "You speak with a keen dislike for their set."

"Yes. Well. I have had my share of bad experiences."

When she didn't elaborate, he said, "But you are gentry, are you not?"

"No. My father acquired his fortune in the textile trade, so my family was never really good enough for the gentry or the aristocracy. Honest work is frowned upon by them, you see, which only makes me loathe them all the more. Both are a class determined to instill their will on everyone, to make demands and rule people's lives. Well, it ruined mine and…I'm sorry. I did not mean to become so incensed, but when I think of Cassandra, Emily, and myself and the heartache we all endured, it angers me, knowing we could be socially accepted if not for all the ridiculous rules."

"I take it you have no intention of ever returning to that way of life?"

"Most assuredly not." She drew a deep breath and expelled it. "I would rather live on a deserted island in the middle of the ocean than have to endure the company of an aristocrat."

Try as he might, Caleb couldn't quite stop her words from slicing away at his chest. It shouldn't matter if she detested his kind, yet it did, whether he wanted it to or not.

Disappointed by the idea of how much she would hate him if she knew him to be a duke, he turned his shoulder toward her and pulled at a loose piece of tile. "I should get back to work," he said, infusing his voice with as much lightness as he could muster.

"Yes, of course. Good luck with that."

She clambered down, leaving Caleb alone. For long moments after, he just sat there, his excitement with his progress and the work ahead completely forgotten. All he could think of was George and the burdens he'd had to live with because of the title.

CHAPTER FOUR

WHEN THEY WITHDREW TO THE parlor
after dinner that evening, Mr. Crawford
took a seat in the corner by the door, allowing
Mary, Cassandra, Emily, and the children to make
use of the sofa and armchairs. A fire burned brightly
in the fireplace, thanks to Mr. Crawford's willingness to chop wood for them. Even though Mary
had told him it wasn't necessary yet, he'd insisted,
and when the temperature had started to drop in
the evening, she'd appreciated his doing so.

"Do you prefer *Gulliver's Travels* or *Robinson
Crusoe* tonight?" Cassandra asked everyone.

"*Robinson Crusoe*," Eliot said, and both Bridget
and Penelope agreed.

Picking up the red leather-bound volume, Cassandra flipped it open and started to read. Mary
leaned back in the armchair with Bridget in her
lap. There was something wonderfully comfort-
ing about the little girl's cheek pressed against
her shoulder as she snuggled closer for warmth.
Daphne sat on Emily's lap while Penelope and
Eliot crowded next to Cassandra.

Discreetly, Mary darted a look at Peter, who'd

chosen to stand next to Mr. Crawford. Shifting her gaze, she met the infinite blueness of the man's eyes. Her cheeks grew warmer, and she deliberately glanced away. He was too great a distraction for a woman who'd chosen to forego a life of romance or passion in favor of one that was sensible and meaningful.

She tried to concentrate on the story, and that went rather well until she heard Peter whisper, "What are you making?"

Unable to resist, she let her gaze wander back to Mr. Crawford, who now sat with a long piece of wood across his lap and a knife in one hand. As she watched, he carved away a few shavings and let them fall to the floor. He muttered something she could not hear and saw Peter's face light up with obvious interest. Whatever was the man doing?

Her eagerness to find out caused her to tap her foot which in turn made Bridget bounce up and down in her lap. The girl squealed repeatedly until Cassandra sighed. "Perhaps I should continue reading tomorrow?"

"Aw! I want to know what happens next," Eliot protested.

Mary bit her lip. "Sorry. I'll try to keep Bridget quiet until you've at least finished the chapter."

Emily smiled as if she knew precisely why Mary could not sit still, and Mary responded with a quelling look. The story continued and seemed to last forever before Cassandra finally marked her spot with a bookmark and Bridget slid to the floor with a thump.

"Let's get you all to bed," Emily said as she

ushered the children out of the room. "You too, Peter."

"Yes, you should go and get some rest," Mr. Crawford told him. He stood and brushed a few shavings from his trousers. When Peter looked ready to argue, Mr. Crawford said, "You'll need it if I am to show you how to hammer in nails tomorrow. Get good at it, and I'll help you make a box for your tools."

"I don't have any tools," Peter murmured.

Mr. Crawford bent his head so he could speak to Peter in a conspiratorial tone. "We'll have to rectify that then, won't we?"

The joy in Peter's eyes was enough to make Mary's heart melt. She could almost cry with pleasure on account of the boy's enthusiasm. He was clearly delighted, and his thoughts had been shifted toward brighter things. Thanks to Mr. Crawford.

"I'll clean that up," Mr. Crawford said, gesturing toward the mess he'd made. "Just show me where there's a brush and a dust pan."

"All right," Mary said.

Cassandra followed them out into the hallway. Her hand caught Mary's elbow, pulling Mary back so she could whisper, "Don't be too long," before saying good night to Mr. Crawford and turning toward the stairs.

Heat flooded Mary's cheeks, and for a quick second she thought of telling Mr. Crawford they could leave it until the morning, but at the same time, she longed to be alone with him.

Careful.

Such folly had cost her dearly before. It had led

to a stolen kiss and her foolish conviction that the man who'd whispered words of endearment in her ear meant to court her and marry her. Instead he'd been ordered to forget her. His father had not deemed her worthy of his son or his title.

Offering Mr. Crawford a hesitant look, Mary told herself this was different because *he* was different. He was just an ordinary man while she... well, she was about as ordinary now as she ever would be.

But that doesn't mean he can't hurt you.

She pushed the warning aside with the solid reminder that they'd only just met and that all they were doing was cleaning the floor. He was hardly going to proposition her in the process.

"This way," she said.

Ignoring the shiver her wayward thoughts caused, she led him into the kitchen and across to a closet next to the pantry.

Mr. Crawford lit the way with a candle he'd brought along from the parlor. The light from it flickered across the walls, trapping them both in an intimate glow.

At her back she could feel the heat of his gaze upon her. Or maybe it was just the flame from the candle. She did not know, but it did cause a slow burn in the pit of her belly and a mad desire to turn and embrace him.

Of course, she didn't. Doing so would be far too improper. And dangerous. So she opened the closet and collected the items they'd come for.

"What are you making?" she asked while she helped him sweep up the shavings a few minutes later.

"A fishing rod," he said.

Surprised, Mary glanced up from the dust pan she held. He was watching her intensely.

"Really?" A more elaborate response failed her.

"It's for Peter," he murmured, and she almost flew into his arms, the compulsion to offer her thanks and convey her gratitude so intense it was hard to resist. "I thought it might distract him," Mr. Crawford continued. "I always enjoyed fishing myself, and in my experience, most boys do."

"You should probably make one for Eliot too," she said.

"I plan to, but Peter will get his first. He seems to need it more."

Mary nodded and bowed her head as she repositioned the dust pan. Mr. Crawford swept additional shavings onto it. "Have you made many such things before?" she asked, her curiosity piqued by this skill of his.

"Not really, but I know what they're supposed to look like, so I'm sure I'll figure it out."

His answer amazed her, and she looked up again. He was closer than he had been before, and he stared right at her with unwavering intensity.

"You're a remarkable man, Mr. Crawford." Not only because he could fix a roof or make a fishing rod out of nearly nothing, but because he chose to devote his spare time to making a sad boy happy.

His hand reached out as if to touch her, and Mary steeled herself for the contact. But then as if catching himself, he withdrew and straightened his posture. "All done," he murmured and offered his hand to help her rise.

She took it without even thinking and gasped

in response to the skin-to-skin contact. He was pleasantly warm and his grip incredibly solid, holding her up when she feared she might fall.

"I..." She wasn't sure what to say. How did one confess to madness or admit to wanting something one ought not to want?

"Will you walk me out?" His voice was level, but his eyes conveyed a need that matched her own.

"Yes." She withdrew her hand and led the way back to the kitchen where she deposited the shavings in the bin before returning the brush and dust pan to the closet.

Mr. Crawford waited by the door, watching her closely as she moved past the shadows to reach him. He didn't say a word, and he didn't have to, for his eyes conveyed what words could not say.

Swallowing, he undid the latch and opened the door to the cool autumn air beyond. A strange reluctance to let him go made her follow him out. Turning to face her, Mr. Crawford reached for her hand, brushing it gently with his fingers before raising it to his lips.

"Until tomorrow, Miss Clemens." He grazed her knuckles, producing a surge of heat at the point of contact and a burst of awareness at her core.

Exhaling, she strove to gather her wits as he straightened, released her hand, and turned toward the cottage. As she watched him go, only one thought rang in her head: whatever her past experiences had been, they no longer mattered because when it came to Mr. Crawford, she wanted more, and she'd happily risk getting hurt in order to get it.

Even though he could not stop thinking about her, Caleb determined to keep his distance from Miss Clemens in the days that followed. Because if kissing her hand had taught him anything at all, it was that he longed to taste her mouth as well. And once he did that...well...other things would surely follow, because where she was concerned, he feared no touch or caress would ever be enough. The physical attraction was simply too strong.

So he stayed away, busying himself with repairs, showing Peter how to use different tools. After all, it was clear now that giving in to temptation would lead to misery for both of them, because while most women dreamed of marrying a peer, Miss Clemens wanted the one thing he would never be: a simple man without a title. And since he liked her too well and respected her too much to suggest a fleeting affair, he had no choice but to resist her.

But the way she cared for the children and the willingness with which she consistently offered to help everyone made him question his ability to do so. Indeed, there were days when he feared he might end up in Bedlam. Like when she'd shattered a glass and sustained a deep cut.

Caleb's heart had fluttered with desperate unease when he'd seen the wound, and had continued to do so until the wound was properly cleaned and the bandage he'd tied around her hand secured to his satisfaction. The need to comfort her afterward had been too fierce for him to ignore, which made him wonder what might have happened if she had not walked away after offering thanks.

Perched on top of the roof, he watched her walk toward the lake with Peter and Eliot by her side. The boys were thrilled with the fishing rods he'd made and used them as often as they could, provided someone went with them.

"Halloo?" a man's voice suddenly called. "Miss Clemens, Miss Howard...Lady Cassandra? Are you home?"

Caleb made his way to the ladder and climbed down to where a handsome young man with inquisitive eyes stood waiting. "May I help you?" Caleb asked.

The stranger looked him up and down and narrowed his gaze. "Who are you?" he asked with the sort of edge to his voice that told Caleb he wasn't pleased with Caleb's presence.

"Mr. Crawford." Caleb stuck out his hand, and the stranger eventually took it, albeit with obvious reluctance. "I'm here to fix the leaking roof."

The other man's expression eased. "Excellent," he said. "I am Mr. Townsend."

"Ah." Caleb recalled Lady Cassandra's brief mention of him when he'd offered to chop firewood. "Pleasure to meet you."

Mr. Townsend gave a slow nod. "Are any of the ladies about?"

"Miss Howard and Lady Cassandra have gone on a nature walk with the girls."

"And Miss Clemens?" Mr. Townsend's interest was evident in the altered pitch of his voice.

Caleb clenched his jaw and reminded himself that he was in no position to get between this man and Miss Clemens. "She's by the lake with the boys. I'll show you the way."

"No need for that." Mr. Townsend waved toward the roof. "I'm sure you have work to do. Wouldn't want to keep you."

The words, "I'm a duke, you ass, so show some respect," tickled Caleb's tongue. He forced them back and strode past Mr. Townsend instead. "Nevertheless," he muttered, intent on ignoring the man.

"You really needn't," Mr. Townsend said, catching up.

Caleb kept his gaze fixed on his destination. "I insist." To his relief Mr. Townsend said nothing further until they arrived at the lake.

He rushed forward. "My dear Miss Clemens, it is so good to see you."

Caleb rolled his eyes and focused on the woman who haunted his thoughts and his dreams. She stood with a pail in one hand and in the other, a fishing rod from which a small flapping creature dangled. Wide-eyed and speechless, she glanced at Caleb, who merely shrugged.

Miss Clemens frowned before redirecting her gaze to her gentleman caller. "Mr. Townsend," she began and handed Peter the pail. "It has been far too long. I was almost starting to think you'd forgotten about us."

Clutching his hands behind his back, Caleb glared at her smiling face. She looked genuinely happy to see Mr. Townsend, which only made Caleb want to strike the man. Preferably in the face.

"Oh no, Miss Clemens," Mr. Townsend assured her, faltering slightly when she steadied the fishing rod against her hip, took hold of what Caleb presumed was a tiny fish, and proceeded to unhook it from the end of the line. "I...er...ah..." Mr. Townsend continued, his gaze darting between Miss Clemens's face and the fish she was trying to release.

Eliot, too, watched in awe, as if the idea of a woman handling such matters was the most impressive thing he'd ever seen. And then, with a flick of her wrist, Miss Clemens sent the fish flying back into the lake where it landed with a tiny plop.

"You were saying?" she asked Mr. Townsend.

Caleb grinned. He had to give her credit for her ability to ruffle the man who now sputtered as if he'd just lost the ability to speak.

"I...er..."

"Yes?" Miss Clemens prompted.

"I hope you can forgive me for staying away so long," Mr. Townsend finally said. "The farm has kept me very busy this past week. Do say you'll forgive me."

Caleb groaned in response to Mr. Townsend's simpering tone, earning a scowl from Miss Clemens. He raised an eyebrow in return.

"Of course I do," she said with a smile.

Again, Caleb felt inclined to bury his fist in Mr. Townsend's face. Until he saw how fake Miss Clemens's smile actually was. It did not reach her eyes or tug at her lips with genuine pleasure.

But Mr. Townsend did not seem to notice,

because rather than take his leave, as Caleb hoped he would, he said, "My sister will be coming to visit next week. I would like for you to meet her, so I thought I'd invite you to dine with us during her stay. Shall we say Thursday at seven o'clock?" He beamed at Miss Clemens as if he'd just bestowed a great honor upon her.

Caleb watched her in anticipation of what she might say. She was biting her lip, hedging a bit as if she wished to decline but did not want to be rude either. "Thank you." She drew the word out, her mind clearly searching for some acceptable excuse. And then she met Caleb's gaze, and her eyes immediately sharpened. "I trust Mr. Crawford is permitted to join us?"

Rendered immobile for a second, Caleb pondered the significance of this request. She wanted him there, which made him feel seven feet tall and ridiculously smug. Especially when he caught the frown on Mr. Townsend's brow and the displeased slant of his mouth. It was as if there had just been a contest between them and Caleb had won, though what he had won, he wasn't quite sure. But it was certainly clear that Miss Clemens did not want to suffer Mr. Townsend's company without his added presence, which suggested she hoped to dissuade him from making advances or getting his hopes up about a possible match between them.

"Well…er…" Mr. Townsend blustered. "Would you not rather ask Lady Cassandra or Miss Howard, if it is a chaperone you require?"

"No," she said. "Considering the late hour, I would much rather have the reliable escort of a man I know and trust."

Caleb's heart swelled. In this strange competition he'd unwittingly entered, it did seem as though he was faring much better than his opponent.

"But he's a laborer, Miss Clemens," Mr. Townsend said. "Does he even own acceptable evening attire?"

"He certainly does," Caleb said with a low growl. He'd visit the tailor in the village if necessary.

"But what about shoes?" Mr. Townsend glared at Caleb's mucky boots.

"Do you wear your best when you're plowing the fields?" Caleb asked. The barb struck. He could see it in Mr. Townsend's eyes.

"Fine," Mr. Townsend muttered. His cheeks had turned ruddy. "As long as you look the part, you're welcome to join us."

Caleb smiled. "How kind you are, sir. I'm already counting the days until we meet again."

"I—"

"Yes, I know. There is a lot for you to see now that we have accepted. Preparations must be made." Caleb took a step forward. "Please, don't let us keep you."

"But—"

"After all, I am sure you want to impress Miss Clemens and your sister with your hospitality. Might I suggest you get started right away?"

Mr. Townsend glanced at Miss Clemens, who immediately nodded. "He does have a point."

"Right." Mr. Townsend tipped his hat in Miss Clemens's direction. "Until we meet again, Miss

Clemens." He started back toward the house, nodding at Caleb as he passed him. "Mr. Crawford."

Caleb waited until the other man was well out of earshot before returning his attention to Miss Clemens, who stood with her hands on her hips and undeniable censure in her eyes. Casting a quick look at Eliot and Peter, she made sure they had their fishing in order before approaching him. It had been days since they had conversed in private, which somehow served to increase the tension as she moved in closer to where he stood.

"He's not a bad man," she said, almost apologetically.

Caleb stuck his hands in his pockets to stop from reaching out and touching her. "Perhaps not," he agreed, "but he's obviously pressing his suit with a woman who's clearly not interested, though I have to wonder why that might be." Now that the man was gone and no longer posed a threat to the misplaced possessiveness Caleb felt toward Miss Clemens, he was able to think more rationally. "Given your position, he could make an excellent match."

"Cassandra and Emily would agree with you there."

Schooling his features, Caleb forced himself to ask the next question. "So then why not take the chance to marry and start a family of your own?"

She shrugged. "Because I want more than a man who's willing to support me."

"What do you mean?"

"Simply that as handsome and kind as Mr. Townsend might be" —a surge of jealousy raked Caleb's spine and he curled his fingers until he clenched his fists—"there's no connection between us."

Caleb's heart thudded against his chest. "You don't desire him," he told her plainly. And then, knowing he shouldn't but needing the reconfirmation, he quietly added, "The way you desire me."

Her gasp stirred the air between them, and he instinctively dropped his gaze to her parted lips. This was madness. He ought to apologize and walk away, but since she did not move, neither did he. Instead, he watched her throat work as she swallowed, the truth in her eyes brightening her gaze as it locked with his and held in a fiery exchange of mutual need.

I want you.

He could practically hear her say it, could feel the charge those words evoked thrumming through his veins and heating his blood. "I want you too," he murmured with brutal honesty, "but ruining you would be a crime, Miss Clemens, so I fear I must refrain."

"I know," she whispered. "It's the worst kind of torture."

Caleb smiled, pleased by her confession even if it did not offer either of them the solution they wanted. But to bed her would be a mistake unless they agreed to marry. A notion that seemed slightly premature considering their brief acquaintance. Not to mention the fact that she would never marry a peer.

"There is some comfort in knowing we feel the same way, I suppose." Stepping closer, he nudged her arm in a playful way. "It's better than the unrequited affection Mr. Townsend is suffering."

A tiny smile pulled at her lips. "I suppose that's true. I just…I wish…" Her hand caught the edge of his sleeve in a hopeless gesture.

"Me too. But no matter how much we want, getting married would be a bit hasty, don't you think?"

She laughed at that. "Oh, indeed. You must forgive me, Mr. Crawford. I did not mean to suggest such a thing."

He laughed as well and took a step back. "I should return to work so I can fix the remaining leaks in the roof before it rains."

"Yes, of course," she said, her voice slightly breathless. "The boys and I will stay here a while. They're both quite eager to catch a trout."

"You didn't tell them there are no trout in this lake, did you?"

"No," she said with a cheeky grin. "Should I have done?"

He shook his head. "As long as they're happily occupied and having fun, I see no reason for it. And who knows? They might surprise you." Adding a wink, he turned about and walked back to the house, strangely satisfied with the conversation they'd had even if it hadn't solved anything between them. But at least they both knew where they stood with each other now. Whether or not they would act on their feelings in the future remained to be seen, but for now he would content himself with knowing Miss Clemens desired him as much as he desired her.

CHAPTER FIVE

"MR. TOWNSEND CAME TO CALL when you were out," Mary confessed to Emily and Cassandra while they enjoyed their afternoon tea together on the terrace. With shawls wrapped around their shoulders, the air was tolerable. They all knew the day would soon come when they would be forced back inside, so they chose to take advantage of what little dry weather remained.

The girls, dressed in smocks, sat at a smaller table nearby with their paints, while Peter and Eliot kicked a ball around on the grass. Overhead, the occasional banging reminded Mary of Mr. Crawford's presence. Their conversation earlier in the day had been both unexpected and enlightening. *I want you too.* Another rush of heat assailed her as she recalled the sensual caress of his voice as he'd said it.

But he was right. For them to act on their mutual desire without her risking her reputation, they would have to form an attachment, and that meant marriage, which was something she'd promised herself she'd avoid.

Besides, how well did she really know Mr.

Crawford? He'd been friends with Cassandra's brother since childhood and was still friends with him today, which ought to vouch for his character. For although she didn't know the viscount very well, having spoken to him on only a few occasions, Cassandra had nothing but praise for her older brother. And the lengths he'd gone to in order to ensure his sister's well-being when their parents wanted nothing to do with her was telling.

"Did he really?" Emily said in response to her comment.

"He even invited me for dinner next week so I can meet his sister," Mary said. She took a sip of her tea and allowed its warmth to soothe her.

"Then his courtship of you is official," Cassandra said.

"Did you accept?" Emily asked.

Mary nodded. "Yes." She lowered her voice to a whisper. "On the condition that Mr. Crawford escorts me."

Cassandra choked on her tea while Emily clasped a hand over her mouth to stifle her gasp. It took a second for them to recover.

Cassandra darted a quick look toward the roof and leaned forward in her seat. "Have you developed a tendre for him? For Mr. Crawford that is?"

"We'd understand if you have," Emily whispered. "He's marvelously handsome. And tall too. I mean, Mr. Townsend is good looking, but between him and Mr. Crawford..." Emily sighed while Mary tried to still the flutter in her belly.

"I don't know," Mary said. Was it a tendre or merely a physical attraction? "I cannot concentrate on anything when he is near. Or even when he's not. Thoughts of him follow me wherever I go."

"I felt that way about Timothy," Cassandra said. "He and I were mad for each other, which is why we chose to give in to passion and live in the moment." She smiled with a mixture of sadness and sentimentality. "I'm glad we did, because if we hadn't, Penelope wouldn't exist. At least through her, a part of Timothy survives."

Mary inhaled deeply. Compared to Cassandra who'd loved and lost, her own romantic complications seemed trifling.

"Would you let Mr. Crawford court you instead of Mr. Townsend, if that were an option?" Emily asked. "Considering your reluctance to marry, would you be open to the idea of becoming Mr. Crawford's wife?"

"I'm not sure." And she knew he definitely wasn't either, or he'd have suggested that option instead of insisting they curb their desire. "I've grown accustomed to my independence, and I enjoy living with you and the children. To give that up is not something I can imagine doing."

"But will you still feel the same twenty years from now, Mary?" Cassandra placed her hand over Mary's. "Can you honestly tell me you would have no regrets?" Mary shook her head with increasing uncertainty. "Then why not embrace the passion you feel and see where things lead?"

"Because the last time I tried that it broke my heart."

Emily nodded as if understanding. "I know," she said, "but unlike last time, you're not a young debutant pinning her hopes on the man who kissed her. You're a grown woman with the freedom to make your own choices now. If you want to marry, there's at least one man eager to have you, and if you don't, then that is fine as well. Furthermore, you have two very loyal friends who are willing to support you no matter what you decide."

"And if it is an affair with Mr. Crawford you want, neither of us would judge you," Cassandra piped up.

Mary squeaked while Emily responded with a giggle.

"You cannot be serious," Mary muttered. "The scandal would be—"

"Nonexistent," Cassandra claimed.

"Think about it," Emily said. "Nobody would have to know."

"Except us," Mary reminded them. She shook her head. "I cannot believe we're discussing this. That you would even suggest it."

"Think of who you are talking to," Cassandra said.

"Well yes," Mary agreed. "I can understand you, perhaps, but Emily?"

Emily pursed her lips. "We are not living sheltered lives anyone. I have read a few books here and there, and I have listened to everything Cassandra has been willing to share. Which is quite a lot."

Mary stared at her in dismay. It was like looking at a completely different person from the one she'd been living with for the past five years.

"And," Emily added, "since I have never even

enjoyed a man's attention, I can promise you, Mary, that if I ever have the chance to spend just one night with a man like Mr. Crawford, I will take it."

The glint in Emily's eyes and the fierce determination in her voice gave Mary pause. Unlike her and Cassandra, Emily had never even been kissed, and while her own experience with kissing had led to disaster, she didn't regret knowing what it was like. Which was probably similar to Cassandra's opinion on lovemaking.

"I don't know if I can," Mary told her friends. She picked up her teacup and stared down into the dark brown liquid. "Five years ago, I fell in love when Wrenwick kissed me. For weeks he courted me in secret, assuring me he would soon make our engagement official. But that never happened, because in the end, he didn't dare oppose his father's wishes." She sighed with lingering disappointment. "It took me years to recover from the hurt I suffered when I realized I didn't matter as much to him as I thought I did." She sipped her tea. "I cannot go through that again."

"Then wait a while," Cassandra suggested, "until you figure out what you want."

"Miss Clemens," Daphne said, drawing Mary's attention away from her friends, "can you please help me paint a kitten so it looks just like Raphael?"

"I can try," Mary said and set her cup down. Rising, she went to admire the girl's work. "But I cannot promise you I will succeed."

"You always say trying is half the challenge already solved." Daphne moved aside and handed Mary her paintbrush. "I'm sure your attempt will be better than mine, anyway."

Smiling, Mary dipped the brush in a bit of brown paint. She'd think of her conversation with Emily and Cassandra later. Right now, all she wanted was a distraction from her ongoing contemplations about Mr. Crawford and the undeniable effect he had on her.

Clouds were gathering by the time Caleb finished attaching the final slate tile to the part of the roof he'd worked on for the last couple of days. The women and the children had retreated inside a while ago, but only after the girls had completed their paintings. He'd paused his work when he'd seen Miss Clemens get up to help Daphne and had felt his heart squeeze in response to the nurturing image she presented. She was good with children and would make an excellent mother one day, if given the chance.

By the time he'd gathered his tools and descended the ladder, rain had started to fall. Looking up at the darkening sky, Caleb could only hope the repairs he'd made so far would hold and that no additional damage would be done to the house during the night.

The fragrant smell of meat roasting in the oven filled his nostrils when he entered the kitchen. His stomach growled in response, his body warming to the sight of Miss Clemens peeling potatoes while Miss Howard chopped vegetables and Lady Cassandra prepared some gravy. The atmosphere was cozy in its inclusiveness. It agreed with him more than sitting at the head of a long empty table while waiting for his meal to be served.

But this was temporary. Eventually he would have to return to Camberly House and resume his duties.

Banishing that unpleasant thought, he removed his damp jacket and hung it on a peg near the door. "Anything I can help with?" he asked.

"You're welcome to set the table," Mary said with a brief glance in his direction.

Caleb nodded and went to wash his hands before going in search of the plates. Stacking them in his arms, he carried them into the dining room. A wry smile tugged at his lips at the thought of a duke performing such an ordinary task. His mother would probably be horrified. He laughed and shook his head. When he'd told her he needed to get away for a while, he'd failed to mention what he would be doing or how he'd be living.

The door opened and Miss Clemens stepped in. "How are you doing?"

"Have a look," he suggested as he placed the last fork in its allotted spot.

She surveyed the table, then looked at him with enough curiosity to make Caleb's stomach tighten. Her gaze grew assessing. "Why are you so good at everything you do?"

He grinned while shrugging one shoulder and locked her compliment away behind his heart. "Experience and self-reliance, I suppose. I've never been opposed to trying new things, and since leaving home ten years ago, I have had to figure a lot of things out on my own. Setting a table properly, however, just requires a bit of attention to detail. Most people can do it if they try."

"I know. But most people might not know to align the edge of the plate with the edge of the table or to place the silverware as precisely as you have done." She tilted her head. "It simply makes me wonder, that is all."

Caleb drew a deep breath. She was right to do so, of course. After all, how many laborers would think to fold the napkins to imitate fans? The foolish effort would likely give him away.

But she chose to abandon the topic in favor of another. Moving toward him while her fingers trailed over the back of each chair, she quietly asked, "Is there a Mrs. Crawford I ought to know about?"

Caught off guard, Caleb blinked a few times before he could answer. He decided to pose a question of his own. "Do you honestly think I would have said the things I said to you earlier if there were?"

A flush filled her cheeks, but she kept her assessing gaze on him. "That is what I am trying to determine." When he didn't respond, she pressed her lips together in a pensive way before saying, "I have misjudged people before."

"Is that why you left London and came to live here?" He had to ask even if she refused to answer.

She dropped her gaze, and Caleb held his breath in anticipation of either enlightenment or disappointment. The only sound filling the room was the rain tapping hard against the windows.

Miss Clemens shifted. Another second passed.

And then, "Yes." Hesitantly, she raised her gaze to his and showed him her mortification. "I kissed a man I should not have kissed and believed him when he said that we would eventually marry."

Everything inside Caleb revolted in response to those words, and yet he forced himself to ask, "What happened?"

"I stupidly assumed our courtship was real, but as it turned out, I was not good enough for the gentleman in question. Or at least that is what his father said when he told me to stay away from his son."

Moving closer to her, Caleb stared down into her upturned face. "I am sorry you were hurt."

She smiled a smile that didn't quite reach her eyes. "It is in the past, but the impact it had on my life..." She shook her head. "I was young and naive and convinced I was madly in love. But even if I'd wanted to consider another gentleman's attentions, none were forthcoming after I became known as a woman who sought to trap unsuspecting gentlemen into marriage."

Confounded by the cruelty she'd been subjected to, he could not think of what to say except, "Who started that rumor? Do you know?"

"The father of the kissee."

Caleb's lips twitched a little. "The kissee?"

"As in the victim of my unrestrained passion." She rolled her eyes and blew out a breath. "Never mind the fact that he kissed me first and not the other way around."

The unfairness tore at Caleb's heart. "I don't suppose you'll tell me the scoundrel's name so I can give him a sound thrashing?"

She smiled just enough to lift his spirits. "It is in the past, Mr. Crawford. Best not dwell on it."

"Right." He could not stand the anger or the jealousy he felt toward a nameless stranger—a man who'd tasted Miss Clemens's delectable lips without valuing the pleasure of it. "You should know that the man was an idiot."

A touch of humor seeped into her eyes. "Really?"

He met her gaze boldly. "All I know is if I had been the one to kiss you and court you, I would not have been able to walk away and forget you."

Her eyes shimmered in the candlelight, and Caleb took a step forward. He had to reach her, touch her, hold her...

Miss Howard strode into the room with a steaming pot of vegetables. Lady Cassandra followed on her heels, carrying a dish with slices of meat neatly arranged next to a row of boiled potatoes.

Caleb flexed his fingers and forced his attention away from Miss Clemens, who was now calling for the children to come and eat their dinner. He went to the table and took his seat between Daphne and Miss Clemens, as he'd done every evening since his arrival. Without even thinking, he placed a slice of roast pork on Daphne's plate along with one potato and a spoonful of vegetables. He then cut up the meat and potatoes for her and removed the steamed carrots from the mixture of vegetables because he knew she did not like them.

"Did you grow up in a large family, Mr. Crawford?"

It was Lady Cassandra who'd asked the question, and Caleb glanced in her direction. "I had three brothers and quite a few cousins who visited regularly."

"Had?" Miss Howard asked.

Caleb strove for a casual demeanor and said, "My oldest brother passed away recently."

"Oh." Miss Clemens jerked in her seat and turned her body more fully toward him. "I am so sorry to hear that."

"We all are," Lady Cassandra said.

"Thank you." He reached for the various dishes and proceeded to serve himself now that everyone else had filled their plates. "His death has made me reflect on some of the choices I've made. When I fell out with our father ten years ago and left England with every intention of putting as much distance between us as possible, I also lost touch with my brother. He wouldn't have known where to find me if he'd wanted to, while I just couldn't bring myself to write and explain what had happened. His relationship with our father was so very different from my own."

"And your other brothers?" Miss Howard asked. "You said you had three in total?"

Caleb nodded and took a bite of meat. "I lost touch with them as well and have recently discovered that they left England shortly after I did for similar reasons. Because our father wanted to control our lives."

"It would seem you've come to the right place then," Lady Cassandra murmured. "The three of us are well acquainted with the pressure demanding parents can place on their children. When my parents discovered I'd conceived out of wedlock, they practically threw me at every available bachelor, desperate to get me married before it started to show. Miss Clemens and Miss Howard share similar experiences."

"I was ignored throughout every Season," Miss Howard said. "When my fate became clear, Papa produced a suitor forty years my senior and told me I'd lost the right to be picky." She pushed her vegetables around on her plate while quietly adding, "I have never cried so much in my life, but then I heard about Lady Cassandra and what her brother had done to help her. When I sought her out for advice, she suggested I come and live with her here."

"I wanted the company," Lady Cassandra said with a smile. "And I have come to appreciate the friendship."

"We're both very grateful," Miss Clemens said. "Had it not been for you, I would probably be living in Scotland right now."

"Scotland?" Caleb stared at her in surprise.

"That is where my parents wanted to send me when they realized my reputation could not be salvaged. Out of sight, out of mind, as my father put it." She stared down at her plate for a moment before stabbing at a potato with her fork. "He wanted to save my younger sisters from suffering the repercussions of my mistake. As a parent, it was the right decision, I suppose, even though it hurt to be cast aside not only by the man I'd thought I'd marry, but by my entire family too."

"But you didn't go to Scotland," Caleb said.

"No. Lady Cassandra and I were friends before her sudden departure from London. We stayed in touch, so I knew she'd made a life for herself here.

I asked if I could come and stay with her for a while and well…that turned into five years."

"Will you stay here too, Mr. Crawford?" Daphne asked.

When Caleb dropped his gaze to her, he found her watching him expectantly. "I don't think I can," he said.

"Why not?" Peter asked, staring at him from across the table.

"Because I was hired to do a job," Caleb explained. "Once that has been completed, I will have to leave."

"I could write to my brother and suggest you take on a more permanent position as caretaker," Lady Cassandra said. "The pay is reasonable, and I know we would benefit from your continued presence."

"The children have taken to you," Miss Clemens said. "And I…" She took another bite of her food, allowing her words to fade.

Caleb felt his heart ache. A bond had been forged between himself and these women, not to mention the children they cared for. He'd made a home here during the brief time he'd spent in their company. But it was temporary. Eventually he would have to return to London and resume his responsibilities there. His position as duke demanded it of him, and to be honest, he could not abandon his mother for too long. Not when she'd recently lost both her husband and her eldest son.

"Thank you. That is very kind of you," Caleb said, "but I'm afraid it's not possible."

"Because…?" Penelope asked.

"That's enough," Lady Cassandra chastised her daughter. "Mr. Crawford probably has responsibilities he would be neglecting by remaining here longer than necessary."

"I have a mother who needs me," he said because it was true, "and I have an inheritance from my father that must be dealt with. Coming here was actually a welcome excuse to avoid having to do so, but I cannot ignore it forever."

"What did he leave you?" Eliot asked through a mouthful of meat.

"Eliot," Miss Clemens chided.

Caleb grinned at the boy who always asked the most forward questions. "Some property, actually. And some money."

"How much money?" Eliot asked.

"That is enough," all three women exclaimed in unison while they stared at Eliot with severe disapproval.

"Sorry," Eliot muttered. He took another bite of his food. "I just—"

A booming crash cut him off, the sound prompting Daphne to leap in her seat.

"It's just thunder," Caleb assured her. Excusing himself he stood and went to the window. "The wind has picked up. And the rain is coming down hard." Light lit up the sky and another crash followed. Leaping out of her chair, Daphne ran to him, and he swept the girl up in his arms, holding her close so she would feel safe. "It's all right," he murmured as she pressed her face into his chest. "You're safe in here."

"But what about Raphael?" the girl cried. "I think he's still out there!"

"Did you forget to bring him inside with you earlier?" Miss Howard asked.

Daphne bobbed her head up and down and cried harder.

"He'll be fine," Miss Clemens assured her. She'd risen as well and was now stroking her hand over Daphne's head in order to sooth her. "Cats are versatile creatures, sweetheart. He'll know to take shelter wherever he can find it."

Caleb stared back out at the trees he could see through the darkness. Their branches whipped from side to side, and then another blast of light lit up the sky. Muffled by the drumming of rain and the howling wind, Caleb heard the feint sound of neighing. "I should check on my horse," he said and lowered Daphne to her feet. "The thunder will have unsettled him."

"You cannot mean to go out in this weather," Miss Clemens said.

Looking at her, he saw the fear in her eyes – fear for him – and he could not stop from taking her hand. He squeezed it quickly before releasing it once again. "Don't worry. This isn't my first thunderstorm, Miss Clemens. I will be back before you know it."

"Watch Daphne for a moment, please," he heard Miss Clemens say as he strode from the room. Returning to the kitchen, he snatched his jacket from the peg by the door and shoved his arms through the sleeves.

Miss Clemens burst into the room, carrying a lantern. "Take this at least so you can see." Her voice was steady but alarm strained her features.

"Thank you." He took the lantern from her,

brushing her fingers as he did so. A charge went through him, warming his insides and jolting his pulse.

"Do you not have a hat you can wear?" she asked with marked concern.

"It is at the cottage." Along with his greatcoat. He hadn't thought he'd be needing either one when he'd come inside earlier after completing his work for the day. "Perhaps you can prepare a hot cup of tea for when I get back and see to it that a warm fire is burning in the parlor?"

"Yes, of course." She caught his arm when he turned for the door, and he paused there on the threshold to look back at her. "Do be careful, Mr. Crawford."

He dipped his head to acknowledge he'd heard her and opened the door. It caught on a gust of wind and swung wide, slamming against the outside wall. Tightening his jaw, Caleb stepped out into the turbulent night, caught the door, and forced it shut before heading toward the cottage where an overhang jutting from the right wall provided shelter for his horse.

CHAPTER SIX

TOO AGITATED TO STAY STILL for even one second, Mary moved around the kitchen. Having lit a fire in the parlor, she kept checking on the water she'd put to boil for the tea Mr. Crawford had requested and looking out the window in anticipation of his return. If only she had a clock nearby so she had some idea of how long he'd been gone. It felt like twenty minutes, but she suspected it was only ten.

"The children are all in bed," Cassandra said, entering the kitchen. "Emily is reading to them from *Robinson Crusoe*."

"It looks as though the world is ending out there," Mary said, ignoring Cassandra's comment because it was impossible for her to think of anything else at the moment. Hugging herself, she forced her gaze away from the blurry window and went to find a teapot.

"He will be all right," Cassandra said. "Mr. Crawford's a strong and sensible man."

"I know that, Cass." Preparing the tea strainer, Mary poured hot water through it and into the pot, busying herself in a futile attempt to keep her mind off the storm outside and the man who was caught up in it. She jumped when another boom sounded overhead and took a deep breath to steady herself. "I know my concern is irrational, but I cannot seem to make it go away."

"Because you care about him," Cassandra said. "Deeply."

Mary closed her eyes briefly. "How is that even possible, Cass? When I decided five years ago never to form an attachment to another man ever again?"

"That was before you met Mr. Crawford," Cassandra told her gently.

Mary stared down at the teapot that now stood waiting. "What am I to do?"

Silence hung in the air for a moment, and then Cassandra's hand touched her shoulder. "You could choose to give Mr. Crawford a chance and see where things lead."

Mary drew a quivering breath. "The effect he has on me terrifies me. I worry it's clouding my judgment and that it will prompt me to make the same mistake I made once before."

Cassandra dropped her hand and fetched a tray which she set before Mary so she could place the teapot and cups upon it. "Having a relationship of any kind puts us at risk of getting hurt, Mary. The key is to determine whether or not the other person is worth that risk."

"How can I possibly know that, Cass?" Mary shook her head. She wanted to believe the best of Mr. Crawford. His actions so far had certainly convinced her that he was thoughtful and considerate, but was that enough to ensure she could trust him?

Cassandra looked at her and smiled. "What does your heart tell you?"

Groaning, Mary scrubbed the palm of her hand across her face. "My heart has been wrong before. I'd be a fool to follow it again." No. This time, she'd use her head, and her head was telling her to be cautious. "And besides, you heard him yourself this evening at dinner. He will leave here as soon as his work is complete. He gave no indication at all that he would have cause to stay."

"Have you given him any, Mary?" Cassandra's gaze held hers.

"Maybe not." But suppose she overcame her fears and told him how much he meant to her. Could she ask him to stay when she knew his mother needed him? "I'm not sure doing so would be in his best interest."

Cassandra sighed. "I hope you're right about that, because the only thing worse than getting hurt is having to live with regret."

The outside door burst open just as she finished speaking, bringing rain and leaves and a sopping wet Mr. Crawford into the kitchen. Water dripped from his hair and ran down his body, pooling around his mud-stained boots. In his arms, he cradled a scraggly clump of shabby fur that meowed with piercing dissatisfaction.

Crossing the floor, Mary brushed past Mr. Crawford and closed the door to shut out the cold. He was shivering badly, and she could see now that his face was terribly pale.

"Come on," she said, applying her most practical tone. "Let's get you warmed up." She pulled

Raphael away from Mr. Crawford and handed him over to Cassandra.

"I'll take him up to Daphne," Cassandra said. "Thank you, Mr. Crawford. She'll be most pleased to know he is well and safe indoors."

Mr. Crawford nodded in a jerky way, and Mary immediately set to work, pulling his jacket from his shoulders and hanging it over the back of a chair near the stove to dry. His shirt, she saw, was plastered to his arms while splotches of dampness stained his waistcoat. Somehow, she would have to get him dry before he caught a cold.

"I've made some tea," she said and went to pick up the tray. "We can have it in the parlor while you warm yourself by the fire."

He didn't respond but she sensed he was following her out into the hallway and toward the cozy room that awaited. Reaching around her, he opened the door so she could enter, his arm grazing her shoulder to spark her awareness.

Mary stepped into the welcoming warmth, and he closed the door behind them to keep the heat in, which of course made her keenly aware of how very alone they now were. She crossed to the small table in front of the sofa and set the tray down while he moved closer to the fire. She poured two cups of tea and offered him one of them.

"Thank you." His voice was low.

Mary watched as he sipped his drink. A sigh of supreme satisfaction rose from deep within his chest, then his gaze met hers, and the smile that followed almost knocked her off her feet. Her pulse leapt and her fingers tingled with the sudden urge to reach out and touch him and offer him comfort.

"Those wet clothes won't do you any favors," she said, not knowing where she found the words to imply something as scandalous as him undressing with her in the room, but it did seem like a reasonable thing for him to do if he wished to avoid getting sick.

He raised an eyebrow. "You want me to take them off?"

"I want to ensure your comfort," she explained while fighting to keep her back rigid and her voice as serious as possible.

With a snort, he set his cup on the mantle and started unbuttoning his waistcoat. "I can think of a few ways for you to do so, Miss Clemens."

Heat ignited in Mary's cheeks, and she instinctively retreated a step. "I'm going to fetch you a blanket," she muttered, backing away even further in the direction of the door.

Mr. Crawford watched her go with an underlying hint of amusement in his eyes. His fingers undid another button on the waistcoat, and Mary fumbled for the door handle somewhere behind her. Finding it, she allowed the escape it offered to calm her nerves.

"I will return shortly," she said with a hoarse whisper she barely recognized as her own. And then she fled into the hallway, desperate for a moment's reprieve from the man who addled her brain and left her longing for his embrace.

"I need a blanket," she told Cassandra and Emily when she met them on the upstairs landing. "Mr. Crawford..." She glanced to one side, too distressed to offer a proper explanation.

"I see," Cassandra said.

Brushing past her friends, Mary hurried into her own bedchamber, threw open the lid of the trunk at the foot of her bed, and pulled out a thick wool blanket she only used during the coldest winter months.

"Well, you'd best go and make sure he gets it," Emily said from her position next to the door. The two women had followed Mary into her room and were both watching her with great interest.

"He was very wet when he came in," Cassandra said. "The sooner he gets warmed up the better."

"Can you manage on your own?" Emily asked with a yawn.

Cassandra promptly yawned as well. "It has been such a long day, and we are both rather tired. In fact, we were just off to bed when you met us in the hallway."

"You were heading toward the stairs," Mary said. She held the blanket against her chest, taking comfort in its warmth.

"Only with the intention of asking you about Mr. Crawford's condition." Emily's expression was too serene to be taken seriously. "As long as you think you can manage without our assistance, I do believe we'll retire."

"I never said—"

"He's welcome to stay on the sofa so he doesn't have to go back out into that awful weather," Cassandra said. "Just tell him to get undressed first so he doesn't leave watermarks on the upholstery."

Mary stared at her friends who were both pressing their lips together in obvious attempts to stifle their laughter. "You're awful," she said. "Do you know that?"

"Hmm…" Cassandra murmured. "I do believe you'll thank us later. Good night."

She left the room with Emily close on her heels. The sound of doors opening and closing nearby could be heard, followed by silence. Mary gripped the blanket harder, squared her shoulders, and strode toward the stairs. Her friends were being ridiculous. *She* was being ridiculous. Mr. Crawford was chilled to the bone and in dire need of her help. That was all there was to it.

But when she opened the door to the parlor without thinking to knock, she saw that there was nothing ridiculous about this situation and that it threatened to become far more complicated than she had ever imagined it could. Because there he stood before the fire just as she'd left him, except he'd not only shucked his waistcoat, but his shirt, boots and hose as well. Indeed, he was completely naked save for the breeches that still preserved what remained of his modesty, and by God if he wasn't the most beautiful man she'd ever laid eyes on in her life!

Granted, his back was turned toward her, but it was the sort of back that was made to be admired. Muscle sculpted it to perfection, dipping inward toward his spine. His shoulders were broad and further accentuated by the well-defined shape of his biceps. Mary's gaze travelled lower to his tapered waistline and the molded shape of his bottom. Her mouth went dry, and it took some effort to tear her gaze away from that part of his body. But to ogle that area was most improper. Certainly more so than it was to admire the rest. So she dropped her gaze further, to the bare calves dusted by dark brown hair and the feet that were firmly planted on the parlor floor.

"You should probably close the door," he said, jolting Mary so forcefully she actually jumped.

Her chin jerked up, and to her absolute horror she saw he was watching her over his shoulder. Heat erupted inside her, and her stomach immediately dropped all the way to her toes. Embarrassed, she turned and closed the door behind her, pausing with her face toward it and her back toward Mr. Crawford for a minute in order to catch her breath and slow the beat of her racing heart.

"Are you all right?" she heard him ask.

"Perfectly," she said with the most unsteady voice she'd ever used.

"I'm sorry if I have unsettled you, Miss Clemens, but I needed to get out of the wet clothes in order to warm up."

"Yes. Yes, of course." She took a deep breath and clutched the blanket even tighter before turning back to face him. "I…er…I brought you this."

His gaze dropped to the blanket. "Thank you."

"And Cassandra says you can sleep on the sofa just as long as you don't get it wet." She forced her feet forward one at a time until she was close enough to hand over the blanket. "It will save you from having to go back out into the storm."

"I appreciate that," he murmured. Accepting the blanket, he unfolded it completely and wrapped it around himself to cocoon most of his body from his armpits to his ankles.

Feeling as though she could breathe again, Mary

went to make herself a cup of tea. "How was your horse?" she asked while taking care not to spill the tea on the table as she poured.

"A little anxious. He doesn't like this kind of weather, but stroking his muzzle for a while seemed to sooth him."

"I'm sorry we don't have a proper stable." She took a sip of her tea and sighed.

"You needn't worry. It is not the first time he's had to endure a storm and it probably won't be the last, but it helps to remind him that I am close by and that he isn't alone."

Taking another sip of her tea she glanced toward him and almost choked. "What...?" she sputtered and coughed at the sight of him holding his breeches and smalls in one hand while keeping the blanket in place with the other.

"You said I had to avoid wetting the upholstery," he said as he hung the pieces of clothing over the fireplace screen next to his shirt and hose.

"Well, yes," she somehow managed to say without stammering or squeaking, "but I didn't expect you to get completely undressed while I'm here with you." The notion of him wearing nothing at all beneath the blanket was simply too scandalous to contemplate. It didn't matter if she couldn't see anything. The knowing itself was enough to put her in a muddled state from which she feared there could be no escape, because now that her mind had ventured down that particular path, she could not stop herself from trying to form a complete image of what she might see if he suddenly dropped the blanket completely.

"Do you ever miss your family, Miss Clemens?"

His unexpected question, coming seemingly out of nowhere, disrupted her indecent thoughts. Blinking, she lowered herself to one of the armchairs. "My family?"

"Do you ever think of trying to repair your relationship?"

"I used to," she said. Shifting in her seat, she made herself more comfortable and took another sip of her tea. "After my anger toward my parents had passed, I considered returning to London for a visit. But then I thought of my younger sisters and the reason my parents banished me in the first place, which was to protect their reputations by adding distance, and I ended up staying away instead."

He took a seat opposite her, and for a brief moment, Mary's discomfort returned at the sight of the blanket parting in order to make space for his legs. But then he asked, "Did they never write to you in all these years?"

Sadness swept in and she quietly shook her head. "I don't believe they know where I am, and even if they did, I doubt they would want to associate with me in any way."

Mr. Crawford frowned. "I find that a very harsh punishment, based on what you have told me with regard to what happened."

"In their minds I was entirely to blame. I brought shame to them and the rest of my family. Getting rid of me was the only thing that made sense to them, I think."

"I hope I meet them one day," he muttered. "And if I were them, I'd hope the opposite."

She couldn't help smiling. "Thank you, but I

have made my peace with that part of my life, and I have come to accept that I will never again be the woman I once was. I've experienced too much."

He watched her closely, intensely, until her skin pricked with awareness. "I think you're probably a better person for it."

"You believe challenges improve a person's character." Not a question but an observation.

"I have no doubt that it did so for me," he said. He drew the blanket tighter and reached for his tea. "As angry as I was with my father when I left home, I was also young and inexperienced, with the kind of cocksure confidence only youth can give you." His lips slanted as he took a sip of his tea. "I raced off to France, certain I'd find someone there who'd love the drawings of houses I wanted to build and hire me straight away. Instead, I was told my ideas were pointless without the necessary experience to realize them – that presenting a mere drawing of an idea to a group of builders would likely lead to an unstable structure."

"So what did you do?"

He grinned. "Well, I sure as hell wasn't going to go back to England and face my father's patronizing glare. So I took a job with a bricklayer first, then with a carpenter who specialized in making window frames, doors, and roofing materials. After a couple of years I began an apprenticeship with a builder who worked on the sort of houses I had designed. He taught me most of what I know today. Also gave me the chance I so desperately longed for to make my own vision a reality."

"He sounds like a good man."

"He's one of the best," Mr. Crawford whispered. The tension in his blanket had eased a little, making it sag in the middle to show off more of his chest.

Mary tried not to look. She liked the comfortable repartee they'd been enjoying these past few minutes and didn't want anything to disrupt it. So she decided to ask a question of her own. "Besides building houses, fixing roofs, and carving fishing rods for little boys, what other things do you enjoy doing?"

He stared back at her from across the small distance between them, and Mary could feel her blood heat in response to the fire now burning in his eyes. "Spending time with you," he said as if any other answer would be absurd.

Warmth filled her heart, and a grin traced her lips. Sinking back against her chair, she nudged him playfully with the tip of her shoe. "Besides that," she said, shoving aside all physical response to that comment. The only way she'd survive staying here with him dressed only in a blanket was if the tone remained light and friendly.

Thoughtfulness creased his brow. "History has always interested me. I'm fascinated by the people who came before us and by their incredible accomplishments. Just take the pyramids, for instance; the Viking expeditions to Greenland; or battles fought by the Romans. There's a wealth of knowledge to be found in the past, Miss Clemens. I always grab any chance I get to learn more."

"You should take a closer look at our library then. We've a few books I'm sure you'd enjoy. Like *The Autobiography of Benjamin Franklin*. I read it myself last year and found it incredibly infor-mative."

"Thank you. I'll be sure to take a look at it. And then perhaps you and I can discuss its contents."

"Perhaps," Mary said. She finished her tea and returned her cup to the tray before rising. "I wish you a good night, Mr. Crawford."

He stood as well and adjusted the blanket, draw-ing it tight around his torso. "Same to you, Miss Clemens." His voice was low and sultry. Desper-ate to resist it, Mary went to the door while hot little embers skittered along her limbs. "Thank you for the tea and blanket."

"You're welcome," she said without daring to look at him again, because she saw where this ended now, and while part of her yearned for his kiss and everything else he was willing to give her, another part screamed in protest, too loud to be ignored.

CHAPTER SEVEN

TO SAY HE'D SLEPT COMFORTABLY on the narrow sofa that was roughly a foot shorter than his body would be a lie, but he did stay warm and he did wake up with the most delightful memory of Miss Clemens's flustered response to his state of undress the night before.

He grinned as he recalled the shock in her eyes when she'd realized he was naked beneath the blanket. Her entire face had turned red. But there had been interest too, a flare of curiosity she'd valiantly tried to hide by affecting a serious tone.

Ah, but he longed to discover the depth of her passion, to be the man who stoked her desire. But then he'd have to marry her because that was what she deserved. So he had to ask himself if he were really prepared for that. Did he know her well enough? She certainly didn't know him, and if she ever did, would she accept him for who he was?

He had no answers but he knew one thing: His parents had married for practical reasons, for duty and convenience, and they'd been mostly estranged from each other. Caleb didn't want that for himself. When he married, *if* he married, he wanted it to be to a woman who would be his friend, companion, and lover.

An image of Miss Clemens stole into his mind, and he immediately stood, eager to get on with the day, assess the damage the storm had caused, and perhaps catch a glimpse of the woman who'd somehow managed to possess his every thought.

When he discovered she'd not yet risen, he went outside to check on his horse. Apollo whinnied when he saw him approach and greedily accepted the carrots Caleb offered. Untying Apollo, he led him to a grassy patch so the horse could enjoy a good breakfast while Caleb inspected potential damage to the house.

To his relief, it was minimal. A couple of tiles had blown off the roof, but he'd been planning to remove them anyway. And a shutter had been torn off its hinges. Caleb found it some distance away on the ground and with both of its hinges missing.

By the time he finished fixing it, he learned that Miss Clemens had risen, eaten her breakfast, and gone for a walk. Since she'd not come to greet him, he could only surmise that she wished to avoid him right now.

"I need to ride into the village," he told Miss Howard, who was giving the children handwriting lessons. "Is there anything you need?"

"Not really. The butcher will be stopping by tomorrow with our weekly supplies, but Miss Clemens does enjoy the strawberry tarts from Wilson's Bakery. If you were to purchase one for her, I believe she'd be very grateful."

Caleb grinned on account of the woman's transparency and promised to keep that in mind. But he'd have to be careful how he went about the purchase since offering gifts to a woman was not deemed appropriate unless it constituted flowers. And even then it would be assumed that intentions were being announced.

In the end, he solved the problem by buying strawberry tarts for everyone even if it did seem like an extravagant gesture for a mere laborer, but he wanted to please the children as well, just as much as Miss Clemens in fact, which was something of a curious thought.

Carrying the box of pastries with him, he visited the tailor next. With only four days until Mr. Townsend's blasted dinner, he had to put in an order for a proper pair of trousers with shirt, vest and jacket to match.

"I'll take this charcoal-colored wool," he told the tailor, deliberately selecting a fabric that wasn't too costly or cheap. "And this black satin for the lining."

"That will be twenty pounds, sir," the tailor said after taking Caleb's measurements.

Caleb promptly produced the necessary sum. "It's a good thing I just got paid then, isn't it," he said to avoid any gossip about a laborer with enough blunt to splurge on a brand new outfit. That was the last thing he needed if he wanted to maintain anonymity. Which he did since the alternative was to have the world intrude upon his privacy with the exact same problems he'd come here to escape.

The strawberry tarts were well received by everyone. Caleb laughed at the sight of the children's eyes as they took in the treats and at their custard-covered mouths once they'd each had a bite. Miss Clemens, he noted, smiled with pleasure as she consumed her tart as if it were the most delicious thing she'd ever tasted.

"I also like going for long leisurely walks," he told her later that day when he found her alone in the garden. She was adding fir branches around the base of the rosebushes next to the house in preparation for winter. Hearing him, she looked up from her crouched position, her expression slightly tense as if she weren't sure whether to stay where she was or run. "Being out in the middle of nature comforts my soul."

"Why are you telling me this?" she quietly asked.

"Because you inquired about my interests, and I only mentioned history. But I enjoy a variety of different things, like chess and whist, provided I have a decent opponent, gothic novels, especially those written by Ann Radcliffe, and gardening to some extent. In France I had a small vegetable and herb box outside my kitchen door. I used to love taking care of the plants and watching them grow."

"Forgive me," she said as she straightened herself and peered up at him, "but did you just say that your interests include Ann Radcliffe?"

"I'm a complex man, Miss Clemens," he said with a shrug.

He added a smile and she laughed as expected, her entire face glowing with unrestrained humor.

"Indeed it would seem that you are," she said. "How very unexpected."

"Because I'm a man?"

"Well...yes...I suppose so, though I hate to admit it. After all, Mrs. Radcliffe's novels are romantic in nature, and her female characters do tend to dominate her stories, taking on the primary roles traditionally held by male characters."

"Yes. But I enjoy her novels because of the psychological suspense, the supernatural elements, and fast-paced action. She's an excellent author. My only regret is the limited number of novels she's written, for I have read them all numerous times."

She bit her lip and hesitated briefly before saying, "I must confess I rather enjoyed *The Mysteries of Udolpho.* That castle gave me chills and had me looking over my shoulder a few times while reading."

Caleb grinned. "I know. There's the bolted door that somehow opens in the middle of the night, strange voices, and even a ghostly apparition. I couldn't put the book down the first time I read it."

"There are similar elements in *Northanger Abbey.*"

"Yes, but that novel focuses more heavily on the romantic relationship between the main characters while the mystery hovers in the background." He pondered that statement for a second. "What I love about Ann Radcliffe is the balance between the two. I never really felt as though I was reading a romance novel. It was more of an adventure story for me."

"I hope you won't take offence to this, but I'm surprised by how well-read you are. Books aren't cheap, and well…you didn't go to university so—"

"Why would you think that?"

She stared at him, and he knew he'd said too much, but he didn't want her forming inaccurate opinions about his level of intellect. More importantly, he wanted her to view him as her social equal.

"I…er…I confess your choice of profession led me to believe you hadn't completed any higher levels of education." Her embarrassment was clear in the tiny frown puckering the skin between her eyebrows and the way she pressed her lips together.

Leaning in, he inhaled the sweet scent of rosewater clinging to her skin. "People are often more than they appear on the surface, Miss Clemens. Also, one doesn't have to have attended university in order to be well read, but I do happen to have done so for a couple of years. I studied architecture, as a matter of fact."

She gaped at him. "But that must have cost your family a fortune!"

"It did." He leaned back so he could study her face more easily. She was clearly having trouble understanding who he was and where he belonged in the world. "You've made a lot of assumptions. For one, you immediately believed I was poor because I choose to work with my hands outside in all manner of weather. But don't forget, Viscount Aldridge is my friend."

He was treading dangerously close to the truth right now, and although he was tempted to confess it, he also knew doing so would make her loathe him. Which was something he wasn't prepared to allow. Not when he enjoyed her company as much as he did. And not when he had no duty toward her beyond the bounds of friendship.

If he kissed her however…

His gaze dropped to her lips, and he drew a shuddering breath. If he surrendered to *that* temptation, he'd have to tell her everything. That sort of intimacy demanded the truth. Which was yet another reason to keep some distance between them.

"Are you saying you're gentry?"

"I'm not saying anything at all, Miss Clemens, besides the fact that there's more to me than meets the eye. Which is also true about you. Tell me, what are your interests, besides the children you care for and your friendships with Lady Cassandra and Miss Howard?" Crouching down, he grabbed some fir from a nearby pile and proceeded to place it as he'd seen her do.

She joined him momentarily and together they worked for a number of seconds before she said, "I enjoy nature walks for the same reason you mentioned earlier. But I prefer Miss Austen's works to Mrs. Radcliffe's, and as far as her works go, I favor *Pride and Prejudice*."

"I haven't read that novel," Caleb said while patting down the fir around the base of one rosebush. "But if it is your favorite, I shall have to give it a try." He glanced across at her and was briefly distracted by the loose tendrils of hair brushing her cheek. His fingers itched to tuck them behind her ear and savor the brief contact such intimacy would afford. He cleared his throat. "If you have a copy, I'd like to borrow it if I may."

She darted a look in his direction and suddenly smiled. "Of course, Mr. Crawford, though I must warn you that it is a very romantic read. It will not satisfy your appetite for the ghoulish."

"Is there at least some amusing dialogue?"

"Certainly there is. Miss Austen wrote with both intelligence and wit. Her stories also have the most wonderful endings, oftentimes with some poor impoverished woman marrying the wealthy man she never thought she could have."

Caleb could see why such stories would appeal to Miss Clemens. They provided her with the happily-ever-after she herself had been denied. Placing the final piece of fir in the flowerbed, Caleb stood and brushed off his hands before offering Miss Clemens his hand. She accepted it and he pulled her up, ever conscious of her cool palm resting securely against his much warmer one.

"I should be finished with the roof by the end of the week," he said, still holding her hand. "Once that is done, I'll replace the rotted planks in the attic."

"How long do you expect that to take?"

He swallowed and tightened his hold on her hand. "Another couple of weeks, I should think."

"And then you'll be gone." She dipped her head, refusing to meet his gaze, but her voice cracked on the last two words, and his heart broke in response.

Without even thinking, he pulled her into his arms and held her to him. "I have to," he said. "But that doesn't mean we won't see each other again."

"Of course," she murmured against his chest.

Her warm breath whispered through him, and closing his eyes, he pressed his lips to the top of her head. He was a duke and she was a woman who hated nobility. So what future could they possibly have together when she would refuse any offer he made? And she'd do so in anger, with the pain of knowing he'd deceived her – something he never would have done if he'd known from the start how fond he'd become of her. But it was too late now. He'd led her to believe he was just an ordinary man, and he'd done so for weeks.

What a fool he was. What a bloody fool.

A shiver went through Miss Clemens, and for one blessed second, she drew him closer. But then she relaxed her hold and withdrew from his arms. "I should go," she said without meeting his gaze.

"Miss Clemens…" He reached for her, but she was already out of his grasp, and then she was gone, back into the house where safety awaited.

"Perhaps you should give Mr. Townsend more of a chance," Mr. Crawford told her a few days later on their way to Townsend's farm for dinner. Seated on Apollo, Mary rode while he walked alongside the horse, guiding him by the reins.

They'd barely spoken since their embrace in the garden, not only because Mr. Crawford had applied himself laboriously to his work but because she'd been unable to face him. Already, she'd been trying to keep a distance after seeing him partially undressed the evening of the storm.

But the embrace had undone her in ways she could not begin to explain. It had awoken something far more potent than desire – something frighteningly close to love. And since he was obviously set on avoiding an attachment with her and determined to leave once his work had been completed, she made an effort to avoid forming deeper emotional ties. Already, the inevitable heartache she'd suffer upon his departure had put her in a dismal mood. And now he wanted her to consider Mr. Townsend? It was too preposterous for words.

"No," she said simply.

"I will agree that he is easily piqued, but I believe that is only because he felt threatened by me, for which you must not blame him since I was not exactly welcoming."

"He insulted you, Mr. Crawford."

"Agreed. But he does seem to hold you in the highest regard." He looked up at her with blue forget-me-not eyes. "My point is, I think he would treat you well."

"Is that the only reason why one should marry? To be treated well?" She tilted her head and raised a brow, daring him to answer in the affirmative.

"Of course not," he said with a sigh. "But it is a start, and he's not exactly bad looking either. On the contrary, I dare say many women would find him attractive."

"A pity I am not one of them," she said with a flat clip to her voice. This really wasn't the sort of conversation she wanted to have with the man who'd won her heart. "Drop the issue, Mr. Crawford. Mr. Townsend's pursuit of me is utterly pointless, and he will come to realize this in due course."

"Then you will never marry?"

Mary trained her gaze on the horizon and gripped Apollo's mane between her two clenched fists. She was suddenly ready to jump off the horse and punch Mr. Crawford as hard as she could muster. Why was he doing this to her? Surely he must have some inkling of her feelings for him? Or did he always flirt with women this way, leading them on only to leave them aching for him in ways from which they would never recover? For a second she imagined a long line of heartbroken women in his wake, each praying for his return while he simply moved on to the next.

Not that there was anything to indicate such a flaw in his character, but because of her own horrid experiences, it was hard for her to control her overeager imagination.

She gritted her teeth. "Probably not," she said in answer to his question. "I will not marry a man I do not care for. Not when I no longer need to do so. And since no other offers are forthcoming," she added, unable to keep her bitterness at bay, "I believe I shall continue to live with Miss Howard and Lady Cassandra for the remainder of my days. I'd certainly rather grow old with them than with some husband I cannot abide."

"Poor Mr. Townsend." When she didn't reply, he said, "He has in the course of one short minute regressed from a man you do not care for to one you cannot abide. Are you certain you would not rather return home instead of enduring an evening that's bound to be taxing on your already strained nerves?"

"My nerves are not strained, Mr. Crawford."

"Then perhaps you'd be kind enough to loosen your grip on Apollo? He's a gentle creature and quite underserving of the pain the pique you are in this evening is likely causing."

Mary expelled a long breath and tried to relax. "I'm sorry. My agitation is caused by what I must tell Mr. Townsend. I do not relish having to inform him there is no future for us."

"Would you rather I tell him?"

Unable to help herself, she laughed at the very idea. "No. That would be terrible."

He grinned at her, and her heart melted more easily than she would have liked. "You're right. He will only believe it if you tell him. But do it after dessert when he's had lots of wine with his meal. It will help lessen the blow."

She shook her head. A smile lingered about her lips. "You are incorrigible, Mr. Crawford. Do you know that?"

"I believe it may have been mentioned once or twice."

They arrived at their destination, and Mr. Crawford reached up to help Mary down. His hands settled solidly against her waist before he lifted her off Apollo. Steadying herself, her hand found his shoulder. Her fingers curled against the muscle, and then she was being pulled toward him, sliding down the front of his body so slowly she could not ignore the solid planes pressing firmly against her own body.

Her feet found the ground, and she swayed, her head too light and her legs too weak to keep her balance. "Stop." She spoke the word softly but firmly even as he kept his hands on her for added support. "I cannot bear it any longer."

Carefully, he eased her away and offered his arm. She stared at it for a second and then shook her head. "Let's not make matters worse for Mr. Townsend by suggesting something that never has been and never will be."

"Miss Clemens, I—"

"No," she told him determinedly. "I am not a toy for you to play with. I am a person with feelings, and you are coming perilously close to hurting them. I will not have it." And with that declaration she marched toward the front door and knocked as hard as she could.

It swung opened almost immediately to reveal Mr. Townsend himself. He smiled broadly at her and welcomed her into his home, ignoring Mr. Crawford's presence in the process. It wasn't until they were shown into the parlor where Mr. Townsend's sister, Miss Frederica Townsend, awaited and introductions had to be made that he bothered to look in Mr. Crawford's direction at all.

Regardless of her own irritation with the man at the moment, Mary could not abide the rudeness. She accepted a glass of claret and took a seat on the sofa next to Miss Townsend.

"My brother has told me nothing but wonderful things about you, Miss Clemens," Miss Townsend said. "He says you run an orphanage no more than a mile from here."

Mary watched Mr. Crawford walk to the fireplace and take up a non-inclusive position there before she glanced at Mr. Townsend who'd seated himself in an armchair directly opposite her. "I wouldn't really call it an orphanage, Miss Townsend. It is a home I share with my friends, Viscount Aldridge's sister, Lady Cassandra Moor; Miss Emily Howard; and the children we've taken into our care."

"How charitable of you," Miss Townsend said.

"I told you she's got a heart of gold," Mr. Townsend said, his eyes fixed on Mary.

Discomfited by the attention, Mary shifted in her seat. "It was actually Lady Cassandra's idea we do so. Considering her daughter's lack of a father, she sympathizes with children who have lost their parents."

Mr. Townsend frowned. "But her daughter's a bastard, is she not?"

A disgruntled snort could be heard from the vicinity of the fireplace.

Mary clenched her jaw. "Your point?"

"Only that Lady Cassandra's daughter lacks a father for a reason," Mr. Townsend said. "While I appreciate Lady Cassandra's kindness toward others, she is a sinful woman who was too easily lured into temptation by the devil himself."

Mary gaped at Mr. Townsend. In all the discussions they'd had, he'd never given her reason to believe that his beliefs would be so strict and so… so…impossible for her to align herself with.

"Our father always warned us of such failings of the human flesh," Miss Townsend muttered.

"I trust he was a very devout man?" Mary asked, forcing the words out past the dryness in her throat.

"He was a vicar," Mr. Townsend said.

Another snort from the fireplace had Mary glancing in Mr. Crawford's direction. "That is what my father wanted for me," he said. "I told him to go to hell and thank God for that."

Miss Townsend gasped while Mr. Townsend glared at Mr. Crawford. "I'll remind you to watch your tongue sir. There are women present."

"Yes, of course," Mr. Crawford muttered. A smirk curled his lips, only easing marginally when he met Mary's gaze. He raised his glass in salute and winked before taking a sip, returning his attention back to the fire.

"I do not believe you ever mentioned your father's vocation before," Mary said for want of anything else.

"It never occurred to me to do so," Mr. Townsend said. "After all, I am the one vying for your hand, Miss Clemens. Not my father."

If his intentions had been dubious before, they were now abundantly clear. Mary steeled herself in preparation for what she intended to say, but then the door opened and a maid announced that dinner was ready.

"Allow me to escort you," Mr. Townsend said, offering Mary his arm.

She wanted to decline, but that would be rude. So she set her hand upon his forearm and gave Mr. Crawford a helpless look. His expression was firm, completely lacking all manner of emotion. Turning away, he offered his arm to Miss Townsend, who accepted with a bright smile that Mary instantly detested.

A tug on her arm pulled her attention back to the man by her side. "You look lovely by the way," he murmured. "Quite healthy."

Of all the compliments in the world…Mary sighed and resigned herself to what promised to be the worst evening of her life. When they reached the dining room, Mr. Townsend helped her into her seat before claiming the chair directly beside her. Mr. Crawford and Miss Townsend would sit across from them with a large floral arrangement placed squarely between them.

"May I offer you some beef?" Mr. Townsend inquired after filling Mary's wine glass to the brim. He held an oval serving dish toward her.

"Thank you," she took a small piece, her appetite lost somewhere between the front door and the parlor.

"I understand you're a laborer, Mr. Crawford," Miss Townsend said once the meal was underway.

"He is more than that," Mary said, unable to stop from refuting Mr. Townsend's ill opinion of one of the most incredible men she'd ever had the pleasure of knowing.

"In what sense?" Mr. Townsend asked with an unmistakable edge to his voice. "He mends houses, does he not? That is, as far as I have been able to surmise, the extent of his skill."

Mary bristled. "You are wrong, Mr. Townsend. Indeed, Mr. Crawford…" She paused when she noted the slight shake of Mr. Crawford's head. He wanted her to keep quiet about his achievements, which made no sense at all, but she would respect his wishes, so she reached for something else to say and eventually settled on, "he made fishing rods for the boys and in so doing has made them both incredibly happy. Peter, the eldest boy and the most recent arrival in our home, struggled with social interaction for a long time until Mr. Crawford managed to pull him out of himself."

"Pull him out of himself?" Mr. Townsend chuckled as did his sister. "Sounds rather peculiar."

"It is the only way I can think to describe it," Mary said.

"The boy had an inward perspective which kept him apart from everyone else," Mr. Crawford said.

Mary met his gaze somewhere over the top of a large pink flower. He understood and that knowledge alone increased her fondness for him. But to what avail? She returned her attention to her plate and ate a few more bites of food. It was actually quite delicious.

She especially liked the caramelized carrots and was just biting into one when Miss Townsend said, "It must be such a relief for you to receive my brother's attentions after being absent from Society for as long as you have been, Miss Clemens. I suspect you must have lost hope on that front, yet here you are, the subject of every conversation he and I have shared since my arrival."

Mary stared across at the young woman who'd seemed so harmless at first sight. She was definitely a few years younger than Mary, which meant she herself would be seeking a husband at present. "Relief is not exactly the word I would use," Mary told her carefully. Whether Miss Townsend was being deliberately cruel or she was utterly clueless about appropriate conversation subjects had yet to be determined.

But then she smiled at Mr. Crawford as if no one else was in the room. Holding the expression, she turned her gaze on Mary, and although her eyes were warm, the words she spoke fell with every intention of causing pain. "While in London, I made some inquiries about the woman my brother had written to me about. I was staying with a family friend there during the Season, you see, and when I mentioned your name, Miss Clemens, there was almost no end to the news about you."

"Please stop," Mary said, since they were the only words screaming inside her head. She had no interest in revisiting her awful past with Mr. Townsend and his jealous sister as her guide.

But of course an end was too much to hope for when Mr. Townsend raised his glass and said, "You may rest assured that I do not blame you for what transpired. Indeed, I believe my sister's investigative skills may be able to clear your name."

"Many people told me that the rumors about you were fabricated nonsense put about by a man who thought you unworthy of his son." Miss Townsend looked at everyone in turn as if she believed herself to be the most fascinating person in the world. "And in all fairness, even you must admit that aspiring to marry a peer was a bit of a stretch."

"My family is one of the wealthiest families in England, Miss Townsend," Mary seethed. "At the time, it did not seem unlikely at all!"

"Be that as it may, my dear," Mr. Townsend said in a sickeningly soothing tone, "You are not titled, which pretty much excluded you from the running right from the start, though I dare say it did not prevent the blighter from stealing a kiss here and there."

"If you ask me, he was a fool for not marrying her," Mr. Crawford announced with a level tone that instantly brought Mary's gaze back to him. He was watching her closely and with so much sympathy she felt like crying.

"His father wouldn't have it," Miss Townsend said.

"Nevertheless," Mr. Crawford murmured. "He should have married her anyway."

Confused by the underlying suggestiveness of his words and distraught by Miss Townsend's relentless pursuit of the subject at hand, Mary stood. Remaining seated and keeping calm had become completely impossible.

"You may take some comfort in knowing they're dead now," Miss Townsend added.

"What?" Mary couldn't even begin to unravel the inappropriateness of such a callous statement. And yet she had to know, "Who is dead?"

"The Duke of Camberly and his son. Both perished earlier in the year."

Losing all strength in her legs, Mary sank back into her seat and slumped against the backrest. Lips parted in stunned disbelief, she stared across at Miss Townsend's bland expression before shifting her gaze to Mr. Crawford, whose eyes now conveyed confounded horror.

CHAPTER EIGHT

G EORGE.
His own bloody brother!

He was the idiot who'd spurned Miss Clemens after leading her on.

Caleb clasped his wine glass and tried to breathe. Not an easy task after learning the woman he wanted would not only hate him for lying to her, despise him for belonging to a set she abhorred, but also loath him for being related to the man who'd cast her aside five years earlier, shattering her heart and sullying her name in the process.

Of all the men in the entire world...

"Are you all right, Mr. Crawford?" Miss Townsend asked. "You look a bit pale."

"Do I?" Surely Miss Clemens looked worse with her vacant stare and trembling lips. If only he could reach out and offer her comfort. But there was a table between them, set with porcelain and crystal, and even if there weren't, what right did he have? He'd promised her nothing. Rather, he'd fought to resist her even as he shamelessly flirted with her, encouraging her to hope.

She was right to demand he stop. He ought to

have left her alone from the start. Except doing so had been impossible, hadn't it? She'd tempted him just as easily as she must have tempted George.

Christ, what a mess!

It was only made worse by the sharp blade of envy slicing away at his heart. For while he hadn't even kissed her yet, George had. He'd known what Miss Clemens's lips felt like beneath his own, what her mouth tasted like and the sounds of pleasure she'd made while enjoying such an intimate embrace.

His grip on the wine glass tightened until a splintering sound pierced the air. Miss Clemens and Miss Townsend both gasped. Caleb stared down at the bleeding palm of his hand, now adorned by shimmering shards of crystal.

A napkin was thrust toward him by Mr. Townsend. "I fear you've upset our guests, Frederica." He dropped the napkin in front of Caleb and turned to Miss Clemens. "Perhaps a cup of tea will restore your nerves?"

"My nerves?" She sounded incredulous and rightfully so. Apparently Mr. Townsend had no common sense at all if he supposed her nerves were the issue.

"Well, yes. You are clearly distraught."

Caleb groaned and proceeded to pull the sharp little pieces of crystal from his hand.

"Of course I'm distraught," Miss Clemens said. "To be anything else after learning that a man with whom I was once well acquainted has recently died would be inhuman, sir." She glared at Mr. Townsend before pinning her gaze on his sister. "And you, to speak of the matter and my indiscretion with so little sympathy is galling."

"Miss Clemens," Mr. Townsend said with a note of warning. "I would ask you to speak to my sister with respect. After all, you and I are to be—"

"What?" Miss Clemens's eyes were blazing now. Mr. Townsend leaned away from her as if deeming her unpredictable. "Married? You have not asked me to be your wife, and yet you assume that I will be even though you and I would make a terrible match."

"Surely you jest," Mr. Townsend declared. "The shock you sustained just now has addled your brain."

"Indeed it has not," Miss Clemens insisted. "If anything, coming here this evening has only strengthened my resolve. I will not attach myself to a man who looks down his nose at others and insults my friends."

"Miss Clemens—"

"No, Mr. Townsend. The answer is no."

Caleb wanted to cheer in response to her brazen bluntness. Instead, he winced as he pressed the napkin Mr. Townsend had given him to his wounds, blotting at the pebbling blood.

"The nerve," Miss Townsend said, earning a withering glare from Miss Clemens.

"Indeed," she muttered, prompting Caleb to smile even as he wondered if Miss Townsend and her brother had registered the subtle barb. "If you would be kind enough to escort me, I would like to return home now, Mr. Crawford."

He immediately straightened in his seat and rose. "Of course, Miss Clemens. I would be delighted."

He followed that statement with a swift half-hearted farewell to his hosts, who remained at the table, most likely too stunned to stand, while he escorted Miss Clemens out of the house.

"Good grief," she said when she was back on Apollo and heading for home. "What awful people."

"At least you got to see the real Mr. Townsend," Caleb said.

"It astounds me to think how badly I have misjudged him." She made a wretched sound. "My parents told me I was naive to think a marquess would want to marry me. I insisted they were wrong, but apparently I do have a tendency to think the best of people. Even when they don't deserve it."

"How could you know what either of these men was truly like before they chose to show you?" Guilt spliced its way through him because he knew he was just another case of what Miss Clemens described: a charlatan taking advantage of her goodwill. But at least if he could make her feel better, then some good would come from the mess he'd created. "Did Lady Cassandra or Miss Howard ever tell you Mr. Townsend was unworthy of your friendship?"

"No. They were actually in favor of him courting me even though I made it clear to them I wasn't interested."

"You see? Everyone was seduced by his charisma. Even I must admit that I never expected him to be quite so insulting. In hindsight, however, the comments he threw my way during his visit last week should have given some indication."

They walked on in silence while dusk turned

to night. Overhead, a blanket of stars glittered like an endless collection of diamonds haphazardly strewn out on navy-blue velvet. The moon, a luminescent disc in the sky, glowed bright across the crisp autumn landscape. Winter would likely sneak up behind them and when it did, the house would have to be ready to withstand the cold.

"Thank you," Miss Clemens said, startling him slightly.

He'd been so busy making a mental list of what remained to be done he'd forgotten he was trying to navigate a dark dirt road while leading a horse along with him.

"For what?" he asked

"For making me feel better."

"It is the least I can do," he murmured.

"You're a true friend," she said, adding to his guilt. "I'll be sorry to see you go. As will everyone else. The children have all taken such a liking to you. Is there really nothing we can do to convince you to stay?"

His heart ached with the longing to simply abandon his duty forever and live out the rest of his days in a house with three spinsters and five lively children. And if George were still alive, he might have been able to do so. But fate had put a limit on his options.

"My mother needs me, Miss Clemens." *The dukedom needs me, Parliament needs me, my estates, servants, and tenants all need me.* "As it is, I fear I've been gone too long."

"I understand."

Apollo clopped toward the garden gate of her home, and Caleb leaned over the side to unlatch it. Once inside, he led the horse back to his spot beside the cottage and helped Miss Clemens dismount. Remembering her earlier request to stop flirting with her, he made a deliberate effort to minimize their contact and stepped away quickly, as soon as she was on the ground.

"Allow me to walk you to the door." Light from behind the kitchen window served as a guide.

"Would you like to come in for a cup of tea or a glass of port?" she asked. Reaching the door, she stopped to look up at him, and in spite of the darkness, expectation and hope were visible in the depths of her eyes.

"Perhaps another time, Miss Clemens." He saw the disappointment before she looked away. "It has been a trying evening, so I think I'd prefer to retire early and get some rest."

"Yes. Of course." She opened the door, paused for a second, and swung back toward him. Before he was able to determine her purpose, she placed a swift kiss on his cheek. "Thank you once again, Mr. Crawford." Her words were soft, whispering across his skin in the sweetest caress. And then she was gone, back into her house, leaving Caleb more alone than he'd ever felt before in his life.

He stood there for long moments after, paralyzed by Miss Clemens's innocent show of affection. Pressing his hand to his cheek, he imagined still feeling her lips, warm against his skin. When he finally managed to move, it was with an urgency he could not explain. He had to get back to the cottage before he did something foolish, like tear the kitchen door off its hinges in order to have her.

Miss Clemens with her golden hair, inquisitive gaze, and boldness had lit a fire inside him that could not be quenched. It strained his nerves and threatened his temper, resulting in nothing but pure frustration. And her chaste little kiss only made it worse. *Damn!* It had quickened his pulse and hardened his muscles in ways that could not be healthy.

Yanking the door to his cottage open, he strode inside, located the tinderbox, and lit an oil lamp to light the small room. Breathing hard, he leaned against the wall and struggled to gain some measure of control. Blood thrummed through his veins, and his mind played tricks on his senses, conjuring images of what could be if they'd both just surrender to their desires. He'd have her out of her gown in a trice, naked on the bed and with her hair fanned out accross the pillow.

And then he'd taste her. Every inch of her perfect body.

Yes, that was what he wanted. Something no other man could claim to have had with her. Something that would only ever be his. Groaning, he snuffed out the light and collapsed on the bed fully clothed, anxious for sleep to claim him.

"There's a dance at the assembly hall on Saturday," Cassandra announced a few days later at breakfast. "I'd love for us to attend."

She'd always enjoyed dancing and socializing, but there had been little time for it in recent years with the children to look after, since it did require getting someone to watch them for a few hours. The village teacher, Mrs. Durham, and her husband had helped with this a few times before. In exchange, they'd received ten pounds, so it went without saying that it was a luxury the three women couldn't afford too regularly.

"It has been a while since the last time we went out to such an event," Cassandra said. "And just imagine how thrilled all the ladies will be if we bring Mr. Crawford with us. I daresay most will swoon at the very sight of him. Don't you agree, Mary?"

Mary licked a bit of jam off her fingers and tried not to cringe at the idea of every woman within a five-mile radius competing for Mr. Crawford's attention. "He may not know how to dance," she said, but as she did so, she knew he probably did. After all, he had a talent for surprising and impressing her in the most unexpected ways.

"A man who climbs about on a roof as nimbly as he does is bound to possess some skill on the dance floor," Emily said with a meaningful look directed at Mary.

When she'd returned from dinner with the Townsends on Friday, she'd told Cassandra and Emily everything. They'd both been just as appalled by Mr. Townsend's and his sister's behaviors as she was, but of far greater interest to them had been the kiss she'd given Mr. Crawford. Both had questioned her about it relentlessly, drawing all manner of conclusions and insisting she must be in love with him already.

She'd denied it and claimed that the kiss was intended as nothing more than friendly appreciation. Which was nonsense, of course. She'd been meaning to kiss him properly, but had lost her nerve on her way to his mouth and had consequently settled on his cheek instead.

"I have to go to the village today to buy some more flour and milk," Emily said. "I'll stop by the school while I'm there and ask Mrs. Durham if she and her husband are free to watch the children on Saturday."

"What's happening on Saturday?" Mr. Crawford asked in a low tone as he entered the room.

His voice sent ripples of awareness through Mary's body and filled her head with the memory of him after she'd kissed him, staring back at her as if he wished to shove everything between them aside and pull her into his arms. But then he'd returned to his cottage, snuffed out the light and gone to bed, and she'd done the same. Disquieted by a peculiar state of unrest, she'd found sleep eluded her every night since. Exhausted, she would drift off hours later and be up once again at dawn.

"There's a dance at the assembly hall," Emily said while Mary stifled a yawn. "We hope to attend."

"Sounds like fun," Mr. Crawford said. He pulled out a chair next to Peter and poured himself a cup of tea. Smiling brightly, he grabbed some toast and started buttering it while humming a merry tune.

He'd adopted this cheerful demeanor for the past three days. Since Saturday morning, to be exact. And just like on each of those days, Cassandra and Emily both raised their eyebrows while looking at Mary. Clearly, they thought this was all due to the kiss she'd given him, but that couldn't possibly be true because he'd grown even more distant than usual since then, addressing her only when absolutely necessary. For the most part, he worked, ate his meals, and retired to the cottage without staying for story time after dinner or even to enjoy a glass of port once the children were put to bed, as he had done before.

Which had to mean that he feared she wanted an attachment, and this was his way of telling her he wasn't interested. She accepted that, because she had to. What she did not like was how much she missed his company. Chatting with him had become the best part of her day. She'd cherished each conversation, even though they'd brought her closer to heartbreak.

"You must join us," Cassandra said. She leaned forward, folding her arms on the table. "Do you dance by any chance?"

Mary coughed and took a quick sip of her tea.

"On occasion," Mr. Crawford said slowly. "Depends who I'll be partnering with."

"Ho! What a fine answer that is," Emily hooted. "Will I do for the reel?"

Mr. Crawford grinned. "It would be an honor, Miss Howard."

They finished their breakfast without Mr. Crawford agreeing to dance with anyone else, and Mary tried not to feel overlooked. A difficult task now that her emotions were fully engaged. And the fact that he chose not to sit directly beside her and continued to avoid being alone with her in the days that followed only made her feel worse.

It was as if she were suffering the same kind of heartache she'd felt five years earlier, except this time she'd nowhere to run – no way of avoiding the man who'd stolen her heart.

CHAPTER NINE

SATURDAY ARRIVED WITH THE FIRST breath of winter. Waking, Mary felt the chill sweep through her the moment she stepped out of bed. Dressing quickly, she hurried downstairs and opened the kitchen door, almost colliding with Mr. Crawford, who stood poised to enter.

"Good morning," she muttered, her breath swirling toward him like mist on the moors.

"Miss Clemens," he said and dipped his head by way of greeting. "What a pleasant surprise."

"Is it?" she asked, unable to hide the pain stealing through her. Setting her mouth, she pushed her way past him and marched toward the pile of firewood kept in a small covered enclosure.

"Of course," he said, sounding surprised. "Why wouldn't it be?"

She grabbed three pieces of wood and hefted them into her arms. "You have been ignoring me." Plain words that could not be misunderstood.

"Have I?"

She blew out a breath, muttered an oath, and started back toward the house, not caring at all if he followed. Entering the kitchen, she set the wood down, filled the kettle with water and proceeded to ready the fire, ignoring the presence she sensed looming somewhere nearby. She absolutely refused to look at him.

"I have clearly upset you," he said, following her into the dining room. When she crouched in front of the fireplace and reached for a log, he stalled her by placing his hand over hers. "That was not my intention, Miss Clemens."

In spite of the hot little embers now sneaking their way up her arm, Mary knew she had to be strong for her own sake. She could not give in just because he filled her with longing. "Then what was it?" she asked.

The edge of his mouth lifted, affording him with a roguish smile. Mary swallowed, refusing to let it affect her, even though it was far too late for that. Her traitorous body already hummed in response to his nearness, calling for him to…to do something besides simply touch her hand.

"It was the only way I could think to resist you after you kissed me." His eyes glittered somehow while his thumb began drawing lazy circles on her skin.

"It was just on the cheek," she whispered.

A gruff sound rose from his throat. "Nevertheless. You should know how I feel since I've told you as plainly as I know how."

I want you too. But ruining you would be a crime, Miss Clemens, so I fear I must refrain.

The words he'd spoken two weeks earlier echoed in her head. She hadn't forgotten, but she'd thought he might have lost interest.

"But that kiss…" he continued. "It tore at every restraint with incredible force. So if I've added distance between us, that is why. Not because I do not want you, but because I want you too damn much."

He stood, gave a curt nod, and strode from the room as if somehow unable to stay and face her for one more second. Trembling, Mary placed the log in the fireplace and watched it ignite as she lit the kindling. Staring into the flames, she allowed a new question to press on her mind: what if you simply surrender?

For the rest of the day, Mary listened to Mr. Crawford banging away in the attic as he removed rotted planks of wood and carried them from the house. He'd completed his work on the roof, so all that remained was for him to fix the attic floor, his presence never forgotten because of all the loud noises he made while he worked.

It was oddly soothing, Mary decided, and strangely unsettling once it ceased. Glancing at the clock she saw it was almost five. They would eat dinner soon, then the Durhams would arrive. Mr. Crawford had probably stopped work for the day so he could freshen up and prepare himself for their evening out. Cassandra and Emily were both in the process of doing so, and she really ought to follow suit if she was to be ready on time.

"You should wear your white muslin gown," Cassandra said. She'd entered her bedchamber while Mary stood by her wardrobe, considering her limited selection of clothes.

"It is too cold for that," she said, eyeing one of the few things she'd taken with her when she'd left London. It was exquisite, too fine for a mere village dance, but also tempting because of the man who would see her wear it.

"You have a cloak," Cassandra said. Mary toyed with the fabric, torn between practicality and looking her best. "If he sees you like that, he'll never forget you, Mary."

There was no point in asking whom she was talking about. They both knew. "I want him so much it hurts," she confessed.

"Then conquer your fear."

Mary sighed. "It is not that simple. He doesn't want to give in to temptation. I...I do not know why, but he is determined to avoid an attachment with me at all cost, Cass." She glanced at her friend, completely unsure of how to proceed. "He doesn't want marriage. That much is certain."

"Is that what you want?" When Mary didn't answer, Cassandra moved closer to her and quietly asked, "Do you love him, Mary?"

Mary blinked. "I do not know. Maybe."

"And you don't think he feels the same?"

She shook her head. "I am certain he does not."

"I think you're wrong," Cassandra said. "The way he looks at you suggests he cares for you deeply."

"Then why not tell me?" Mary asked.

Cassandra chuckled and reached past Mary to retrieve the white muslin gown. "As you have told him?" Mary bit her lip in response to that pointed remark. "Perhaps he is just as afraid of doing so as you are."

"But he's leaving," Mary said. She accepted the gown Cassandra offered and held it limply between her hands.

"Have you given him a reason to stay?" Mary shook her head slowly. "Get dressed and I'll do your hair. I want Mr. Crawford to be rendered speechless the moment he sets eyes on you."

She was stunning. So stunning it took Caleb a moment to find his tongue when she entered the dining room. Dressed in layers of sheer white muslin with tiny puff sleeves and a décolletage so low it showed off more skin than it hid, Miss Clemens looked divine. Even the children took notice with Daphne likening her to a princess and the boys staring at her with the kind of wonder one felt when coming face to face with a goddess.

Stepping closer to her, Caleb offered his arm and guided her to her spot at the table. "You are a feast for the eyes, Miss Clemens," he whispered close to her ear while helping her into her seat.

She inhaled deeply, drawing his attention to the swell of her breasts which rose like delectable treats placed on daring display. Unable to resist, he brushed his knuckles across her back before removing himself to his own seat. There were children present, for Christ sake! He had to stay on his best behavior, or he'd be damned to hell for all of eternity. Which was probably what he deserved by now, all things considered.

"Will you dance with Mr. Crawford tonight?"

Penelope asked Miss Clemens after taking a bite of her food.

"If he asks," was Miss Clemens's reply. She smiled prettily at the girl before taking a sip of her wine.

"I have every intention of doing so," he said, meeting Miss Clemens's gaze. "The waltz perhaps, if at all possible."

Her cheeks colored and she lowered her lashes, giving her attention to the food on her plate. She didn't look at him for the rest of the meal, but Caleb knew with instinctual certainty that the dance they would share was at the front of her mind. It was as if every interaction they'd had with each other since his arrival, each glance, each touch, each intimate conversation, had been leading to this, pushing them forward until they collided. And they were destined to collide, no matter how hard they tried to fight it; the pull between them was simply too great.

For the past week he'd been struggling with what he'd learned during dinner with the Townsends. Discovering George had kissed Miss Clemens had been difficult to accept. But then he'd reminded himself that George hadn't cared about her. And as angry as that had made him, it had also put everything into perspective, because it meant that the kiss George had shared with Miss Clemens would never be as meaningful as the one he would share with her. And he *would* kiss her. He'd decided that much this morning when his resolve had crumbled in response to her accusation. In spite of what he'd said before, she'd somehow managed to convince herself that he didn't want her.

Well, he would prove her wrong on that score and see where that led. To a whole heap of trouble, no doubt, but he cared for her enough to be willing to take that chance now. Even if she ended up hating him for it.

They set out an hour later, walking the mile to the village with a couple of lanterns to light the way. When they arrived, it was to the sound of music and chatter spilling through the entrance to the assembly hall.

Stepping into a narrow foyer, Caleb helped Miss Clemens, Miss Howard, and Lady Cassandra remove their cloaks. He handed them over to the man in charge of the cloakroom before leading all three ladies into the large open area where a country dance was already underway. Along the periphery of the room stood clusters of people, some watching the dancing and others in deep conversation.

The tune picked up and clapping ensued, carrying the dancers along in a jaunty rhythm. Caleb grinned, liking the spirited atmosphere. "Shall we?" he asked, gesturing toward an area that wasn't too crowded yet.

With Miss Clemens on his arm, he led the way forward while Lady Cassandra and Miss Howard trailed behind. Several heads turned in their direction as they moved through the room, the interest keen and rightfully so, considering Miss Clemens's stunning appearance. She shone like a diamond tonight. Just the honor of having her on his arm was enough to make him stand taller and smile.

"Lady Cassandra, Miss Howard, and Miss Clemens," a young woman said by way of greeting after making her approach. She'd brought a friend with her and both were now staring at him expectantly. "Will you introduce us to your friend?"

"This is Mr. Crawford," Lady Cassandra said when Miss Clemens and Miss Howard both remained silent. She introduced the young women as Miss Richards and Miss Nutley.

Caleb bowed his head politely. "A pleasure," he said, causing both women to giggle in the most annoying way imaginable.

"He's so handsome," Miss Richards told Miss Clemens in a way meant to imitate a whisper without being even a little bit discreet in the process. "Wherever did you find him?"

"Oh, we didn't," Miss Clemens said without batting an eyelash. "Mr. Crawford found us."

This resulted in another round of giggles. "How delightful," Miss Nutley remarked, as if he were some oddity at a fair. Remaining civil was turning into a chore.

"Tell me, does he dance?" Miss Richards asked.

Caleb opened his mouth, prepared to remind the woman that he was right there and perfectly capable of answering her questions himself. But Miss Clemens beat him to it, her entire body leaning forward as if poised for battle, like the figurehead on the prow of a ship steering into a storm.

"I know you're both a little short sighted, ladies, and since you've obviously left your spectacles at home, I feel it my duty to inform you that Mr. Crawford is still standing right here beside me." She smiled sweetly. "You may pose your questions directly to him."

"Well," Miss Richards exclaimed.

Caleb reckoned that smoke might start rising from the top of her head any moment. Her friend didn't look much happier, but he was vastly amused by the set-down. He raised an eyebrow at the two women who stammered a little before turning away and removing themselves to the other side of the room.

"A little protective of me, Miss Clemens?" he couldn't resist asking.

She gave him a cutting look. "Hardly."

Chuckling, he gave his attention to the dance floor. The country dance had ended and a reel was beginning, so he turned to Miss Howard and bowed. "I believe this is our set." He held out his arm, and she readily took it. As he steered her away, he turned and winked toward Miss Clemens and was wonderfully pleased when he saw she was laughing.

"That was rather harsh," Cassandra said. "But very effective."

"They deserved it," Mary said, "and Mr. Crawford didn't seem to mind."

"On the contrary, he enjoyed every moment of it. And why shouldn't he when you staked your claim so vocally?"

"I did no such thing." Mary crossed her arms and groaned when she saw Mr. Townsend. He was walking toward her with purpose. She decided to be polite. "Good evening, sir."

He stopped in front of her. "Miss Clemens.

Lady Cassandra. How fortuitous it is to find you here."

"Oh?" In spite of his easy tone and warm expression, she would not forget how poorly he'd treated her and Mr. Crawford.

"I've been meaning to call but feared you would turn me away." When neither she nor Cassandra denied such a possibility, he said, "I wish to apologize and ask for your forgiveness. The things my sister and I said to you were wrong. Our conduct was both embarrassing and inexcusable."

"It really wasn't your best moment," Mary agreed. "I confess I was rather surprised to discover such a distasteful side to your character."

Mr. Townsend winced. "Yes...well..." He scratched his head and glanced about, eyes narrowing and brow furrowing as he looked toward the dance floor. "That man has a very unpleasant effect on me."

Following his line of vision, Mary saw Mr. Crawford guide Emily while executing perfect steps. "That man is my friend, Mr. Townsend." She frowned and wondered where he might have learned to dance so well. Perhaps he'd taken lessons with Viscount Aldridge as a child?

"Again, my apologies." He took a step closer. "I meant no disrespect."

"If that were true, you would choose your words with better care."

Cassandra snorted and Mr. Townsend gave her a disapproving look. "Of course," he said, attempting a smile that looked far from genuine. "I quite agree. Perhaps we can make a fresh start?"

Mary's mouth dropped open. "A fresh start?" As

if either of them could forget what had happened or that he'd proposed and she had refused.

"Give me the chance to prove myself, and I can assure you you'll marry me eventually."

"You're very optimistic," Cassandra said.

"It is the best way to be," Mr. Townsend told her.

"As long as it doesn't turn into delusion," Cassandra shot back.

Mr. Townsend glared at her and apparently decided not to counter. Instead, he returned his attention to Mary. "So what do you say, Miss Clemens?"

"I don't like your assurance, sir," Mary said.

He stared at her while Cassandra snickered. "I beg your pardon?" he asked.

"That I will eventually marry you," Mary explained. "It's a little distressing since I have no desire to do such a thing and never have."

"But surely…" Mr. Townsend shook his head and looked suddenly helpless. "Marriage is what all young women wish for. It is unnatural not to do so, and considering your age, I would have expected a bit more enthusiasm and gratitude on your part."

"Mr. Townsend." Mary honestly wasn't sure what to say to him anymore. Except, "Why do *you* wish to marry *me*? Your determination to do so at this point has me at a complete loss."

In the background, the music faded, and she could see the dancers bowing and curtseying to each other behind Mr. Townsend. He pressed his lips together, and his gaze, which had been so steady until now, filled with sudden uncertainty.

A pause followed until Mary thought he might never answer. She saw Mr. Crawford and Emily begin to leave the crowded dance floor, when Mr. Townsend decided to say, "During her time in London, my sister learned that you are more suited to be my wife than I ever would have imagined."

Mary blinked. "What on earth are you talking about?"

Mr. Townsend pressed his lips together. "Perhaps we ought to discuss this in private, Miss Clemens?"

Absolutely not. She had no intention of being alone with this man.

Calculating the time it would take Mr. Crawford and Emily to reach the spot where she stood, she told Mr. Townsend. "There is no need for that. You may speak openly in front of Lady Cassandra."

Mr. Townsend gave Cassandra a fleeting glance and cleared his throat. He paused for a moment before bluntly saying, "I am naturally referring to your dowry, Miss Clemens. Apparently, it still exists and will follow you into marriage in the event that—"

"I think I would like you to leave now," Mary clipped. Of course her dowry of ten thousand pounds was to blame for Mr. Townsend's increased attentions recently. The only problem being she had not wanted Mr. Crawford to know, because if he ever did offer for her, she wanted his decision to be made without money as the incentive. But it was too late for that now. He'd reached them faster than she'd expected and had heard every word.

"Just think of all the good we can do together with those funds," Mr. Townsend prattled on. "The farm could get a new stable, and I could even purchase that parcel of land I've—"

"Enough," Mr. Crawford cut in. "Miss Clemens has made her position clear. Please respect the lady's wishes and walk away."

Mr. Townsend turned to Mr. Crawford and looked him up and down as if assessing his opponent. "I…" he tried, but the strength had left his voice, and his dogged expression had waned.

"Go," Mr. Crawford told him. He jutted his chin in the direction of the door.

Casting one final look in Mary's direction, Mr. Townsend turned on a sigh and removed himself from their vicinity. Whether or not he left the assembly hall itself, Mary did not know, but she was glad her interaction with him was over.

"Would you like some wine?" Mr. Crawford asked.

Cassandra and Emily nodded, as did Mary. "Yes, please," Mary said.

Leaving them, Mr. Crawford went to purchase four glasses. He was barely out of sight before Miss Amanda Partridge, the youngest daughter of a landed gentleman who lived nearby, came to greet them. She was accompanied by a handsome man with tawny hair and bright blue eyes.

"I hope we're not intruding," Miss Partridge said. When Cassandra assured her they weren't, Miss Partridge gestured toward the man to her left. "This is my brother, Mr. David Partridge. I don't believe you've been introduced."

Mr. Partridge took a small step forward and

bowed. "It is an honor," he said. Straightening, his eyes sought Mary and a welcoming smile immediately followed. "When my sister told me of your kindness and dedication toward the children you've taken in," he said, slowly sliding his gaze toward Emily and Cassandra, "I was thoroughly impressed."

"My brother donates to a couple of orphanages in London," Miss Partridge said. "He's very invested."

"I'm sure the children are grateful," Mary said. Being the cynical sort, she could not stop from adding, "But in my opinion, giving money is easier than doing the actual work."

To her surprise, Mr. Partridge's smile broadened. "A woman who speaks her own mind. If you ask me, there are too few of your kind in the world. Will you do me the honor of partnering with me for the next set?"

"I..." Mary was too confounded for words.

"I think I'm going to start being more blunt," Emily said. "The men apparently love it."

"Come, Miss Clemens." Mr. Partridge offered his arm. "It looks as if the cotillion is about to begin."

Accepting his invitation for the sake of politeness, Mary allowed Mr. Partridge to lead her onto the dance floor. She'd spoken with his sister a few times over the years when their paths had crossed in the village. Miss Partridge had always been pleasant, which had made it impossible for Mary not to like her.

Mr. Townsend was pleasant, too, until you got to know him better.

Recalling the reason for his interest in her, Mary considered Mr. Partridge more assessingly.

He guided her forward in time to the music. "Whatever are you thinking, Miss Clemens? Your scowl suggests you'd rather be elsewhere."

"I'm sorry," she said and skipped to one side. "May I ask an indelicate question?"

"They are my favorite kind."

She smiled at him, liking his sense of humor. "Do you know who I was before I came to live with Miss Howard and Lady Cassandra?"

"I'm afraid not, Miss Clemens. Should I?"

She shook her head. So he wasn't after her dowry then. At least that was something. "It doesn't really matter. I am far more interested in knowing why you and I have never met before."

"I spend most of my time in Dorset where I manage a property on behalf of my grandfather. He lost most of his vision a few years ago and life has been a challenge for him ever since."

They continued chatting while they danced, and Mary decided she liked Mr. Partridge at least as much as his sister.

When they eventually rejoined the others, Mr. Crawford was waiting with a stony expression. He handed her her glass of wine and extended his hand to Mr. Partridge.

"Good to meet you," he said. "I'm Mr. Crawford, the man hired by Lady Cassandra's brother to fix the roof on the house where she, Miss Howard, and Miss Clemens live."

"Ah, so you are a craftsman," Mr. Partridge said. "I have always admired people who can make things with their hands, whether it's mending a fence or building a house. Plus, there is something to be said for being able to work outside, not to mention the sense of accomplishment I'm sure you must feel."

"There certainly is," Mr. Crawford agreed.

"David always complains about being stuck in his study," Miss Partridge said.

"I hate every second of it, but responsibility demands it." He scrunched his face to suggest dissatisfaction. "Except when I'm checking up on the orphanages. They have become a welcome escape from the tedium of ledgers and property management."

"I imagine coming here and spending time with your sister is also a reprieve," Emily said.

"Of course," Mr. Partridge said. "Here I am free to relax, to go for a ride or a pleasant walk, to enjoy an evening out with friends." Leaning forward, he added gravely, "Except when Mama is pressuring me to get married."

Mr. Crawford sighed heavily and with what seemed to be sympathetic understanding. "A mother intent on seeing her son wed will likely drive every man to madness at some point in their life."

Mary stared at him with a sudden need to know more. Because although she knew it was probably pointless, she wanted to understand this man who'd become the focus of all her thoughts. She wanted to know who his mother meant for him to marry, and she, God help her, wanted to be that woman.

"Since all of you come from well-respected families, I thought it prudent that my brother get to know you better during his stay," Miss Partridge said, in response to which all heads swiveled in her direction. "Perhaps an attachment will be made, and if not, then at least David will be able to tell our mother he has tried."

"But," Cassandra put in, "while our families may have respectable reputations, we do not. Indeed, knowing us in any capacity could result in scandal."

Mr. Partridge and his sister shared a look and then laughed. "I believe you're worth the effort," Mr. Partridge said, his eyes meeting Mary's. She held his gaze for a second before shifting it to Mr. Crawford, who was watching her with a pensive frown.

It was as if she'd just materialized in front of him, and he was trying to figure out how she'd done it. "You're absolutely right," he said.

She noted the look of surprise in Mr. Partridge's eyes. He took a step back, and Mr. Crawford stepped forward, his handsome face filling her vision and prompting her heart to beat a bit faster.

"I believe it is time for our waltz, Miss Clemens." Mr. Crawford's voice was low and intimate. It pulled Mary toward him and banished all else from her mind. She placed her hand on his forearm and met his gaze, connecting with him in a way she'd never connected with anyone before, as if both existed beyond the realm of reality, their souls embracing even as their bodies walked toward the dance floor.

They took their places while the musicians played the opening notes. And then Mr. Crawford was pulling her to him, his hand settling neatly against her back as he drew her into the dance. A moment of startled surprise made her gasp in response to having him so wonderfully close. And the way he moved…it was as if he'd been born to dance, his elegant steps so smooth she felt like she was gliding.

"I like Mr. Partridge and his sister," he said while leading her in a wide turn. "They're unpretentiousness gives them credit."

"It is unusual for people of their class to be without airs," Mary agreed. "Perhaps it is a result of growing up in the country and with no other gentry nearby. Most of their interactions will have been with ordinary people."

"Do you believe such an upbringing to be a prerequisite for humbleness?"

"Possibly, though I do think life-altering experiences can have a similar effect."

His hold on her tightened as he spun her about. "As was the case for you and your friends?" Before she could answer, he said, "That would imply you were high in the instep before you came here. Having gotten to know you, I very much doubt that could have been the case."

"Granted, there are exceptions," she admitted. A warm shiver erupted at the base of her spine as he curled his fingertips into her back.

"Even for earls, marquesses, and dukes?"

"I don't believe so," she said, recalling the peers she'd once socialized with. Each and every one had believed the world was at his feet. "Being raised amid wealth and with servants to tend to your every need creates certain expectations. It spoils you."

"Would you say that there was a time when you were spoiled as well?" His eyes sought hers, holding her captive and demanding the truth.

Mary thought back on her family home in Mayfair, to the shopping expeditions she'd enjoyed with her mother and sisters, the expensive gowns filling her wardrobe, and the diamond earbobs she'd been gifted on her fourteenth birthday.

"Absolutely. But leaving all of that behind in favor of a simpler and sparser life has given me more freedom than I ever had before," she tried to explain. "It is as if material things and the desire for more held me hostage."

"Losing it made you realize what truly matters," Mr. Crawfurd murmured.

His insightfulness went straight to Mary's heart. "It brought everything into perspective," she said. "As hard as it has been, I cannot imagine ever going back to an idle life. What Mr. Partridge said earlier about how your work must give you a sense of deep accomplishment resonates with me. I have never felt more useful or necessary than I have these last five years."

The music started to fade, causing Mr. Crawford to slow his pace. "You are an extraordinary woman, Miss Clemens. Don't ever let anyone else tell you otherwise." They came to a halt, and he slowly released her, stepping back so he could bow while she curtseyed.

"Thank you," she said, "not only for the dance but for the conversation. You're pretty extraordinary yourself."

"Words I'll hold close to my heart," he said, smiling at her in a way that weakened her knees and left her slightly breathless. He offered his arm and escorted her back to the rest of their group while she began wondering if Emily and Cassandra had a point. Perhaps giving in to desire would be worth it if Mr. Crawford would be hers, if only for a brief moment in time.

CHAPTER TEN

IT WAS ALMOST MIDNIGHT BY the time they returned home to a quiet house. After paying the Durhams and seeing them off, Caleb had prepared to bid the three women good night when Lady Cassandra invited him to stay for a cup of tea in the parlor.

"Mrs. Durham was kind enough to prepare a pot for our return." She peeled off her gloves and placed them on the small table near the stairs. "Get yourselves settled and I'll bring the tray."

"Allow me to help," Miss Howard said and hurried after her friend.

Caleb turned to Miss Clemens and gestured toward the parlor door. "Shall we?"

She nodded and preceded him into the room where she took a seat on the sofa. He decided to sit beside her even though he probably shouldn't. But he wanted to be near her. Especially after watching Mr. Partridge convey his keen interest in her. Caleb liked the man well enough, but he'd be damned if he was going to let him swoop in and steal Miss Clemens away.

She fidgeted with the skirt of her gown. "I

enjoyed this evening," she said. "We don't get out nearly enough. Doing so was fun."

"It certainly was," he agreed. "I especially liked dancing with you, Miss Clemens."

She blushed, which pleased him, for it reminded him of how easily he affected her. She had not blushed a single time while dancing or conversing with Mr. Partridge. Caleb had paid close attention.

"You must have attended many such events before, considering the skill with which you danced," Mary said. "I was quite impressed."

"Careful now, Miss Clemens. You're in danger of turning your compliment into an insult." He smiled wryly, dispelling any embarrassment she might have felt in response to his comment. Leaning back, he stretched out his legs, and glanced at the door. "They're taking a really long time with the tea."

"Hmm..." For whatever absurd reason, he wanted to change the subject, and she decided to let him. "I'll see what's keeping them." She stood and crossed the floor. "I won't be long."

He snorted as she opened the door, and when she stepped out into the chilly hallway, she heard him say, "I've heard that before."

Grinning, she hurried into the kitchen where she found Cassandra and Emily deep in conversation.

"— there were someone like that for me," Emily said. "Not that I...Oh! Mary!"

"I see you are both enjoying your tea," Mary said directing a look at the two half-empty cups on the counter.

Cassandra bit her lip. "We thought you might like some time alone with Mr. Crawford."

"Really?" Marching forward, Mary picked up the tray they'd prepared and raised an eyebrow. "Well?"

Both women glanced at each other and promptly downed the remainder of their tea. "It has been a long day," Emily said. She stretched and rubbed her back.

"It certainly has," Cassandra agreed with a yawn. "I think I'm off to bed."

Mary stared at the pair of them. "You cannot be serious."

"Good night, Mary," Emily said, passing her on her way to the door.

"I can see right through you. You're so transparent," Mary called after her as she disappeared into the hallway.

"Enjoy your tea," Cassandra said as she, too, headed for the door. "And please apologize to Mr. Crawford for our inability to join the two of you."

"I shall do no such thing," Mary told Cassandra's back.

Her friend merely laughed while she hurried off, leaving Mary alone in the kitchen with a tea tray in her hands. Sighing, she walked back to the parlor, took a deep breath, and opened the door.

"What happened to Miss Howard and Lady Cassandra?" Mr. Crawford asked when it became clear that the two would not be joining them.

"They're being held for treason," she said and

set the tray on the table before him.

He grinned. "Indeed. On what grounds, if I may ask?"

Picking up the teapot, Mary proceeded to pour Mr. Crawford a cup. "Conspiracy to cause a scandal."

"How intriguing." He sipped his tea while she filled a cup for herself. "What sort of scandal are we talking about exactly?"

"What do you think?" Her voice was testier than she'd intended, and her hand shook because of her overstrained nerves, causing her to spill a few drops.

"I'm hoping it's the sort that will give me the chance to kiss you."

Her head shot up, her gaze locking with his. "Mr. Crawford!" Good grief, her face was probably hot enough to roast a chicken if she stood close enough to it.

The cheeky man simply smiled with all the rakish charm in the world. "Tell me you haven't thought about it, and I shall apologize straight away for offending your sensibilities."

Mary swallowed. Rendered speechless and completely immobile, she searched her mind for an appropriate response. And failed, because to deny it would be dishonest, and she wasn't a liar.

Mr. Crawford's smile broadened with understanding. He patted the spot beside him on the sofa. "Come sit with me, Miss Clemens, and let us enjoy our tea."

Mary eyed him warily. The way his eyes glittered when he said, "Let us enjoy our tea," made her wonder if it might be a euphemism for something else.

In a way she hoped so, but at the same time she feared for her heart. And yet, if it were a choice between one kiss with Mr. Crawford and no kiss at all, would it not be better to know what it was to enjoy such intimacy with him—if only one time?

Making her choice, Mary picked up her cup and went to sit beside him. She took a long sip of her tea, savoring the soothing effect of the hot liquid as it slid down her throat and warmed her insides.

"I'm afraid of where this will lead," she confessed when he took her cup from her trembling hands and set it aside. But the real truth was she feared where it wouldn't lead because he had no intention of staying.

"Where would you like for it to lead?" he asked as he raised her hand to his lips and proceeded to kiss every knuckle.

"I..." Her breath caught as sensation took hold, scorching her skin in the best way possible. "I'm not sure."

"Mary," he said, the unexpected use of her given name forging a closeness she'd never experienced with anyone else before. "There are things I must tell you – things about me you're not going to like."

"Such as?"

He stared down at their joined hands. "I'm not who you think me to be."

She'd no idea what he was talking about, but it certainly wasn't getting her that kiss she now wanted more desperately than she did her next breath.

So she twisted around in her seat and faced him.

Leaning in, she raised her hand to his cheek. "You're a kind, thoughtful, hardworking man, Mr. Crawford. Whatever you may have done before I met you, please know that it will have no bearing on my high regard for you."

"I could be a criminal," he warned.

She smiled and shook her head with conviction. "That's impossible."

But maybe he had a fiancée he'd promised himself to. If that were the case, she didn't want to know, because once she did, she would have to walk away and never look back. And since that wasn't what she wanted to do, she closed the space between them and pressed her lips to his.

Stunned by her unexpected forwardness, which had in effect prevented him from confessing, Caleb sat completely immobile for a moment while options and their potential outcome played out in his head. But then her mouth moved against his, and whatever hope there had been of easing her away and insisting she listen to him first was outweighed by the need to reciprocate.

So he wound his arms around her and pulled her roughly against him, using her stunned little gasp to deepen the kiss in the most provocative way. Groaning in response, he pressed his hand against her back and held her to him. Her mouth was sweet and delicious, her body so soft and pliable it threatened to make him go mad. Hell, he was half mad already, the feel of her fingers threading through his hair inciting a want beyond any he'd ever experienced before. It brought every wicked fantasy he'd had about her these past few weeks into sharp focus.

Her skill was not what he would have expected, considering this wasn't her first kiss. It was innocently hesitant, which made him wonder what his brother had been thinking, even as he took pleasure in knowing that the two had not shared a wild passion-infused experience. It had not been like this, that was for sure, and the added information only made his heart beat faster.

Drawing her lower lip between his teeth, he nipped at the tender piece of flesh and delighted in the faint little moan of pleasure she made. She was just as desperate as he, following his lead and responding in kind until she drove him to distraction.

"Mary," he murmured against her jaw before kissing his way down the column of her neck.

"Yes," she murmured. She dug her fingertips into his scalp and arched against him, offering herself to his ministrations.

Tight with need, Caleb pressed his mouth to the curve of her shoulder. His breaths were coming hard and fast, his blood roaring through his veins in furious pursuit of more. Christ, she was beautiful, but she was also innocent and respectable and he could not – would not – take that from her.

Not until they were married.

He kissed his way down to the swell of her breasts and licked the edge of her décolletage. A devilish grin pulled at his lips when he heard her whisper his name. Marriage had been a vague idea lately, enhanced by his increased fondness for her. Now, after tasting her like this, it had become a necessary course of action from which he could not retreat.

She shifted closer, her body increasingly rest-less as she pushed against him with greater fervor. His mouth found hers once more, kissing her as if he were drowning and she were his lifeline, as if he'd just crossed the desert and she were the water that would quench his thirst. Her hands slid down his neck and across his shoulders as they moved to his front. And then they were delving beneath his jacket, her fingers working the buttons of his waistcoat.

Caleb caught her wrist and leaned back, undone in a heartbeat by her dazed expression and kiss-bruised lips. Her hair was partially down, with several loose tendrils falling softly against her cheeks. She looked so delicious and ready for more that he almost wanted to die, knowing he could not allow it.

"We mustn't," he told her even as his brain screamed for him to ignore his conscience and play the scoundrel.

"But…" Her voice was so bloody sensual, he feared he'd embarrass himself in the worst way possible. "I just want to touch you."

Oh God!

Of all the things she could have said.

Taking a moment, Caleb closed his eyes and fought for some measure of deeply held control. "If you do," he told her carefully, "there will be no stopping me, Mary. I will want more. A lot more. Do you understand?"

She was quiet for a while. "Yes," she whispered. "I do." Leaning forward she pressed her mouth to his once more and then whispered against his lips, "I want the same thing."

He would deserve a medal one day for turning away such a wonderful offer. But he had to, for her sake, because he knew she did not know what she asked for. Not when the plainest kiss with his brother had managed to break her heart. If he were to bed her before she knew the truth about him, there was no telling what that would do to her.

"Not here," he said, searching his brain for a way to dissuade her. "I will not be the man who takes your innocence on the parlor sofa in a fit of passion, Mary. You deserve better than that."

She flinched and drew away slightly. Giving her attention to the floor, she quietly said, "This isn't a decision I made lightly, but I am looking at a life devoid of passion. All I wanted was to experience every possible facet of it at least once. With you. So to say I deserve better is absolute rubbish, Caleb, for there will be nothing better for me."

Her voice shook with emotion and to his dismay, she swiped at her cheeks with the palms of her hands. Damn him, if he hadn't just hurt her anyway by trying to do the honorable thing. She stood before he was ready for her to do so, before he could think of the right thing to say. And then she was at the door, her hand poised on the handle.

"Thank you for the kisses. They're the best I've ever known."

"Mary." He was on his feet and moving toward

her, desperate to get her back in his arms. "It's not that I don't want you. Surely you must realize that. But my regard for you—"

A sob had her looking away from him. "I'm too proper for a casual bit of sport, aren't I?"

"It's more than casual. This is your innocence we're talking about."

She looked at him with watery eyes, and Caleb's gut wrenched in response. "And I would happily give it to you," she said fiercely, "if only to know what a night in your arms might be like."

"Mary…" Words failed him.

"Good night," she said as she pushed down on the handle and opened the door. "I trust you can let yourself out."

And then she was gone, leaving Caleb with a sinking feeling deep in his chest. He glanced at the sofa where passion had reigned for a few glorious minutes. Raking his hand through his hair, he turned away from it and made his way out to the kitchen and back to his cottage. Tomorrow he'd give her the explanation she deserved and hope she'd still speak to him after.

CHAPTER ELEVEN

HOW COULD SHE EVER FACE Mr. Crawford again? The question pressed on Mary's mind when she woke the next morning and recalled what had happened between them. The way he'd kissed her had made her previous experience with Wrenwick seem unschooled and immature. Even now, her body thrummed with the memory of Mr. Crawford's touch. The way his mouth had moved across her skin, gentle yet somehow aggressive as well, had been intoxicating. He'd called to the wanton inside her, a creature she'd not even known existed, and she had answered by offering herself to him in the most elemental way possible.

Groaning, Mary flung one arm over her face. Because rather than accept, he'd told her she deserved better, which was just another way of saying he wasn't interested in *that*, most likely because he didn't want the attachment such intimacy usually led to.

She'd thought of telling him she'd make no demands, that no matter what happened he'd have no obligation toward her or any potential child. But by then the amorous mood had cooled, and the idea of tackling such details had seemed exhausting.

A knock sounded at the door. Suspecting who it was, Mary answered with a groan.

"I brought you a cup of tea," Cassandra said.

Mary listened to the sound of her friend closing the door and crossing the floor. The bed dipped moments later, and Mary peeked out from under her arm and met Cassandra's gaze.

"Did something happen with Mr. Crawford last night?" The question was gently posed without the slightest judgment.

Mary wasn't sure what to say, except, "We kissed."

"And?" Cassandra prompted.

"It was spectacular," Mary admitted, "until I flung myself at him like the worst sort of light-skirt, and he told me I deserve better."

"Mary..." Cassandra cupped her cheek and stroked it lightly with her thumb. "That just means he's a descent man."

Mary scrunched her whole face and cringed. "Exactly!"

Cassandra paused. A couple of seconds passed, and then understanding dawned in her eyes. "You're worried your forwardness may have altered his opinion of you?"

"How could it not?" Turning her face away, Mary stared at the wall.

"Because of how much he obviously likes you. Whenever he looks at you, his eyes light up." Cassandra shifted and the mattress rocked against her weight. "He's also a man in his prime, Mary. To suppose he'd be put off by any physical response

on your part would be absurd. Rather, I imagine
he was striving to protect you, because although
I know I've been encouraging you to let passion
guide you, losing your innocence is no small
matter. I think you would have regretted a quick
tumble in the parlor, and I am convinced Mr.
Crawford knew this as well, even if you disagree."

"I'm not so sure I do anymore." Expelling a
tremulous breath, Mary sat up and leaned against
the headrest. She accepted the tea Cassandra gave
her and took a long sip. "At the time, I was desperate to remove every barrier between us so I
could feel his hands on my skin. The need to be
touched by him, to join with him in the most
basic way, was so overwhelming it robbed me
of all common sense." She shook her head, still
stunned by the powerful effect he'd had on her.
"It was as if I were starved, and he were the key
to my survival."

Cassandra smiled. "I know what you mean."
She tilted her head. "Don't you think he felt the
same way?"

Remembering, Mary could not deny the possessiveness of Caleb's embrace or the scorching
hot kisses he'd placed against her skin. "Maybe,"
she allowed.

"Maybe?" Cassandra gave her a dubious look.

Mary sighed. "It doesn't matter."

"Of course it does, Mary. Right now, it is the
only thing that matters considering the subject
we're discussing." Inhaling deeply, Cassandra
held the breath for a beat before expelling it. "His
reaction to your" —she waved a hand— "over
eagerness and your absolute certainty that he now

thinks you a harlot."

"Have you seen him yet this morning?" Mary asked, deliberately circumnavigating that comment.

Cassandra nodded. "He rode into the village just before I came to see why you're still in bed. He said he needed to run a few errands and purchase more nails for the planks in the attic."

"So there's no risk of seeing him if I come down for breakfast?"

"No."

Mary rolled her eyes. "You could have said so when you walked in ten minutes ago, Cass. I'm so hungry I might eat you if you're not careful."

Cassandra laughed and scooted back so Mary could rise. Cassandra's laughter faded and she seriously asked "Do you realize how silly you're being?"

Mary paused in the process of opening her wardrobe. She stood there, completely still, staring at her dull collection of drab-colored clothes. To one side, hung the white gown she'd worn last night.

"Yes," she said, answering Cassandra's question, "but the embarrassment I feel is crippling."

"I can see that, Mary. But ignoring Mr. Crawford isn't the answer." Cassandra went to the door and opened it slightly. "Not when he wants to talk to you. I believe he said there was much for the two of you to discuss when I quizzed him about what happened."

Mary turned toward Cassandra with a sharp inhale, but her friend was already slipping out into the hallway and then the door was closing, and before Mary knew it, she was alone.

Sighing, she picked out a moss-green gown with long sleeves and a square shaped neckline. It was simple yet elegant and suited her well, which was perfect, for although she wasn't ready to face Mr. Crawford just yet, she did want to look somewhat attractive when she eventually did.

So she put on the gown and combed her hair, styling it in a simple updo that left a few stray strands framing her face. Her stomach fluttered as she gazed back at her reflection. If only she didn't care what he thought about her appearance. She shook her head. Better yet, if only she hadn't fallen in love with a man who would soon be leaving.

Caleb didn't really need to go into the village to buy nails, but he did get the feeling that Mary would appreciate his absence when she eventually decided to come down for breakfast. Additionally, he and Apollo both enjoyed the vigorous ride across the fields, a longer route than the road had to offer, but it settled his mind and filled his lungs with fresh air.

"Whoa," he said, slowing Apollo from a gallop to a trot. Leaning forward in the saddle, he stroked the horse's neck and proceeded to steer him onto the road that would take them into the village. Perhaps he'd buy more strawberry tarts while he was there. They'd certainly put a smile on Mary's face last time he'd brought them back with him. She'd especially liked that he'd bought enough for everyone.

The edge of his mouth hitched with satisfaction. Everything looked brighter today. The grass was greener, the sky a deeper shade of blue. Even the birds sang merrier tunes than they had yesterday. Before she'd kissed him.

Caleb's chest grew tight just thinking about it. It was as if there weren't enough room inside him to contain his heart, which had more than doubled in size since that wondrous moment when she leaned forward and placed her mouth against his.

Everything had changed in that instant. *He* had changed, from a man who believed he could simply go back to London and the duty awaiting him, to a man who would never go anywhere again without Mary Clemens by his side.

Granted, there was a problem. The very messy and potentially damming problem regarding his true identity. She would not absolve him easily, but he hoped she would understand his reason for being dishonest. He was sure if he reminded her that she would not have spoken to him at all had she known he was a duke—never mind George's brother—she would forgive him without hesitation.

Whether or not she'd accept his proposal, however, was quite another matter, but he chose to be confident with this as well. After all, she clearly cared for him, and she must know he cared for her as well. Together they could be happy. He was absolutely convinced of the fact even though he knew persuading her might be tricky considering her aversion to the aristocracy in general and the deep responsibility she felt toward the children who lived at Clearview.

Perhaps if he suggested they spend most of their time in the country, she would agree more readily? As it was, he preferred the simpler life to whatever it was he'd experienced in London for six months before coming here. He really had no desire to return to that at all, even though he knew he had to. Already, he'd been gone far too long, to the point where he now expected to receive a letter from Aldridge every morning, informing him that his mother or his secretary required his immediate presence. It had been two months after all, so he wouldn't be surprised to learn that their patience with him had run out. Especially not with Christmas only a month away.

An idea sprang to life. Maybe he and Mary could invite Miss Howard, Lady Cassandra, and the children to celebrate with them at Braxton House in the Cotswolds. He was certain his mother would love seeing the grand estate filled with people and to be surrounded by boisterous laughter. They'd go ice skating on the lake and drink mulled wine in the evenings. It would be perfect, and the more he thought about it, the more he looked forward to it. But first, he would have to speak with Mary and make his confession. After that, everything else would fall into place for the simple reason that it had to.

It was a novel concept that lasted the hour it took him to purchase strawberry tarts and ride back to Clearview, where he found another horse tied to the fence outside. It wasn't the one Mr. Townsend usually used, which suggested someone else had come to call. Mr. Partridge perhaps?

Leading Apollo back to his spot by the cottage,

Caleb dusted off his boots and removed his hat before heading to the house. He entered through the kitchen as usual and made his way toward the parlor from which voices could be heard, primarily that of a man he had not seen in ten long years. He froze for a second to listen more carefully. His chest tightened and his breath caught in his throat. It wasn't possible. His ears must be deceiving him, yet he knew the voice so well there could be no doubt.

With shaking heart he opened the door and sought out his brother, Griffin, his face a near copy of his own, save for the paler-colored eyes and a new scar adorning his cheek.

"I'll be damned," Caleb muttered. For a good long second he just stood there staring while Griffin grinned back at him. And then somehow he forced his feet into motion while Griffin stood and came toward him as well. A split second later they embraced each other, and it was as if all the years apart fell away.

"It is good to see you too," Griffin muttered. He patted Caleb's back before stepping aside and flippantly adding, "Your Grace."

Caleb stiffened. He glanced at where Lady Cassandra and Mary were sitting, the former looking curious while the latter had schooled her features into something completely unreadable. "What have you told them about me?' he asked his brother in a whisper meant only for Griffin's ears.

Griffin looked confused. "I don't follow."

That did not bode well. Caleb gritted his teeth. "I mean—"

"We know who you really are," Mary said, "and

I daresay you owe us a bloody good explanation."

Her emotions had never been as conflicted as they were right now. Anger, disappointment, and love warred inside her, confusing her to no end. She needed to know why he'd done this to her – to *them*. Perhaps then she could find a way to forgive him for the lies he'd told since the moment he'd presented himself as a common laborer who'd come to fix the roof.

She still hadn't fully recovered from his brother's arrival. When the knock had sounded at the door and she'd gone to open it, she'd had no doubt as to the identity of the man facing her. He looked almost identical to Caleb, except for a few distinguishable features, and the clothes of course, which were a great deal finer.

He'd asked if the Duke of Camberly was in, to which Mary had responded with a startled snort. Her first thought was that he had to be joking, but then he'd launched into a lengthy explanation, and Cassandra had arrived, and somehow they'd all ended up in the parlor with a tea tray before them.

She stared at Caleb – Mr. Crawford – the Duke of Camberly – and wondered for the thousandth time how he'd managed to fool her so thoroughly. And to think that he'd carried on doing so after discovering that the man who'd broken her heart was his very own brother!

"Mary, I…" He blinked, looking utterly lost and slightly helpless.

Her heart longed to take pity, but her brain refused to allow it. So she crossed her arms and straightened her spine. This was not at all how she had imagined their next encounter after what had occurred between them last night. She'd believed she would blush and avert her gaze while he'd try to charm her into additional kisses. But now... A lump rose in her throat. She wasn't sure she would ever want to kiss him again.

"Perhaps you should have a seat," Cassandra suggested.

Mary glared at her in an effort to say that the cad deserved to stay standing, but Cassandra answered with a quelling look and offered the dastardly man some tea to boot. His brother returned to his own seat with a lot less enthusiasm than he'd shown moments earlier.

"Thank you," Caleb muttered. He glanced at the vacant spot on the sofa beside her but chose an armchair instead. Mary breathed a sigh of relief. Leaning forward, he rested his forearms against his thighs and gave his attention to the table before slowly saying, "When I returned to England eight months ago, it was with every intention of proving my worth to a father who'd always insisted I lacked common sense and usefulness. Instead, I discovered that he and my older brother had perished in a fire shortly before my arrival."

He looked up, directly at Mary, and the pain and regret she saw in his eyes twisted her heart until it ached. "I wasn't raised to be a duke, and I never wanted to be one. That was George's fate, not mine." He shook his head and expelled a tortured breath. "Living in France, away from the wealthy elite, just building and fixing things with my hands, was a wonderful way of life. When I inherited the title, I tried to do my duty, to be the duke I was expected to be. But I hated every second of it, every moment spent in my study dealing with problems pertaining to others, the acquisition of funds necessary to keep my estates running, and my mother's increasing persistence I take a bride and set up a nursery. It was exhausting and not at all conducive to my own happiness. So I planned my escape, and Aldridge mentioned this house and the need it had for repairs. It seemed like the perfect opportunity for me to return to what I enjoy doing while taking a much needed break from the pressure of being a duke."

Mary sympathized, yet she could not forget the extent he'd gone to in order to deceive them. "You told me your father was in Lord Vernon's employ."

"No," he told her gently. "I merely said Viscount Aldridge and I have been friends since childhood. You surmised the rest."

"But—"

"I also said that you'd made a lot of assumptions about me."

She frowned. "Yes, but it never would have occurred to me that they'd all been so utterly wrong. And don't you dare try suggesting it's my fault I did not see through your theatrics when you obviously came here with every intention of pulling the wool over all of our eyes."

"I'm sorry." He looked at Cassandra, including her in the apology before returning his attention to Mary. "But if I had been honest, I never would have gotten to know you. And that would have been a terrible shame."

She knew he was right. If he'd introduced himself as any kind of aristocrat, they would never have agreed to let him live in that tiny cottage and work on their roof. She cringed just thinking about it while acknowledging that she would have judged him on the basis of his title alone and his relation to the man who'd hurt her.

However... "You encouraged certain liberties between us after discovering the man who rejected me, the man who led to my family's banishment of me, was your very own brother." She clapped a hand over her mouth, unable to stop the sudden outpouring of distress. "How could you do that? How could you possibly think things would end well between us when you chose to keep that from me? Did you think you'd just leave, and I'd never find out?" She realized then that this was the part of his betrayal that hurt the most. It wasn't just that he'd made her fall in love with a man who did not exist, but that he'd imagined he'd get away with it.

Rising, she clenched her hands until her nails dug against her palms. Caleb and Griffin stood as well, as was polite.

"I never wanted to cause you pain," Caleb said.

He sounded sincere, but perhaps that was due to his wonderful acting skills. She no longer knew what to believe, except that she could not trust him. "It's too late for that." She started toward the door.

"Mary. Please." His voice beseeched her, forcing her to look back.

Realizing her mistake, she squeezed her eyes shut and fought for strength. "I'm sorry," she said as she opened her eyes with renewed resolve, "but if you've proven anything to me at all, Your Grace, it is that I was correct to believe the worst of the aristocracy. Or at the very least, one particular branch of it. Now, if you will excuse me, I would like to put as much distance between you and myself as possible." She nodded toward Caleb's brother. "It has been enlightening, sir. I thank you for giving me the facts your brother failed to provide." And to Cassandra, "The tea was excellent as always. I'm sorry I cannot stay."

She quit the room to the sound of Cassandra telling Caleb not to pursue her, for which she was truly grateful. Because lord help her, as crushed as she was at the moment, she feared she'd forget about every reason she had to resent him if he touched her. And if he kissed her…Well, she'd melt in his arms, and her heart would break just a little bit more. So she marched into the kitchen and grabbed a heavy wool shawl from the back of a chair. It was Emily's, but Mary knew her friend wouldn't mind her borrowing it.

Opening the door, she stepped into the brusque afternoon air. Gone was the morning sun, replaced by a light drizzle and a thin, ghostly mist. Ignoring it, Mary, wrapped the shawl tightly around her shoulders and walked out onto the grass. She passed the birch trees and rhododendron bushes, putting them all between herself and the house as she crossed toward the lake. The ground was soggy beneath her feet and water hung from every plant leaf, dragging them down in a droopy effect.

Mary drew a quivering breath and stepped closer to the water's edge where the raindrops were forming rings on the surface. Helplessly, her gaze fell on a thin piece of wood, half-hidden in the grass. Moving nearer, her lips began to tremble as soon as she saw what it was: a fishing rod Caleb had made, forgotten by one of the boys. She bent to retrieve it and felt the first tears spill onto her cheeks. How could he do this to her? The cruelty, whether intentional or not, was beyond compare, for she loved the man who'd taken the time to help a boy no one else had managed to reach. But the man who'd lied to her was someone else altogether. She could not equate one with the other, and because of that painful dilemma, she felt her throat close on a sob even as her heart broke in two.

CHAPTER TWELVE

"WILL SHE EVER FORGIVE ME?" Caleb asked Lady Cassandra. He'd wanted to go after Mary and make her listen. But her friend had warned against it, and he had reluctantly agreed to take her advice.

"I don't know," Lady Cassandra said. "More tea, Lord Griffin?"

Griffin resumed his seat and held his cup toward Cassandra. Resuming his own seat, Caleb leaned back and pinched the bridge of his nose. He wasn't prone to getting headaches, but one was definitely coming on right now.

"There has to be something I can do," he muttered, voicing his most desperate thought in spite of its futility. "If I can only make her see that all I wanted was to be an ordinary man again."

"But you're not ordinary, and you never will be," Lady Cassandra said. "And while I will admit that you owed us nothing when we were just three women who happen to own the house on which you are working, you should have told Mary when you decided to pursue her in earnest."

"I tried to but then she kissed me and I got carried away and then we argued and well...here we are," Caleb said without even bothering to hide the miserable state he was in.

"Oh Christ," Griffin murmured. "You've been romancing Miss Clemens." He shook his head and laughed even though there was nothing amusing to be found in this awful situation. "No wonder she's so upset."

"She wouldn't be if you'd kept your mouth shut, Griffin." Caleb gave his brother a meaningful look. "Did Aldridge not tell you I left London for the sole purpose of seeking anonymity?"

"Well, yes. But I don't think either of us expected you to keep your true identity secret from his sister or her friends when all have a similar situation to yours."

Caleb stared at his brother and saw Lady Cassandra doing the same. "I beg your pardon?"

Griffin looked at them each in turn. His expression grew increasingly befuddled. "Am I the only one here who has noticed that each of you has sought to escape the aristocratic world for one reason or other. My point is these women are of your social class, Caleb. The idea of you hiding your identity from them just seems kind of pointless."

"They wouldn't have let me stay if they'd know who I really was." In the years that had passed since his last encounter with Griffin, Caleb had forgotten how dense his brother could be.

"Really?" Griffin didn't sound convinced. He looked to Lady Cassandra. "Would you really have turned away Aldridge's friend?"

"Of course not," Lady Cassandra said. "This

house belongs to my brother. My friends and I live here at his discretion, so if he were to let any friend of his stay here, we would hardly have been in a position to deny the request."

"You see!" Griffin's eyes gleamed while his smile looked annoyingly smug.

Caleb pressed his lips together and scowled. "Miss Clemens would never have given me a second glance if she'd known who I really was," he argued.

Griffin shrugged. "Perhaps you're right. But maybe you're not. In any event, she's not giving you a second glance now, that much is certain. If you'd been honest from the start, however, she might have grown to like you eventually, regardless of whatever prejudice she has toward your title. And then it would have been because she'd gotten to know the man you truly are instead of whatever fabrication you've been offering her since you arrived here."

Caleb blinked. Perhaps he'd misjudged Griffin's wisdom.

"He does have a point," Lady Cassandra interjected.

"I didn't offer any fabrication," Caleb protested. "I'm still the same man she's been getting to know these past two months."

"With one important distinction being that you're now a duke worth more than fifty thousand pounds as opposed to the penniless laborer who fixes roofs for a living," Griffin said. "Ironically, most women I've known would so much rather have the former instead of the latter. Most would be overjoyed to discover your newly elevated position."

Not Mary though. "Miss Clemens is different."

Lady Cassandra grinned. "That she is, Your Grace, but you mustn't lose heart just yet. Not if you truly want her, though I would like to ask about your intentions before we go any further."

Caleb smiled because here at last was a question he could answer without hesitation. "I mean to marry her, my lady."

Lady Cassandra raised an eyebrow. "Indeed? And has Miss Clemens given any indication that she would be willing to consider such a possibility?"

"Well, she...I mean...that is..." He cleared his throat, ignored Lady Cassandra's deepening frown and Griffin's low chuckle, and decided to try again. "Not in exact terms, but—"

"You see," Lady Cassandra said, "Miss Clemens was put off marriage five years ago when your brother decided she was good enough to flirt with and kiss but not to wed."

"He was an ass," Caleb grumbled. "At least where Miss Clemens was concerned."

"Unfortunately, he has also made your quest for Miss Clemens's hand so much harder. And then on top of it all, you turned out to be everything she has spent five years running away from: a man who cannot be trusted."

"I wanted to tell her," Caleb said. "I was prepared to do so, but she stopped me and..." He pushed his fingers through his hair and stared down at the carpet. "She thinks I played her for a fool now, doesn't she?"

"Wouldn't you, if you were in her position?"

As much as he hated it, he had to nod in agreement. "I believe I would."

"So then the question remains," Lady Cassandra said after a pause. She waited for him to meet her gaze before continuing. "What are you going to do about it?"

The immediate answer that came to mind was, "I've no idea." Instinct told him to chase her as fast and as furiously as he could muster, but common sense warned against doing so. "She needs time to come to terms with what she has learned," he said, unsure if what he was going to do was the right way forward. "Perhaps it would be easier for her if I went back to London."

Lady Cassandra's eyes widened. "You mean to leave?"

"Absence does make the heart grow fonder," Griffin said as if reciting Shelley or Byron.

Caleb cast him a frown to which Griffin responded with a mischievous smirk. "Why did you come to find me?" he asked. "I can only assume Mama requested you do so because you would not have left London for any other reason. Not after years of being away. There would be too much catching up to do, too many friends to see." For while Caleb had always enjoyed time away in the country, Griffin had yearned for the city, while Devlin had felt himself drawn to the sea.

Predictably, Griffin dipped his head in acquiescence. "You are correct, dear brother. Mama was concerned about you and rightfully so, considering she hasn't heard a word from you since you left with no indication of when you'd return. And Aldridge refused to give you up until I got back.

Had to threaten him with a duel before he agreed to tell me the truth." Griffin fidgeted with his sleeve. "I assured him you'd forgive him."

Caleb snorted. "Not very likely, considering the result of his divulgence."

"You cannot blame my brother for your own idiocy," Lady Cassandra told him bluntly. "This entire mess is of your own creation, Camberly, so I ask you again, what will you do to fix it?"

"As we discussed, leaving might be for the best," Caleb said.

Lady Cassandra's mouth dropped open. "As we discussed?" She gave an incredulous laugh. "It's no wonder you're rubbish at this when you make assumptions so easily. *We* discussed nothing. *You* had an idea, and *I* have yet to decide if it is any good or not."

Caleb sighed. "If I stay, I will be the problem that refuses to go away. Mary will be forced to face me whether she wants to or not, which is part of the reason why she ran from London in the first place. But if I go, I give her control. She will have the power to decide whether she wishes to see me again and when."

"That…" Lady Cassandra stared back at him for a lengthy moment. "I think that's very thoughtful and honorable of you, Camberly. I also believe it could work in your favor and win back her trust, if done correctly."

Caleb leaned in, as did Griffin. "What do you propose?" they both asked in unison.

The edge of Lady Cassandra's mouth lifted into a devious little grin. "A courtship unlike any other."

Emotionally exhausted, Mary started back toward the house, fishing rod in hand. She wasn't sure what she would say to the duke when she saw him again since nothing she'd thought of so far could properly convey her heartache. Worst of all, she feared there was nothing he could ever say or do to make things right between them again.

Wishing he'd left the house while simultaneously hoping he was still inside, Mary entered through the kitchen, returned the shawl she'd borrowed to the chair on which she'd found it, and approached the parlor. She still had no answers when she opened the door and almost collided with Cassandra, who was coming the opposite way with the tea tray in her hands.

"Oh. There you are," Cassandra said, steadying herself against the doorframe. "I was just thinking I'd come out and look for you if you weren't back in another ten minutes."

"I needed some time to think and to simply process everything that's happened this afternoon."

"Of course. That makes perfect sense." Cassandra stepped past her and walked toward the kitchen.

"I see His Grace has left the parlor," Mary said with a quick glance inside the room. "And he took his brother with him, I take it?"

"Indeed he did."

Mary couldn't believe it. "They can't both stay in that small cottage. There's not enough space, never mind an additional bed."

"Oh, you needn't worry about any of that any longer, Mary. His Grace and his brother have both returned to London, so everything can finally go back to normal."

"But…" Mary's stomach twisted in a most unsettling way. It couldn't be true. Surely. "He has not completed his work in the attic yet, Cass."

"Actually, he says he did so last week and was only staying on because it was hard for him to leave you. But then you said what you said and well, here we are."

"But…he didn't even bid me farewell."

"He wanted to," Cass said, "but with the weather being what it is and darkness sure to set in within the next couple of hours, they wanted to be on their way, so I said I'd tell you on their behalf."

Their behalf. Not his.

Mary didn't like it at all.

"But—"

"That's three buts in under a minute, Mary." Cassandra set the tray down and turned to face her. "Are you certain you wanted him to leave?"

"I never said anything about him leaving," Mary said, surprising herself with the level of her indignation.

"What's going on?" Emily asked as she poked her head through the doorway. "The children are hoping for warm milk and biscuits, so I've come to prepare some."

"Mary's having second thoughts about asking the Duke of Camberly to leave," Cassandra said. She handed Emily a pot to heat the milk in.

"I never…" Mary blew out a breath of frustration and counted to ten. "I never told anyone to leave."

"It was implied," Cassandra said.

Emily glanced at Mary as if observing a painting that hadn't come out right. "Did she not like the part about Mr. Crawford being a duke?"

"Not particularly," Cassandra said out of the corner of her mouth.

"Because he lied to me," Mary told them both. She pulled the biscuit tin off the shelf and began placing biscuits on a plate with angry little movements. "He knew I hated his kind, so he deliberately hid it from me."

"Actually," Emily said, "he didn't know that at all when he met you."

"Very well. He learned of it along the way, but that does not change the fact that he deliberately hid it from me."

"Do you think there's a chance that by the time he realized how much he liked you, it was too late to tell you the truth?" Emily asked.

"It's never too late," Mary insisted.

Cassandra leaned her hip against the counter. "According to what he has told me, he tried to be honest, but you apparently stopped him."

"Oh, really?" Mary grimaced. "And when exactly…" A tiny memory surfaced. She swallowed and looked at her friends. "Last night. He was going to tell me last night before we kissed, but I was too impatient. I stopped him." How on earth could she have forgotten? "When we parted ways, he said we would speak today, that there was much for us to discuss, and I'm now convinced this is what he was talking about."

"But then his brother showed up and ruined his chance to be honest," Cassandra said.

Emily poured the milk into the pot and set it on the stove. Stirring the contents, she looked at Mary. "I think you've both made mistakes. The question is whether or not they're too big to forgive."

Sinking onto a stool, Mary propped her elbow on the counter beside her and leaned her head against her hand. "I honestly do not know. I mean, he lied to me about everything."

"Are you sure about that?" Cassandra asked. "Or is this your wounded pride talking?"

Mary tried to be objective, and as she did so, she realized something. "Maybe not everything." She bit her lip and thought back on all the conversations she'd had with Caleb these past two months. "Letting me think he was someone he wasn't was wrong, although I suppose I can understand why he did it. But when we talked, he was honest. He told me about his time in France, about seeking his father's validation. I don't think he lied when he told me which books he preferred or how he wished he could choose the life he wanted instead of the one thrust upon him by fate. All along, I believed him to be the sort of man who would happily flirt with a woman but never consider marrying her. I accepted this. But what if the constant restraint he showed when we were together was the product of fear? Maybe he just wasn't sure how to deal with the prejudice he knew I would have against him when I eventually learned the truth." She stared at Cassandra and Emily, who were both watching her closely. "What if he were trying to protect me from getting hurt?"

"So you accepted the idea of him not being the marrying sort," Cassandra said.

Of course that was the part she would focus on. "It made sense based on a few things he said."

"What intrigues me is that you contemplated foregoing marriage in favor of having an affair," Cassandra continued.

"Upon your recommendation, if I may remind you," Mary told her.

Cassandra nodded. "Yes, but I made that suggestion because I thought you were utterly opposed to the idea of marriage and were facing a long life ahead without knowing what passion can feel like. But you actually took a moment to wonder what it might be like to marry Camberly. Didn't you, Mary?"

Emily gasped. "Did you really?"

Mary glanced at the ceiling and finally nodded. "For a second or two. Until he refused to have his wicked way with me in the parlor." Emily and Cassandra both snorted with laughter. "It became quite clear in that moment that he wasn't the sort of man who robbed a woman of her innocence unless he intended to make her his wife. As you both know, he refused to let things escalate, which can only mean that he had no intention of suggesting a permanent attachment."

"There are a dozen other reasons why he would refuse such an opportunity, Mary. We've been over several of them already," Emily said, "like the fact that he would not bed you unless he could do so honestly, or how he probably believed you were averse to marriage, which we all know you have been until you met Camberly."

"I do not wish to be a duchess," Mary told them both adamantly.

"What if you must in order to be his wife?" Cassandra asked. "Would you be willing to make such a sacrifice if he asked it of you?"

"I…" She could not think let alone speak.

"The question now," Emily said, "is whether or not you love him enough to forgive the deception and share your life with him."

Mary winced. "He hasn't even asked me to do so, and I doubt he ever will now." She stood and went to the door. "Mr. Crawford is gone forever, and I must accept that. I'm going to see if any of the children are up for a game of cards. I'll tell them their milk and biscuits are on the way."

Mary headed into the hallway and paused for a moment to compose herself. Weeping would get her nowhere. So she squared her shoulders, blinked back the tears, and went to the library. The children who awaited her there would help fill the gaping void inside her, but forgetting the man who'd caused it would be another thing altogether.

CHAPTER FOURTEEN

WHEN CALEB AND GRIFFIN RETURNED to London two days later, their mother was waiting.

"Finally," she said, rising to greet them when they entered her private apartment. "I was so worried when I did not hear from you, Camberly. It has been two months."

"My apologies." Stepping forward, Caleb kissed her lightly on the cheek. "Work kept me busy until recently."

"Work?" She stared at him in dismay. "What sort of work could possibly demand you remain in Cornwall for such a long time without so much as a word to assure me of your wellbeing?"

"He was in pursuit, Mama," Griffin said. Brushing past Caleb, he kissed their mother's cheek as well before offering Caleb a sly smile.

The duchess's eyes widened. "In pursuit of what?" she asked.

"I was mending a roof," Caleb said, deliberately avoiding the question. "Viscount Aldridge's roof, to be precise. It was a personal favor."

"Good heavens." She sank slowly onto her

chaise. Caleb and Griffin seated themselves in a pair of silk upholstered armchairs with blue and silver stripes. The duchess looked at Caleb as if seeing him for the very first time. "I wasn't aware you knew how to do that."

"I did mention that I helped build houses during my time in France."

"Well, yes," she said, "but I thought you managed such projects. It never occurred to me you might have been one of the laborers! Good grief, whatever will people think if word gets out that the Duke of Camberly is nothing more than a drudge? The scandal will have no end, and your marriage prospects will likely dwindle, no matter the title."

Caleb winced. This was why he'd gone to France in the first place. His parents' unwillingness to accept him for who he was. Their constant judgment and ridicule.

"I think many young ladies admire a man who works hard," Griffin said, coming to Caleb's defense.

"Of course they do," the duchess squeaked, "managing estates and making investments, not balancing on a roof or wielding a hammer. Dear God, the indecency of it, Camberly!"

"It's what I enjoy," he told her calmly.

She gave him a look that suggested he hadn't a clue about what he enjoyed. "Don't be absurd. Nobody wants to do such things. That is why those of us who can afford it have servants."

Caleb inhaled deeply. This conversation was starting to grate. "I'll accept that a lot of people might not, but I am different. I am—"

"A duke," his mother provided, "and as such your place is in the study behind your desk or at your club or even at a gaming hell if you so desire, but it is not on top of a roof." She sank back against the corner of her chaise with a look of complete exhaustion. "Can you imagine if I suddenly decided I like scrubbing floors or mucking out stables?"

Griffin grinned. "Now there would be a sight to behold."

The duchess glared at him before shifting her gaze back to Caleb. "Your duty is to maintain the fortune your forefathers have amassed, add to it if you can, and secure the lineage by marrying well and producing heirs. The more the better, I say."

"And if that is not what I want?"

She pressed her lips together and turned her head sharply toward the corner of the room. "Your father and brother are both dead, Camberly, and you are the next in line. It is not what any of us wanted, but it is what it is, and we must all learn to live with it."

"Duty before all else," Griffin murmured. He gave Caleb an apologetic glance.

Caleb clenched his hands. "What about happiness?"

The duchess sniffed and he saw to his surprise that her eyes had begun to shimmer. "The dukedom is bigger than we are. It will exist long after we are forgotten, but it also demands sacrifice and dedication, and I have certainly done my part, as has your father."

"By marrying for convenience rather than love," Caleb said, voicing his knowledge of his parents' unhappy union for the very first time.

"If you turn your back on the duty your title demands, it will all have been for nothing," his mother said with a tremulous voice.

"It must end somewhere," Caleb told her gently, "or would you have all our descendants be just as unhappy as you have been most of your life?"

He could see that the question gave her pause, and he took that opportunity to reach for her hand. "Doing what I love doesn't mean rejecting the title."

"But the gossips will tear you to shreds. Your reputation will be ruined and…and…"

"And what?" He tightened his hold on her hand and waited for her to meet his gaze more completely. "Why does any of that matter? I'm a duke, Mama. I do not need the *ton's* approval or care what they choose to say about me."

"If only I could be as blasé about this as you," she said. "If only I had an ounce of your courage."

"You'll have my support and protection along with my love," he told her sincerely. "But if you stand in the way of my happiness, you will have my resentment as well, just as Father always did."

"He only wanted what was best for you, Camberly."

Caleb shook his head. "No. He didn't. If he had, he would not have stopped paying for my education at Oxford when he discovered I'd switched my religious studies to architectural ones."

Sighing, the duchess slowly nodded. "I think you may be right." She pressed her lips together and frowned. "We've ruined your life, haven't we?"

He smiled at her warmly. "Don't be silly, Mama. I'd never allow you to do that. I'm much too stubborn and bent on doing what I want regardless of who disapproves."

"You were a fine example for Devlin and me," Griffin said. "You gave us both courage to pursue our own dreams."

Caleb stared at his brother in surprise. "Truly?"

Griffin nodded. "Had it not been for you I'd have gotten a commission, and Devlin, poor sod, would be wearing a wig to court."

"Your father did think it prudent to have a barrister in the family," the duchess said, "though I will admit turning you into a soldier, Griffin, would have been a tragic mistake." She looked at each of her sons in turn. "I hope you can both forgive me and your father for being so wrong about both of you."

"Of course we can," Griffin said even though Caleb knew it wasn't that simple. He would never forget his father's last words to him. *You're nothing, Caleb.* They would probably haunt him for the rest of his life.

Pulling her hand away from Caleb's, the duchess stood and went to the window. Parting the drapes a bit more, she looked out and said, "Will you at least consider marrying?"

"Mama," Caleb began.

She turned away from the window and clasped her hands together before her. "It is a reasonable question."

"Indeed it is," Griffin said, adding that extra bit of commentary he loved providing.

"There is someone," Caleb confessed. He

watched his mother's face brighten. "But it is complicated and will require your full coopera- tion."

"Oh yes!" She was swiftly back on the chaise and beaming with expectation. "Who is she?" Tilting her head, her expression grew pensive. "Consid- ering where you have been these past months, I assume she's country bred? Not that I would con- sider that a hindrance. Much of the gentry resides outside the big cities, but do give me a name, for I am about to expire from sheer curiosity."

"So I see," Caleb told her dryly. He cleared his throat and glanced at Griffin, who was looking thoroughly amused. "Perhaps you can call for some tea?"

"Of course," his brother agreed. Rising, he went to the bell pull.

"Her name is Mary Clemens," Caleb said while watching his mother closely for any reaction she might have to that particular name.

The duchess frowned. "How odd."

"What is?" Griffin asked.

"As I recall, your brother, George, was once attached to a certain Miss Clemens. She wasn't right for the position, however, so your father put an end to the brief romance and encouraged George to look elsewhere."

Caleb almost stopped breathing. His hand clutched at the armrest, and he felt his teeth gnash together. A heavy hand settled against his shoul- der. "Careful now," Griffin warned.

"She. Wasn't. Right. For. The. Position?" He could barely get the words out he was so enraged all of a sudden.

The duchess blinked. "Not everyone is cut out to be a duchess, Camberly. It takes a certain kind."

Dear God, he was going to do or say something he would soon regret. To prevent that, he squeezed his eyes together hard and tried to slow the beats of his racing pulse. "Is that what you truly believe?" He had to ask.

"I don't think it's an easy job. It certainly hasn't been for me." She gave him a wary look before adding, "That said, however, I must point out that unlike you, George would have been a traditional duke, which means that he would have needed a traditional duchess if either of them were to maintain their sanity. His Miss Clemens would have been ruined by this way of life in the end."

Caleb bristled. "*His* Miss Clemens."

"Well, yes. She was a very simple, plainspoken girl from what I understand, and while that may have charmed your brother for a moment, she would have been wrong for him in the long run." His mother drew a deep breath and expelled it. "But you're different, Camberly. You're no ordinary duke, so I'm sure the woman you choose to marry will be perfectly suited to you."

"She's the same, Mama."

The duchess looked lost. "I beg your pardon?"

"George's Miss Clemens and my Miss Clemens are one and the same."

The duchess's mouth dropped open. Silence ensued. And then, "That cannot be."

A knock at the door followed, and a maid appeared with a tea tray. "I see you read our minds," Griffin could be heard saying from the position he'd recently taken next to the fireplace.

"Is there anything else, Your Grace?" the maid asked and set the tray on the table.

"No," the duchess said without looking away from Caleb. "That will be all for now."

The maid bobbed a curtsey and left the room. Griffin returned to his seat. He looked at Caleb and then at their mother. "Perhaps we should add some brandy to that teapot. You both look as though you could do with the fortification."

It took a week before the duchess was ready to listen to reason. For the first three days, she refused to discuss Mary entirely, changing the subject each time Caleb raised it. On the fourth day, when Caleb insisted that only Mary would do when it came to marriage, the duchess enumerated all the ways in which he was wrong.

"Her father is in trade, Caleb," his mother began. "As a duke, you ought to be marrying within your own ranks. And let's not forget that your brother courted her first. When word gets out, people will talk and scandal will follow."

"My mind is made up," he'd countered. "I love her, and that is all that matters."

She'd sighed in response and walked away, but he'd seen her resolve begin to waver.

By mid-December, after listening to Caleb's added explanations and his assurance that if she failed to support him in this, he'd never forgive her, she finally agreed to offer her assistance. Caleb reckoned she only wished for him to stop waxing poetic over Miss Clemens at every available opportunity, which was fine by him. Just as long as the end result was to his satisfaction.

"The carriage is ready," he told his mother one Monday afternoon at half past two. "Shall we depart?"

She nodded and went to collect her reticule. "Are you absolutely certain about this?" she asked while he assisted her with her cloak a short while later. Murdoch handed her her gloves.

"Absolutely," Caleb told her.

She proceeded to put on her gloves and accepted the arm he offered. It had started to snow that morning, so the steps were slippery even though the footmen had just brushed them clean.

"You do realize you're setting all kinds of wheels in motion by doing this," the duchess added as they proceeded toward the awaiting carriage with the Camberly crest adorning each side. "If you change your mind—"

"I won't," he told her firmly.

"Well, then," she said as he handed her up. "I hope it turns out as you hope, for if it does not, your life will not be the only one ruined by all the tumultuousness you're going to cause."

"Thank you, Mother," he told her bluntly, "I am aware."

"Did it ever occur to you that going back to Clearview and simply asking Miss Clemens to marry the man you are might be the best option?" she asked when he was comfortably seated on the opposite bench. The carriage rocked as it took off, and she reached for the leather strap by the window to steady herself. Her chin was slightly raised in the same defiant tilt she'd affected since he'd first suggested marrying Mary. It reminded him that she still wasn't completely convinced the union would be a success, even though she'd agreed to help him.

"Of course I've thought of that. Endlessly, in fact, but I fear she might refuse if I take that course."

"And she won't if you force her to face everything she once fled?" His mother shook her head. "Honestly, Camberly, I fail to understand you sometimes."

"I know." He smiled at her, and she, he was happy to see, smiled back in return. "She must accept the title I hold before she can have the man she wants, Mama. The only place I can prove that to her is here, in London, where all her heartache began."

"Very well, Camberly. Let us ensure her swift arrival then, shall we?"

He settled against the plush velvet squabs. "I would not go to all of this trouble unless I was absolutely certain this is the woman I want to spend the rest of my life with," he said after a while. The carriage tilted as it rounded a corner and slowed to allow for an increase in traffic. "It is important to me you know that."

"I do," she told him gently. A soft smile followed. "Your father wronged Miss Clemens most grievously when he put out those rumors about her. It was badly done, and I...I did not approve of his actions though I understood his reasoning."

Caleb's chest contracted at the thought of Miss Clemens at the center of ill-intended gossip, of her sudden rejection, not just by the man she thought she'd formed an attachment with, but by Society as a whole. "Do you think George cared for her?"

His mother nodded. "I know he did, for he told me so right after giving your father the set-down he deserved. But it was too late by then. Word was out that Miss Clemens was a scheming fortune huntress, and by the time he reached her house to check on her, she'd already left town and…well, I suppose Aldridge must have been under strict orders from his sister not to disclose a thing, because George never did find out where Miss Clemens had gone, and as you know, he never considered anyone else, or he would have married."

"So he loved her?"

"In his own way, I suppose he did." Caleb's mother gave a sentimental chuckle. "He was always more emotionally restrained than you, Griffin, and Devlin. George was the quiet and serious one, while you three ran roughshod through the house. Drove your father and me mad for the most part."

"Is that why George was the favorite?" Caleb asked. He'd made peace with this notion years ago, but he was still curious to know the truth of it.

His mother gaped at him. "There was never a favorite, Caleb," she said, using his given name instead of the title due to surprise, no doubt.

"He received all the attention and all the praise."

His mother grimaced. "I think your memory is slightly skewed. Your brother was the heir, Camberly. Your father put tremendous pressure on him, and all that attention you're talking about…

those were extra lessons he received in agricul-
ture, book keeping, and lord knows what else.
As for the praise, George worked hard because
he was a perfectionist and because he wanted to
make your father proud."

"I think he succeeded," Caleb said.

"He did, but I also know he hated every second
of it just as much as you hate it now."

Caleb's gaze snapped onto hers. "He never said a
word." Surely George would have mentioned that
at some point, wouldn't he?

The duchess shook her head. "Consider the age
difference between you for a moment. By the
time you were ten, he was off to Eton where he
made his own set of friends. After that, he moved
in separate circles from you, Griffin, and Devlin,
though I do know he wished you'd had more in
common – a way in which to connect. He told
me once that he always felt as though he was very
alone. You three had each other, and he was by
himself."

"And then he met Miss Clemens, only to be told
he could not have her." Caleb sighed. He'd always
envied George, but not anymore. The carriage
drew to a halt and he straightened himself. "The
mistakes we make," he murmured as he opened
the door and alit. He helped his mother down.
"Let us try to put an end to that habit."

"You know he meant well," the duchess
remarked, accepting his escort.

Caleb wasn't sure if she spoke of his father or his
brother. All he could hear in the ensuing silence
was the age-old saying that the road to hell was
paved with good intentions. They were like

blisters beneath the soles of his feet, but as long as he got to marry Mary, he did not really mind. And as wrong as he knew it was, he appreciated his father's interference in George's affairs right now, because if George had married Miss Clemens, then Caleb would never have been able to have her, not even with George being dead and buried. For that was the law – a man could not wed his brother's widow.

They climbed the steps leading to the tall front door of a pristine white townhouse. Caleb reached for the shiny brass knocker and gave it a few hard raps. He glanced at his mother, who looked every bit the graceful duchess, chin high and eyes facing forward so she would be sure to meet the butler's gaze directly the moment the door opened.

It did so quickly, allowing Caleb a direct view of an elegant foyer with white marble floors and a massive arrangement of roses adorning a table set directly against the far wall. His mother glanced at him and raised one eyebrow before returning her attention to the man who'd opened the door. He was a middle-aged fellow, somberly attired in a pair of black trousers with jacket to match.

"Yes?" He inquired with a noticeable raise of his chin.

"Are Mr. and Mrs. Clemens at home?" Caleb asked. "The Duke of Camberly and his mother, the duchess, would like to have a word with them if it's no inconvenience."

The butler stared at them. He blinked and then stared at them some more before collecting himself and granting them entry. "Please wait here a moment," the butler said after showing them into a parlor dominated by subdued pastel colors. Here, hydrangeas appeared to be the theme, for they featured in every picture on the wall and in several porcelain figurines.

The butler retreated, leaving Caleb alone with his mother.

"It seems they have good taste," she remarked. She did not have to add, *even though they're new money*, for him to know it was implied. "I like what I've seen so far."

"Not that it really matters," Caleb told her.

She gave him a pointed look. "You may not think so, but let me assure you that when you marry Miss Clemens, you will be grateful if her family is the sort you can get along with without too much difficulty."

"Perhaps," he agreed for the simple sake of ending the discussion.

Arguing about his future parents-in-law was the last thing he wished to be doing the moment they entered the room. He glanced at the clock and noted the time. Ten minutes had passed since their arrival, and the Clemenses had still not arrived to greet them.

"Do you think they're deliberately keeping us waiting?" Caleb asked his mother when another ten minutes had passed.

"That would be rather rude, but given our family's effect on their daughter's life, understandable, I suppose."

Caleb drummed his fingers against his armrest. Perhaps this meeting would not be as easy as he had expected. He cleared his throat and was considering calling for a servant to bring them some tea when the door opened and the Clemenses walked in.

"Your Graces," Mrs. Clemens said by way of greeting. Her voice was curt while still managing to sound polite.

Her husband, who followed her into the room, executed a bow in concert with his wife's curtsey. "I hope you'll forgive the wait," he murmured. "We were not expecting callers."

Caleb, who had risen the moment Mrs. Clemens had entered the room, stepped forward and offered his hand. Mr. Clemens eyed it as if uncertain, but eventually shook it without too much hesitation. "Please, let us sit," Caleb suggested. "There is a matter we wish to discuss with you."

"Oh indeed?" Mrs. Clemens arched a brow. "One would think there was nothing left to be said between us."

Ah, so the lady was holding a grudge.

Mr. Clemens gave his wife a look of warning. "I'm sure the duke and his mother have come for a reason. The least we can do is hear them out."

Mrs. Clemens seemed to consider this before nodding her agreement. "Very well. Shall I ring for some tea?"

"Please do," the duchess said. "I fear this may take some time. So sorry to impose on you like this without any notice, but my son is very eager to move things along, so here we are."

"And we are both eager to know the reason for it, Your Grace," Mr. Clemens said. He waited for his wife to sit before lowering himself to one of two available armchairs. Caleb sat in the other.

"I have come to discuss your daughter's future,"

Caleb said.

Two pairs of eyes widened, and then Mr. Clemens frowned. "Really?" He glanced at his wife, who was now biting her lip as if trying to stop herself from blurting out an insult. "Edith is a charming young lady," Mr. Clemens said carefully. "Well educated too, I can assure you of that. Her mother and I are both very progressive and thought it wise to ensure she'll not bore the man she eventually marries. But considering our previous experience with your family, I regret to inform you that I cannot in good conscience allow you to court her. Even if you are a duke."

"In that case you need not concern yourselves," Caleb said, "for Edith is not the daughter to whom I refer."

Mrs. Clemens appeared to relax while Mr. Clemens's eyes took on a bewildered look of confusion. "But who else is there? Sarah and Lilly are both married, so I don't quite—"

"I am speaking of Mary," Caleb said more sharply than he'd intended. To think the man could not recall having a fourth daughter was so astounding it made his nerves tighten to the point of snapping.

"After five years we'd hoped the business with your brother would be in the past," Mrs. Clemens told him tightly. "We told Mary at the time that it was unwise to set her cap for a marquess, but of course we hoped, as all parents do, that our daughter would aspire to greater things than we ever could." She glared at Caleb. "My husband wrote to your father at the time and apologized for Mary's transgression."

"You sent her away," Caleb told her while matching her frigid stare. This was not going as he had hoped.

"To protect our other daughters from being ruined by association," Mrs. Clemens explained. She swallowed hard and dropped her gaze. The fight appeared to go out of her, leaving a seemingly unhappy woman behind. "We did not have the power to fight a duke's influence. Sending Mary away felt like the only viable option at the time."

"Your coming here and inquiring after our daughter," Mr. Clemens said slowly, directing Caleb's attention away from Mrs. Clemens, "may have given us the wrong impression. I hope you'll forgive any assumptions made on our part. All things considered, we really ought to have known better than to suppose that you, the brother of the man our Mary tried to trap, would have any interest in—"

"Please." Caleb held up a hand, quieting the man. "This has nothing to do with my brother or the unfortunate rumor my father started in order to chase Mary away."

"I…er…I see," Mr. Clemens said even though it was clear he saw nothing. His wife appeared equally stumped.

"You do realize your daughter did nothing wrong?" Mary had never said much about her parents' reactions to what had happened, save for their intention to remove her to Scotland so her sisters would have better chances of making agreeable matches.

"Um…" Mrs. Clemens wrung her hands. "Your

father was a duke, Your Grace. A highly respect-able gentleman."

"What reason would we have had to suppose he would be dishonest?" Mr. Clemens asked.

Caleb could think of a dozen, the first one being that Mary was one of the most direct people he'd ever known. She wasn't a liar.

"So you believed him and the rumor he spread, over your own daughter's word?" Caleb's mother asked before he could manage to do so.

"Does it really matter?" Mrs. Clemens asked. She looked at each of them in turn. "We had no power to dispute what was being said. Only your brother could have done that, except he left Town shortly after and didn't return until the following Season."

Rising, Caleb crossed to the fireplace and stared down into the flickering flames while struggling to keep his anger at bay. He drew a deep breath and expelled it before turning back to face the people he hoped he'd soon be related to. "Even so, I daresay it would have made all the difference in the world to Mary if her family had believed her."

Guilt stole into the Clemens's eyes and Mrs. Clemens even dabbed at hers with a handkerchief Mr. Clemens produced from his jacket pocket. "We don't even know where she is," he said.

"She is safe and happy and living among friends," Caleb assured them.

"So you have seen her?" Mrs. Clemens's eyes brightened.

"Indeed, I have recently returned from a two-month stay at Clearview, which is where your Mary resides." A maid entered with a tea tray, and Caleb waited until she'd departed once more before strolling back to his chair and resuming his seat. "During my…sojourn there, I had the pleasure of becoming well acquainted with her. We became friends and I…" He paused for a moment while Mrs. Clemens served tea.

She glanced up at him with visible hesitation. "Sugar or milk?"

"Neither," he said, thanking her for the cup while his mother added a lump of sugar to her own. "The fact of the matter is, I fell completely in love with her."

His comment caused Mr. Clemens, who was in the process of picking up his cup, to jerk so violently he spilled most of the contents. His wife thrust a napkin toward him while staring at Caleb with wide-eyed dismay. "So you've come to ask for her hand?" she asked.

Caleb glanced at Mr. Clemens. who'd finally managed to mop up most of his tea from the table. "It is a bit more complicated than that."

Mr. Clemens discarded the soaking wet napkin on the tray and turned to Caleb. "In what sense?"

"In the sense that I did not tell her I was a duke or the brother of the man who once broke her heart."

"But why?" Mrs. Clemens asked with incredulity.

Caleb took a moment to explain the circumstances under which he'd first met Mary and why it had been so difficult for him to tell her the truth later on. "I fear she may never forgive me, but if there's even the tiniest chance she might, then I'll take it."

"My son is the Duke of Camberly," the duchess said. "That cannot change, and although he may wish to embrace the same sort of life your daughter has grown so fond of, away from Society and its responsibilities, he will still have estates to manage and tenants to look after. There is also his seat in Parliament to consider, which means he will have to spend part of his time in London, no matter how much he prefers the country."

"In other words," Mr. Clemens said, "Mary would have to accept this in order for the marriage to work."

Caleb nodded. "And I think getting her to do so will be easier if we show her that she can belong here again. Which is the crux of my visit today. I would like you both to apologize to her for making her feel unwanted."

Mr. Clemens shook his head. "We only—"

"Additionally," Caleb said, cutting him off, "I want you to invite her for Christmas. Tell her she is welcome to bring her friends and the children they care for. Be convincing."

Mrs. Clemens stared at him. "She will never agree, Your Grace. We...we haven't even heard from her in all these years. Not one word!"

"Of course you haven't, because it was never up to her to reach out. It was up to the two of you. Her parents. And do not tell me you failed to find her when I know well enough that your inability to do so is due to lack of effort on your part." Picking up his teacup, Caleb took a long sip and set it back down. "Now you have another chance to do right by Mary, as does my mother."

"I mean to make reparations by having the truth

printed in the Mayfair Chronicle," the duchess announced.

"Truly?" the Clemenses asked in unison.

"Invite your daughter for Christmas," Caleb said, "so I can proceed with the next part of my plan."

"Which is what, Your Grace?"

Caleb tugged on the sleeves of his jacket. His lips twitched with the thrill of pursuing the woman he wanted. "To court her as if every future happiness depends on her accepting my proposal."

CHAPTER FIFTEEN

"THERE IS A LETTER FOR you, Mary," Emily said when she came to the table at luncheon.

They were having chicken soup, which helped warm them on this particularly freezing December day where even the fire burning in the grate seemed insufficient. Cassandra was placing hot bricks near the children's feet for added comfort while Mary filled their bowls.

She looked up in surprise and wondered if it might be from *him*. It had been two and a half weeks since Caleb's departure and still her body felt numb. No matter how hard she tried, she could not stop thinking of him, which only caused her to question everything she'd said and done until she could no longer stand it. The pain was too much. She longed to escape it but didn't know how. What she did know was that Caleb had made her feel more alive than ever before. And that the moment he'd left, the part of her that smiled and laughed and enjoyed having fun had withered and died.

"It looks like it's from your parents," Emily said.

The ladle Mary was wielding clattered against the soup tureen. "What?"

Emily placed the sealed piece of paper bearing her address and theirs on the table in front of Mary. She drew a sharp breath, and her hand reached out, her fingers carefully sliding across her mother's elegant script to ensure it was real. And then an awful thought struck her. They'd no idea where she was because she'd never told them. So if they'd gone to the trouble of uncovering it now after all this time, it had to be because something terrible had happened.

Heart racing, Mary snatched up the letter and held it to her breast. "Will you please excuse me for a moment while I read this?"

"Of course," Cassandra said, looking only slightly alarmed. "We'll make sure the children eat every last drop of this tasty meal you've prepared. Including the carrots."

Daphne made a face and Eliot said, "Yuk!"

Mary felt a bit of the tension ease and thanked her friends before quitting the room. Drawing her shawl more tightly around her shoulders, she went to the kitchen where heat still radiated from the stove. She took a deep breath and steeled herself for the worst before breaking the seal and unfolding the letter.

Our dearest Mary,

Your father and I must express our sincerest apologies for the way in which we have wronged you. It has recently come to our attention that we were mistaken in our beliefs regarding what happened between you and the Marquess of Wrenwick. His brother, the new Duke of

Camberly, has set the story straight, laying all blame at his own father's feet.

After all these years, we can only pray you will find it in your heart to forgive us for not believing you at the time and for asking you to leave your home. We understand you have since made a comfortable life for yourself with two dear friends and that the three of you have bestowed your generosity upon a few orphans.

In an effort to broker peace between us and prove to you how sorry we are, we would like to invite all of you to spend the upcoming holiday season with us in London. Our house, as you know, is spacious enough to allow it, though some of the children may be required to share a bedchamber.

Your sisters send their love and best wishes, too, along with every hope of seeing you again very soon. Please let us know, or simply arrive. We are all ready and eager for your return.

With everlasting love and affection,
Mama and Papa
P.S. We will cover the cost of a hired post-chaise.

Sniffing, Mary brushed the tears from her cheek with the back of her hand, only to find herself crying harder. A sob lodged itself in her throat, struggling against the lump that had formed. She'd dreamed of this moment five years ago, of them coming to their senses and realizing just how greatly they'd wronged her. She'd dreamt of them missing her so much they'd hire investigators to find her, but then the weeks had turned into months, and the months had turned into years, and she'd lost hope.

Her body shook, not from cold but from violent

emotion. She'd thought she'd stopped caring, but the letter had brought it all back, and the words… the words went straight to her heart, melting it as easily as the sun would melt butter. Inhaling deeply, she reread the letter and cried a bit more before managing to regain her composure.

Caleb had done this. He'd gone to her parents and told them everything, and now they wanted to see her. She inhaled deeply. He was trying to make things right between them by clearing her of any wrongdoing with his brother. But as much as she appreciated the gesture, it didn't change the fact that he'd deliberately played her for a fool.

She knew she probably looked a fright when she returned to the dining room, and Cassandra's and Emily's concerned expressions confirmed this. "What has happened?" Cassandra asked.

Emily set her spoon aside. "Is everything all right?"

Peter slurped and Eliot belched, sending all the children into a fit of laughter which earned them a sharp reprimand from Cassandra.

Mary nodded. "Yes. We have all been invited to spend Christmas in London with my parents."

"Really?" Cassandra asked with some surprise.

Mary nodded. She bit her lip. "I'm not so sure it's a good idea," she said. Hurt from their ill-treatment still clung to her like a heavy wool cloak.

"May I?" Cassandra asked. She held out her hand, and Mary reluctantly handed her the letter. After reading it, she met Mary's gaze with bewildered curiosity. "Is this not what you have been waiting for, Mary? For your parents to apologize and beg your forgiveness?"

"I no longer know," Mary confessed. "It has been so long. I do not feel the same desire to see them again as I once did."

"They are your parents," Emily reminded her. "And what of your sisters? You said you used to be close."

Mary winced. She'd missed Sarah, Lilly, and Edith most of all after leaving London. It was her own fault she hadn't stayed in touch with them, because she'd feared they would tell their parents where she was hiding. "True," she muttered. "I have to admit I long to see them again."

"Then let us accept your parents' offer," Cassandra implored. "Besides, the children will have a better Christmas there than they're bound to have here. We cannot deny them that for any reason."

A small smile tugged at Mary's lips. "You are too manipulative, Emily."

"So it's settled?" Emily asked while everyone in the room seemed to hold their breath.

"Indeed," Mary said. "We are going to London for Christmas."

The children whooped in response, their happiness cementing the rightness of Mary's decision in her mind. It would likely be a strained reunion, but she'd do it for them. As for Caleb… She wasn't sure how she'd respond if she saw him during her visit to London and could only hope the attraction she felt for the man would not cloud her judgment in any way.

They arrived three days later, exactly one week

before Christmas Eve. After descending from the carriage, Mary had started helping the children down when the front door opened and a flurry of silk and lace launched itself in her direction. Before she knew what was happening, she was being embraced by her mother, who seemed stronger now than ever before, her arms squeezing Mary as if she meant to crush her.

"Thank God you are finally here," her mother exclaimed, heedless of who might happen to see. "You cannot imagine how much I have missed you."

"It cannot be more than I," another feminine voice said. "Or I," someone else remarked.

With barely a chance to catch her breath, Mary was helplessly pulled from her mother's arms into her sister, Edith's, embrace and then into her father's. It was overwhelming and much more frantic than she would have expected. It also banished the indifferent demeanor with which she'd intended to greet her parents and filled her heart with warmth instead.

"This is Miss Howard and Lady Cassandra," she said, introducing her friends as soon as she had the chance to. She gestured to each of the children in turn, "And here's Daphne, Bridget, Penelope, Peter, and Eliot."

"How delightful," Mrs. Clemens said. She leaned forward and smiled. "It is a pleasure to meet all of you."

"Come," Edith said, motioning for the children to join her. "Cook has prepared cream puff pastries and hot chocolate for you to enjoy."

Wide-eyed and full of wonder, the children followed her up the front steps and into the house while Mr. Clemens paid the driver, who helped two footmen retrieve the luggage from on top of the carriage.

"Let us go in as well," Mrs. Clemens said. She gestured for Emily and Cassandra to precede her and Mary.

"Where are Sarah and Lilly?" Mary asked her mother as they followed Emily and Cassandra into the foyer where Faulkner, the butler, stood waiting. He produced a rare smile as he welcomed Mary.

"Oh heavens," her mother exclaimed, "your sister, Sarah, married four years ago, and Lilly made a match of her own a couple of years later. They've both got homes to run and children to look after."

"Children?" Mary could scarcely believe it although she knew she ought to. After all, it had been five years, but Sarah and Lilly were both younger than she, so the idea just hadn't occurred.

"They wanted to be here when you arrived," Mary's mother continued, "but I thought it might be a bit much after the long journey you've had, so I told them to let you get settled first and that we would see them soon."

Mary took off her gloves and handed them to Faulkner so she could untie the ribbons of her bonnet. "Will tomorrow be possible?" she asked her mother. Her father, who'd entered the foyer behind them, closed the door, stepped around them, and gestured for Cassandra and Emily to follow him toward the back of the house.

"Yes. I believe so," her mother said. She took Mary's bonnet and set it on a nearby table. Linking her arm with Mary's, she guided her in the direction everyone else had gone. "We will have them over for tea to start. I'll send a note over straightaway, inviting them both."

"Thank you, Mama," Mary said. She placed her hand over her mother's. "I'm sorry I never wrote to tell you where I was or how I was doing."

Her mother's lips quivered ever so slightly, and it took a bit longer than usual for her to respond. When she did, her voice was but a whisper. "We're sorry too. Exceedingly so. Your father and I said some regrettable things and...to think we even considered sending you to Scotland weighs heavily on my conscience."

"You did what you thought was best for the rest of the family," Mary reminded her.

Her mother did not look convinced. "Camberly was furious with us when he came to explain everything. He could not fathom how we, your parents, had failed you when you needed us most. I've never felt smaller than I did while faced with his censure."

"He chastised you and Papa?" Mary could scarcely believe it.

"Most effectively." Mrs. Clemens turned to face her, revealing the deep ache of regret that dimmed her eyes. She squeezed Mary's hand, and the lines of concern creasing her brow eased. "Thankfully, you are here now and that is what matters." She found her vigor again and said, "There is so much for us to do, especially with the children. Do you think they'll enjoy going ice skating on the Serpentine?"

Mary smiled with genuine feeling for the first

time in weeks. "I know they would, Mama."

"There is also the National Gallery and the Hunterian Museum," her mother continued. "Oh, they will love the Irish Giant. He is quite a curiosity. And then of course there is…"

Mary failed to hear the rest of her mother's ideas as they entered the sunroom. The children were busily devouring their creampuffs with unencumbered pleasure while grinning in response to her father's account of some naughty deed he recalled from when he was their age. Heart swelling with joy, Mary went to join them. She selected a pastry for herself, and offered her cup to her mother, who filled it with steaming hot chocolate.

She was home again at long last, and it felt better than she would ever have imagined possible. If she did happen to come across Caleb during her visit to London, she would have to offer her thanks.

"I cannot believe you have married Baron Huntingham," Mary told her sister Sarah the next afternoon. After taking tea together, Mr. Clemens had suggested that everyone go for a walk in the park. The children raced ahead while Cassandra and Emily called for them to slow down and walk. Leaning close to her sister, Mary whispered, "You always told me you found him too arrogant."

Sarah laughed and turned to glance at her husband, who walked a few paces behind them. He was keeping company with Lilly and her husband, Mr. Gilford, while Esther kept pace with Mr. and Mrs. Clemens.

"That was my initial opinion," Sarah confided, "until we discovered our shared interest in minerals. He promptly invited me to see his collection, and we have been inseparable ever since."

"So you have finally found someone with whom to talk about rocks," Mary said. The ache she'd felt after Caleb's departure from Clearview returned. How she missed discussing all manner of things with him. How she missed his smile.

"I suppose so," Sarah said. "And Lilly has married the gentleman farmer she always hoped for, so she can now spend her days with as many sheep as she can count."

Mary grinned. Lilly's fondness for sheep had always been something of a curiosity. "From what I gather, Mr. Gilford is no ordinary farmer." He was handsome as sin for one thing and for another, Mary had seen him watching his wife as if he wanted her for dessert.

"He has vast amounts of land and at least fifty farmhands to help take care of it all." Sarah lowered her voice to scandalously add, "And Lilly tells me he is exceedingly virile and eager to keep her in the bedchamber." A snort of repressed laughter followed. "It is my understanding she is very happy indeed."

Sighing, Mary watched Cassandra and Emily catch up to Peter and Eliot who were both in the lead. Words were exchanged, which made Mary smile. She didn't have to hear what was being said to know Cassandra was sternly insisting they not run off again.

"Does motherhood agree with you?" Mary asked her sister while she continued to watch the children she'd grown to love. Daphne and Bridget had somehow managed to climb onto a large decorative rock, while Penelope appeared to by trying to climb a tree.

"Of course," Sarah said. "It is the best thing in the world."

"I look forward to meeting your daughters one day." Because of their very young ages, Sarah's and Lilly's children had remained at home with their nurses.

"And so you shall, but first I would like to hear about you and what you have experienced these past five years," Sarah said.

"Yes, you must tell us everything," Lilly said, catching up just in time to hear what Sarah had told her. "There must have been some admirers along the way. A gentleman farmer perhaps?"

Sarah snorted. "They're not all as fit as yours, Lilly."

Mary thought of Mr. Townsend. "Or as pleasant," she remarked.

"Oh?" Both sisters asked with interest.

"I will admit there was one who was very persistent in his pursuit of me," Mary said, "but his character was lacking, so I turned him down."

"I'm sure there will be others," Sarah said. "Especially now that you are back in Town. Granted, many families have gone away to the country for the holidays, but some are still here, and with our yearly Christmas ball coming up, I know for a fact there will be at least three eligible bachelors present. Considering the Duchess of Camberly's article in the Mayfair Chronicle this morning, your reputation will be restored and—"

"Thank you, Sarah, but I am really not eager to form an attachment," Mary said. When her mother had pushed the paper under her nose and forced her to read it, she'd been stumped by the duchess's admission of guilt on her late husband's behalf. But as much as Mary appreciated the sentiment and the effort Caleb must have gone to in order to make it happen, she wasn't as excited by the prospect of having her reputation restored as she knew she should be. "Unfortunately, I believe it is too late for me, regardless. At five and twenty I am well past my prime."

"Oh, you mustn't say that," Lilly admonished. "Plenty of women bear children well into their thirties, so it is not as if you've lost your chance to start a family."

"I don't know," Mary hedged. "It is not so simple."

They caught up with Cassandra and Emily, who had managed to gather the children together in one energetic clump. "We weren't sure whether to hire skates or continue walking," Cassandra explained.

"That depends on what everyone wants," Mr. Clemens said. "Those in favor of skating say, 'aye!'"

A chorus of 'ayes' followed, and Mr. and Mrs. Clemens both laughed. "I think it is unanimous," Mrs. Clemens said. She crossed to the stand where skates could be rented and proceeded to make the necessary arrangements.

Soon after, they were all gliding along the length of the Serpentine while Mr. and Mrs. Clemens watched from the lakeside. Grasping hold of Daphne's hand, Mary helped the girl keep her balance as they followed the rest of the group.

"Can I try to skate on my own now?" Daphne asked after a while. "I would like to try and do what Peter is doing."

Mary sought out the boy and saw he was spinning around while staying in place. "You might fall," Mary warned, knowing that this was why Daphne had always been hesitant on the ice, because she'd once hurt herself badly after losing her balance.

"I know," the girl said, "but I am not going to get any better unless I take that risk."

Impressed by her wisdom, Mary released her hand, and the girl skated over to Peter. She waited for him to stop spinning, then asked him to show her how it was done, which he proceeded to do with a surprising amount of patience for a boy his age.

"Miss Clemens," a deep voice called, and Mary's heart promptly lurched in response while her pulse began to flutter with jittery discomfort.

Turning, she saw the man to whom the voice belonged. Caleb was skating slowly toward her with a warm, welcoming smile, while his deep blue eyes reflected the late afternoon sunlight. God, he was handsome, his hair slightly mussed with careless abandon in a way that took her back to the days he'd spent fixing the roof of Clearview House, to a time when he'd been just a man. A very charming, endearing, and thoroughly intoxicating man.

Mary tipped her chin up as he slid to a halt beside her. She'd known she might meet him if she came to London; she just hadn't though it would be quite this soon.

"Mr. Crawford," she said, deliberately greeting him as she had grown accustomed to doing before she'd learned of his title. "You are looking very well."

"As are you." Dropping his gaze, he raised it slowly, sliding it up the length of her body until she pulsed with awareness. Pausing on her lips, he reminded her of the kiss they had shared, provoking a spark that charged straight through her. His eyes met hers. "Have you been in Town long, Miss Clemens?"

Mary started. The question was posed with unexpected casualness. Was he not aware of the effect he had on her? Had he not felt the same? "We arrived yesterday."

"And how long will you be staying?"

He caught her hand as if it was normal for him to do so – as if his touch did not set her soul on fire. Oh God, she was losing her mind. Or perhaps she already had? "Three weeks, I should think," she managed to say.

Skating slowly in a wide circle, Caleb pulled her along with him. "Are you visiting your parents?" He drew her toward him, turning her slightly until they were hip to hip. Skating forward in tandem, he slid his arm around her waist, holding her closer than most would deem proper.

"We've made amends," she said. "Thanks to you, in part, from what I understand."

"I merely offered some necessary clarification," he murmured, close to her ear.

"Did you also ask your mother to writer the

article printed in the Mayfair Chronicle this morning?"

"I confess, I may have suggested she do her part in compensating for the way our family has treated you." He quietly added, "We are all very sorry indeed."

She ought to be angry, furious even, for the lies he'd told. But how could she be when he was doing all in his power to right a wrong that wasn't even his own? It just proved him to be a better man than she wished to give him credit for.

Swallowing her pride, she said what needed to be said. "Thank you, Mr. Crawford." She angled her head and caught his gaze while the world drifted by around them.

"It was the least I could do." He straightened himself and stretched out his arm, breaking the intimacy by adding an appropriate measure of distance between them.

Mary tightened her hold on his hand and held on tight. She did not want to lose him again, but at the same time, how could she trust him? *Because he tried to tell you the truth*, she told herself as they skated further away from her family. But if he'd really cared about her, would he not have made sure she knew, no matter what? *No.*

He was scared.

Just as scared as you are right now.

The thoughts in her head were crowding her brain, but when she and Caleb finally slid to a halt and he turned her to face him, there was one that stood out more than the rest.

"You hurt me more than your brother ever did," she said. "Perhaps that puts things in perspective."

Sadness stared back at her, so bleak it threatened the pleasure she'd found in seeing him again. "I know and I am sorry. If I could go back with what I know now, I would do everything differently."

"How?"

"I would be honest with you from the start and hope you would love me anyway." Her throat closed and words failed her. "But perhaps we can start again." Hope brimmed in his dazzling eyes. It lifted Mary's spirits and filled her with a renewed sense of longing. "I know I have a lot of unacceptable qualities, like being a duke, for example. But if you will permit me, I would like to show you that I can still be the man you knew at Clearview, no matter what title I hold."

"I don't know." She had to think clearly about this, and being so near him was muddling her head. "My appetite for dukes has been sated, I'm afraid."

He smiled in spite of the anguish in his face. "Allow me to call on you tomorrow, Miss Clemens. We'll spend the day together, and I will show you my favorite places in London."

To tell him no would be unbelievably difficult. And besides, she really did not want to. What she desired most of all right now was to tell him yes. So she nodded. "Very well, Mr. Crawford. Tomorrow it is. But I cannot promise you'll get the result you seek. My heart still hurts, and my mind is urging me to be cautious."

Without commenting, he skated backward while executing a perfect bow. Mary laughed into the palms of her hands when he added a wink. Turning about, he called over his shoulder, "Be ready by ten!" He bent his knees and pushed himself forward to increase his speed as he skated toward the far bank.

"Who was that?" Sarah asked from directly behind Mary's left shoulder.

Startled, Mary spun around, attempting to face her. She almost lost her balance in the process and had to be steadied by Lilly and Edith, who were there as well, looking just as curious as Sarah.

"Mr. Crawford," Mary said. Her sisters raised their eyebrows in a silent plea for more information. "Very well. He's more correctly known as the Duke of Camberly."

All three pairs of eyes widened.

"You are acquainted with His Grace?" Sarah asked in dismay. "The brother of the man who caused you to leave for only God knows where five years ago?"

"I would have thought you'd be angrier with him than you appear," Edith said.

"It's complicated," Cassandra said, somehow materializing at Mary's right elbow. She'd brought Emily with her. "Mary mistook His Grace for a common laborer when they initially met."

"So did you," Mary said. Feeling crowded, she skated away from her sisters and friends, but of course they chose to follow.

"Ah, I begin to grasp the bigger picture," Sarah said at Mary's back. "You fell for him without knowing who he really was, and now you want the laborer rather than the duke, which poses a bit of a problem since you cannot have one without the other."

"Thank you, Sarah," Mary muttered. "I have

managed to figure that much out on my own."

"I don't see the issue," Penelope said. Somehow she was now there as well, skating alongside Mary. Looking down at her, Mary saw that the other children were not far behind. "Mr. Crawford is handsome and kind. He knows how to fix things too, which I imagine would be rather useful," Penelope said.

"He rescued Raphael from that awful storm," Daphne added.

"And he makes a brilliant fishing rod, Miss Clemens," Peter shouted across the heads of the other children.

"I like how he smells," Bridget yelled.

Mary had to agree. His spicy scent was a wonderful mixture of cedar, bergamot, and sandalwood. Her heart thumped wildly when she thought of the way it infused her senses whenever she was near him.

"I have agreed to meet him tomorrow," she said in order to placate Caleb's supporters. "Depending on how that goes, I may or may not choose to see him again."

It was the best she could do for now. Because although he'd been charming as always, and she'd wanted to forget all the rest, she had to consider the state of her heart. It was still recovering from his deceit, so if she decided to trust him now and he betrayed her again, she feared she would never survive it.

CHAPTER SIXTEEN

CALEB ROSE THE NEXT MORNING at seven. By eight he was freshly shaved and dressed. He descended the stairs and entered the dining room where breakfast awaited. His mother was, as he'd expected, already seated at the table. What he did not expect was to find Griffin there too.

"You are up early," he told his brother as he pulled out a chair and took his seat.

"Good morning to you too, Caleb," Griffin muttered while chewing his food. He took a quick sip of coffee to wash it down before saying, "You're looking very crisp today."

"And so he should," the duchess said. "If he is to win Miss Clemens, effort must be made." She caught Caleb's eye. "Have you decided where to take her for your outing?"

Caleb poured himself a hot cup of tea and reached for the toast. "I've a few places in mind." For some odd reason, he didn't want to share the specifics, except when it came to his choice of restaurant. "I'm thinking of The Grotto for luncheon."

"Oh, she will love that, I'm sure," the duchess

exclaimed. "It's so romantic."

"As I recall," Griffin drawled, "there's a private corner behind the stairs. I took a young widow there years ago. It was very secluded and perfect for—"

Caleb cleared his throat and gave his brother a pointed look, reminding him that their mother was present and might not want to hear of her son's liaisons. He knew the spot he referred to and had already booked a table there.

"That list I prepared for you, Caleb," the duchess began while drumming her fingers lightly next to her plate. "Perhaps I can use it after all, for Griffin's benefit."

"What an excellent idea, Mama." Caleb grinned. It was high time his brother got a feel for some of the pressure he'd been forced to endure since becoming a duke. "I'm sure there's a lady on it who will suit him perfectly."

"What list?" Griffin asked with undeniable alarm. "A lady suited for what, exactly?"

"Marriage, dear brother," Caleb said without bothering to hide his amusement. "Mama has made a painstaking selection of the best potential brides in the land."

"Then you should pick one," Griffin croaked. He looked as though his cravat was cutting off blood to his head.

"But I am to marry Miss Clemens," Caleb explained. He was enjoying this. It reminded him of when they were lads and they used to prank each other. Before they'd fallen out with their father and gone off in separate directions.

"That has yet to be determined," Griffin said.

He'd bolstered himself and was now firing back. At the head of the table, their mother hid a mischievous smile behind her teacup. "She might refuse you, so you may want to wait on handing that list to someone else."

Caleb's smile faded. "If I cannot have Miss Clemens, I will not marry at all." He looked up with a sudden spark of inspiration. "So there will be all the more reason for you to do so, Griffin, since your son could be my heir."

"My son?" Griffin sputtered.

"Stop it," the duchess demanded, though she did so with laughter in her voice. "You will both marry in due course, of that I can assure you."

Caleb noted that he wasn't the only one glowering at her. "Being married is the unhappiest state a person can be in, Mama," Griffin said. "Just consider yourself and Papa."

The words were out before Caleb could manage to kick his brother or toss a napkin at him or do something to halt the hurtful words. Shaking his head disapprovingly, he looked at the duchess, whose humorous expression had faded into shadowy lines. "You are right. We were miserable with each other. Your father kept countless mistresses over the years while I..." She pressed her lips together and gave both her sons a devastated look. "I was gifted with four wonderful boys and for that reason alone, I do not regret marrying him for a second. We might not have understood each other very well, but becoming a parent was worth every sacrifice.

"What I want for you most of all is for you to know the joy of holding your own child in your arms and marveling over the miracle of life. It is the most remarkable thing in the world, and if you are fortunate enough to experience it with someone you care for, then you will have gained more wealth in this lifetime than would ever fit in the Camberly coffers."

The duchess had clearly changed her opinion on marriage in recent weeks. It occurred to Caleb that her love for him and desire to see him happy had a lot to do with this, so he reached for her hand and gave it a squeeze in a silent conveyance of affection.

A moment of comfortable silence passed between them, until Griffin spoke. "You do realize a man can father a child without having to get himself leg-shackled, do you not?"

"Griffin Nathanial Finnegan Crawford," the duchess said in the most authoritative tone Caleb had heard her use since his childhood. A shudder went through him, and when he glanced at his brother, it appeared as though he was shrinking. "You will not suggest such things while under this roof, nor will you think it. Is that clear?"

"Perfectly," Griffin said with a downcast gaze. "I beg your forgiveness, Mama."

The duchess heaved in a lungful of air which had the effect of increasing her height by at least one inch. "It is almost nine." She looked at Caleb. "I suggest you finish eating so you can be on your way."

Caleb downed the remainder of his tea and stood. Griffin apparently intended to follow, but the duchess reached out and grabbed his hand. "Stay," she said, forcing Griffin back into his chair.

He gave Caleb a helpless look of desperation that begged for his interference. Instead, Caleb went to the door, wished them both a wonderful day, and left the pair to discuss whatever it was they would be discussing. Caleb no longer cared. He was far more interested in courting Miss Clemens.

After a quick stop at a nearby hothouse, Caleb arrived at Clemens House exactly five minutes before ten o'clock and was granted entry by the butler.

"Look who it is," Peter called, spotting him from the top of the stairs and storming down them to fling his arms tight around Caleb's waist. Thankfully, Caleb had the foresight to raise the bouquet of flowers he'd brought above his head so they wouldn't be crushed.

"Mr. Crawford!" Another pair of arms wrapped around one of his legs, and although he could not see the imp, he recognized the voice as Daphne's. The rest of the children were soon upon him as well, hugging him from all sides while the butler made a hopeless attempt at reinstating order.

"Good heavens," the older and far more mature voice belonging to Mrs. Clemens exclaimed. "Leave His Grace alone. The poor man can barely move!"

Laughter followed and Caleb glanced toward the stairs where Mary now stood assessing the scene. Dressed in a lilac gown with lace and satin trimmings, she looked both expensive and enticing, like a box of caramels from Gunter's Tea Shop, just waiting to be unwrapped and savored. But most of all, it was her dancing eyes and joyful smile that drew him.

Christ, she was beautiful, and God, how he wanted to prove himself worthy. He could not muck up this second chance she'd allowed him, or he'd never forgive himself for it.

Returning his attention to the little beasts clinging to him, he pinched the nearest one within reach. Bridget squealed and leapt right off him, allowing better access to the rest of the brood, who giggled and screamed as he tickled them each without remorse until they acknowledged defeat and retreated to another part of the house with Mrs. Clemens close on their heels. The butler, who looked unsure about how to handle the ruckus, excused himself and vanished through a nearby doorway.

"They adore you," Mary said. She'd reached the bottom of the stairs and was now gazing up at him with inquisitive eyes. She pursed her lips in a teasing way that rendered him utterly speechless. "I wonder why."

Intent on affecting her just as viscerally as she affected him, he took a step forward so his chest could graze her breasts as he leaned in to whisper, "They recognize a fellow troublemaker when they see one, Miss Clemens." Inhaling deeply, he allowed her scent to stir his blood without the slightest remorse.

He stepped back in case someone happened to chance upon their scandalous closeness and held up the roses he'd brought along with him. "These are for you," he said, appreciating her dazed expression and lovely pink cheeks.

Blinking, she accepted the offering and excused herself for a moment so she could hand them over to a maid. When she returned, she'd managed to regain her composure, which Caleb appreciated since he could not wait to make her lose it all over again.

"Will you be bringing a chaperone with you?" he asked for the sole purpose of taking her reputation into account.

She bit her lip. "I asked Mama if she thought it necessary, and she has insisted that a woman of my age and situation does not require looking after with the same sort of diligence a debutante would." Twitching her nose in the most adorable way, she pensively added, "I believe she wishes to allow you every opportunity you require in order to convince me to marry you."

Caleb decided he was starting to like Mrs. Clemens immensely. Next time he called, he'd bring roses for her as well. "A fine plan if you ask me," he said and offered his arm. As he led her through the front door and out to the awaiting carriage, he quietly murmured, "One I'm more than ready to execute to the best of my abilities."

She sucked in an audible breath, and Caleb's body tightened in response to the sensual sound. Hell and damnation, they'd only just started their day together, and already she had him wondering how much she would protest if he chose to abandon his carefully crafted plan to court her and simply whisked her off to a bedroom somewhere.

"Mr. Crawford?"

Caleb blinked and realized he must have handed her up into the conveyance without even noticing. Shaking his head to dislodge the dazed effect she'd had on him, he climbed up and took the opposite bench as propriety demanded. But it wasn't all bad, for although he was too far away to touch her except with his foot, he could now take his time to admire her face, her hair, the perfect slope of her neck where it joined with her shoulder, the swell of her breasts, and her narrow waist.

Setting his hat beside him, he cleared his throat, crossed his legs, and prayed he'd survive the day.

"I like your carriage," she said while looking out the window at the buildings they were passing. "It is very grand, is it not?"

"My father commissioned it," Caleb said. "He loved flaunting his title with material things."

"And you don't?" She shifted her gaze to him, and he saw she was genuinely curious to know his answer.

"I find there are more important things in life than carriages with silk velvet seats and gilded trimmings." Placing the palm of his hand on the bench, he stroked the plush surface with his thumb. Deliberately lowering his voice to an intimate tone, he said, "Like you, for instance. I would sell everything I own if that were the price you demanded of me."

"Would you really?" Just a whispered question with the promise of complete surrender.

He halted the movement he was making. "I am still the same man who pulled rotted floorboards out of the Clearview attic, who helped you prepare the roses for winter, who—"

"Crafted fishing rods for the boys and saved Raphael from what Daphne insists was certain death." She met his gaze, and he held his breath. "But you are also a whole lot more, and that is the part that concerns me, Caleb."

Hope spilled through him at the sound of his given name spoken for the first time since their falling out. "I cannot rid myself of the title, Mary. I shall always be a duke, and if you marry me, you will become my duchess." Seeing the disheartened look in her eyes, he hastened to say, "But that doesn't mean we have to allow it to change who we are or who we want to be. If anything, the title should open a world of possibilities to us. It should allow us to choose the paths we want to follow."

"What do you mean?"

She looked too skeptical for his liking so he forged ahead. "There is no rule book demanding I must live on one of the Camberly estates. We can buy a small cottage if that is what you desire and enjoy a peaceful existence there without any servants. It could be on the Yorkshire moors, if you wish."

A reluctant grin teased at her lips. "The Yorkshire moors?"

"Or anywhere else of your choosing. We can even remain at Clearview House if Lady Cassandra and Miss Howard allow it. I certainly don't object."

She opened her mouth to speak, but his comment must have struck her dumb for not a single word emerged. And then the carriage drew to a halt, and the door was swung open. Caleb alit and helped Mary down. She looked thoroughly befuddled, which was just as it should be.

"Have you ever been here before?" he asked.

She stared at him for a second, then glanced at the narrow timbered building that stood before them in the cobblestoned street. "No. I have not."

Pleasure surged through him, followed by eager excitement. "Wonderful," he said, feeling much like a young boy about to show off his favorite toy to his friend. He led her toward the door and opened it for her.

Mary stepped into the tiny foyer, and Caleb followed, brushing past her so he could address the man who welcomed them. "Two tickets please," he said, placing the necessary entry fee on the counter.

"What is this place?" Mary asked. She glanced about in search of a hint.

Caleb accepted the tickets and parted a thick velvet curtain that hung to his left. "A miniature museum with miniature things," he replied and waved her through the narrow opening.

"How intriguing." Mary entered the next room and immediately went to study the first thing she found on display. Leaning forward, she stared through a magnifying glass while Caleb waited for her reaction. She took a sharp breath and Caleb smiled. "There is a painting of Leonardo da Vinci's *Last Supper* on a grain of rice, Caleb. Have you seen it? It is absolutely incredible!" She returned her attention to the rice, shifting her gaze to study the grain both with and without the magnifying glass. "I don't know how the artist did it. I really don't."

Moving toward her, Caleb stepped so close his hip touched hers. When she didn't shy away, he glanced around to ensure that they were completely alone, and then placed his palm lightly against her waist and leaned forward over her.

"I imagine he must have clamped it in place somehow and used very fine brushes, no more than a hair or two thick." Leaning down further, he allowed his chest to connect with her back while his hand stroked gently against her waist.

"What are you doing?" she whispered.

"Just trying to see." His voice stirred the hairs at the nape of her neck, and for some bizarre reason he was tempted to lick her, right there on the sliver of skin between the collar of her pelisse and hairline.

Instead, he pulled back and tried to slow the thunderous beat of his heart. "Look here," he said. "There is a portrait of Henry the Eighth on a pinhead."

"Really?" She pushed him aside without any apology, and Caleb allowed it, both pleased and amused by her delight over the exhibit.

"Shall we move on?" he asked moments later when she'd thoroughly perused three more items, and he'd started wondering if studying the rounded shape of her bottom each time she leaned forward might put him in physical danger. "There is an upstairs section as well."

She flew past him and hurried up the steps while he laughed at her exuberance. "It says this one is from China," she called, directing him toward her. As he approached, he recognized one of his favorite pieces.

"Impressive, isn't it." There was a whole village on a mountaintop carved from a piece of bone smaller than a penny.

"It ought to be impossible," she said. Straightening herself, she glanced around the small upstairs area. It was pristinely kept, with polished wood floors and crisp white walls. "All of this…" She struggled to find the right words and eventually shook her head in surrender.

"It is a testament to man's ability to accomplish whatever he sets his mind to," Caleb said. "I have loved coming here since my nurse first brought me and my brothers years ago. I cannot have been more than six years old at the time and just as enthralled as you by the wonder of it all. Later, when I grew older, it gave me the courage to choose my own path – the path my father refused to allow – because I realized that if an artist could paint *The Last Supper* on a grain of rice, then I could bloody well go and build houses if that was what I wanted." Reaching up, he brushed a stray lock of hair from her cheek. "Anything is possible if you are determined enough, Mary. I have complete faith in that."

"I don't want a cottage in Yorkshire," she said, "and I am not sure if staying at Clearview would be right either."

"What do you want then?" God help him, he'd find a way to give her whatever she asked for.

She bit her lip and took a deep breath. "Do you have an estate to spare?"

Intrigued, he slowly nodded. "I have three, as it happens."

"Would you consider…" She crossed her arms

and started pacing while giving him the occasional glance. Caleb watched, increasingly curious to know her idea. She suddenly drew to a halt and faced him boldly. "What would you say to creating a larger sanctuary for children in need?"

"You mean an actual orphanage?"

"In a way. I suppose so. Yes." She tipped up her chin and waited for him to respond.

Caleb took a moment to do so. "I wouldn't be opposed. In fact, I think it is a fine way of putting the dusty old edifices to some good use."

The smile she gave him was radiant. It threatened to knock him right off his feet. "That is good to know," she said with an added nod to convey her approval.

"Does that mean you might want to marry me?"

She gave him the sultriest look he'd ever seen. "Maybe," was her answer. Relief coupled with endless yearning fizzed in his veins. "If you ask me, that is."

"I plan to," he assured her though he'd leave her guessing as to when. They descended the stairs and exited the museum. "Are you ready for luncheon?" He ushered her forward and opened the door to the carriage. "The Grotto was one of my favorite restaurants before I left England. Have you ever been?"

"No. I cannot say I have."

He leaned in and touched his lips to her cheek to banish the cold. "You are in for a treat then, Mary, for there is no other place quite like it."

CHAPTER SEVENTEEN

M ARY'S ENTIRE BODY WAS TYING itself into tight little knots of unsated need. Every heated look and sensual touch made her want to reach out and grab Caleb and never let go. She wanted to feel his lips against hers again, his hands on her body, caressing in ways she could only imagine. And she wanted to run her hands over him, too, and explore the rippling muscles she'd seen on his arms when he'd stood shirtless before her at Clearview during the rainstorm. She wanted to slide her fingers across his broad back and clasp his solid shoulders.

But can you trust him?

He lied to you once. Most egregiously.

This was true. But it was also true that he'd tried to warn her, that he was at heart an honorable man with no more desire to be a duke than she had to be a duchess. But law of inheritance had determined his fate, so if she wanted a life with him by her side, then that was the price she must pay.

Did she love him enough to do so? To ignore her aversion and marry into the very society that had mocked her and shunned her and made her leave London?

The answer was yes. Yes, she did. Especially when he was prepared to go against all expectation and give her the world. "A cottage," she murmured bemusedly as she climbed into the carriage. Only a simple man with simple needs would ever suggest such a thing with the kind of eagerness he had shown.

She watched him take the seat opposite her and suddenly wondered if in his effort to please her, to make up for what he had done, he was putting aside his wants in favor of hers. "We could do something else," she began, drawing his attention. "We could hire staff to run the orphanage while we live elsewhere on the estate. In a cottage like you suggested."

A slow, affectionate smile tugged at his lips. "Is that what you want?"

"It is not all about me, Caleb. It is also about you and what your wishes are."

His smile widened. "My wishes will be fulfilled the moment we are wed."

As much as she appreciated such a selfless notion, she would not let it distract her. "But would you prefer to live in a cottage or in a grand manor?"

"Honestly?" She gave a firm nod. "My home in France was small, consisting only of one bedchamber, a parlor and a kitchen. I was very content there, as I was in the cottage I lived in at Clearview." Leaning forward, he reached for her hand. "I do not need or want anything beyond that, except you and your happiness."

"That is a very roundabout answer and not very

helpful."

He grinned. "Very well. If it were entirely up to me, I would pick the cottage, but I fear my estates do not have any, except the ones already inhabited by the caretakers."

"Then you must build one," she said. It wasn't something she had thought of until this very instant.

He stared at her. "Build one?"

"Yes." She was warming to the idea of it already – especially if it would allow her to watch him roll up his shirtsleeves and show off his arms. "It makes perfect sense, does it not?"

Caleb blinked. "I suppose…" He refocused his gaze on her. "You would support me in such an endeavor?"

"Of course! Why wouldn't I?"

He chuckled in an almost bashful way that stole into her heart and prompted it to expand. "No one has ever done so, Mary. Not my father or my mother."

"Only because they have preconceived ideas of what the son of a duke is expected to do. But I am more progressive and far more open to new ideas."

An eyebrow rose and his eyes darkened to glistening shades of blue. "Is that so?"

A shiver scraped the length of her spine in the most delicious way possible. She nodded and made the effort to voice her remaining thoughts on the matter. "We can stay in the main building until the cottage has been completed, if that is agreeable to you. And we will go to London each spring so you can attend to your parliamentary duties. I shall not deny you that, and besides, the occasional ball might not be so bad."

"You do realize I have not yet proposed?"

"And I have not given my answer either, but that is just a small formality at this point, don't you think?"

"Indeed I do, Miss Clemens." He raised her hand to his lips and pressed a kiss to her kid-skin-covered knuckles while gazing into her eyes. *You'll always be mine*, they seemed to say, and that thought alone made her belly swirl like champagne being poured into glasses.

The carriage slowed and they exited onto the pavement. "We'll be a couple of hours, Charles," Caleb informed his coachman while Mary braced herself against a sudden gust of icy wind. Tiny snowflakes danced through the air, melting the moment they hit the ground. "If you would like to take a break and return for us later, please go ahead. I do not want to keep you out in this chill."

Thanking him, Charles tipped his hat and urged the horses onward. Caleb put his arm around Mary and hastened her toward the restaurant door. A waiter opened it wide to grant them entry, and Mary stepped forward, into the dim interior where hundreds of candles cast shimmering light across the limestone walls.

"Welcome, Your Grace," a finely dressed man said. "Your table awaits. This way please."

He led them toward a circular stone staircase where niches filled with lighted candles illuminated the stone steps. Reaching the bottom, he showed them to a table tucked away in a private corner behind the stairs. Again, candles scattered about on every available surface produced a golden haze of flickering light that faded into darkness. It was without a doubt the most romantic place Mary had ever visited, perhaps the most scandalous too, considering the seductive atmosphere.

"Some wine?" the man who'd shown them to their table inquired once Caleb had helped Mary take her seat and he'd lowered himself to the opposite chair.

"Do you prefer red or white?" Caleb asked Mary.

"Red, I should think."

Caleb nodded his agreement. "One bottle of Château Lafite please, Mr. Jarvis."

"Excellent choice, Your Grace." Mr. Jarvis handed them each a crisp piece of parchment containing the menu and went to see about the wine.

"May I make a recommendation?" Caleb asked as soon as they were completely alone.

Mary looked up from the list of delicious foods. "Of course."

"The lamb was excellent last week when I came to ensure that the standard was still as good as I remembered. For dessert, I suggest trying the profiteroles."

"Are you fond of sweets yourself?" she asked, setting the menu aside.

He quirked his lips and deliberately held her gaze for an extended moment before quietly saying, "I am fond of you."

Caleb appreciated the color rising in her cheeks,

further accentuated by the candles which afforded her with a lovely pink glow.

"That is not what I was asking, Caleb."

"I rather think it was," he said. Her blush deepened as she timidly dropped her gaze. He loved flirting with her, making her lose her composure, and seeing her nerves reveal the profound effect he had on her.

Mr. Jarvis returned with the bottle they'd requested and filled their glasses. He then took their order of food before leaving them alone once more. It was hard to believe it was only a little after noon. The muted lighting seemed to trick the brain into thinking it was late in the evening, which was one of the things he'd always enjoyed when coming here. Not only did the place have excellent food and an atmosphere fit for seduction, it also allowed for the nonexistence of time since the hour was always the same here, morning, midday, or night.

Caleb picked up his glass and waited for Mary to do the same. "So what do you think so far?"

"You were right," she said, clinking her glass against his. "It *is* unlike anything I have ever experienced before. I love the mood." She twisted in her seat and glanced about, the movement tightening the bodice of her gown in a way that would make any man lose his wits. "The element of respectability mixed with a splash of salaciousness invites a certain lapse in propriety."

God help him. If she said anything more, he would have her against the wall and to hell with whoever happened to see them. He drank his wine, gulping down half his glass in a desperate attempt to control his baser needs.

"I'll need to dig a foundation," he said, latching onto the first non-sexual thought that entered his head, hoping it might cool his ardor.

She knit her brow. "I beg your pardon?"

"For the cottage," he explained. "How big shall we make it?"

"You mentioned only one bedroom before, and that is sufficient for us don't you think? If we ever have guests we can put them up in the manor."

"But what of the children?" he asked her seriously, for it was quite possibly the most important question after asking her if she would be his wife.

"What do you mean?" She tilted her head and regarded him with a puzzled expression, as if he'd just told her he bathed in milk and wore gloves to bed. "We already agreed they would be in the manor as well."

He smiled at her sweetly and slid his chair so it was perpendicular to hers. Taking a moment, he moved his plate and silverware, too, before leaning into her warmth and murmuring, "I was speaking of our children, Mary." Running his knuckles down the length of her arm, he listened to the cadence of her breathing alerting him to her full awareness. "We will have at least five, I suspect, so that is a minimum of three bedchambers if we are to be comfortable. More, if you want each child to have his or her own."

"I…er…"

Mr. Jarvis returned at that moment, saving her from having to respond to his pointed allusion to the passionate marriage he intended for them. Their plates were set before them and Mr. Jarvis excused himself once more. Caleb cut his lamb while Mary did the same.

"Would you like to have a small garden of your own?" he asked. "One separate from the estate's?"

She chewed her food and washed it down with some wine before answering. "I do not know. It is not something I have even considered."

"You took excellent care of the roses at Clearview, so I thought you might have an interest there."

"I do love flowers," she admitted. "And herbs are very useful."

"Vegetables too," he said and popped another piece of meat in his mouth. It melted on his tongue, leaving behind a rich, smoky flavor infused with mint and cracked pepper.

"We can make a vegetable and herb garden just like the one you had in France." A smile of enthusiasm animated her face. "What shall we put in it?"

"Tomatoes are my personal favorite, but we should also have some cucumbers, runner beans, and all manner of root vegetables like carrots and beetroots." They were planning their domestic future together, and Caleb was enjoying every second of it. This was so much better than parents making all the important decisions for a bride and groom because this was after all *their* life, not their parents', and Caleb had every intention of making sure they lived it as they chose. On their own terms.

But that did not mean there weren't practical issues to consider.

"I would like to discuss the settlement with

you," he told her once they had finished their meal. Mr. Jarvis had been to remove their plates and refill their glasses, and they now awaited dessert. "When we attended the assembly, Mr. Townsend brought up your dowry."

Mary nodded. Her eyes had grown distant, and her expression was now guarded. "It consists of ten thousand pounds."

"That is no small sum."

She scoffed. "Mr. Townsend was more than eager to put it to good use on his farm." She lowered her gaze and proceeded to study the edge of the table. "How do you intend to spend it?"

Realization dawned and he reached for her hand, clasping it firmly between his own. "I have no need for your fortune," he blurted with every intention of making her see that all he wanted was her. "My intention is to grant you full control of your dowry, so you may use it as you please."

Raising her head with a jolt, green sage eyes stared back at him in wonder. "But as my husband, you will have every right to control it."

"Control is the last thing I want," Caleb said. "And you are an intelligent woman, Mary, so I know you will spend your money wisely."

"You are..." Her lower lip started to tremble, and he saw to his sudden dismay that tears had pooled against her lashes. They shimmered like dew drops caught in the early morning light, and they made him ache with an overpowering need to pull her into his arms and just hold her.

"Handsome and roguish?" he offered and waggled his eyebrows.

To his immense satisfaction she laughed. "That

too, but I was going to say the most wonderful man I have ever known."

"Because I am letting you keep what ought to be yours?" He hoped there was more to it than that.

She shook her head quickly. "Because you are kind and considerate. I have known it ever since you brought a branch into the Clearview parlor and whittled it into a fishing rod for Peter."

Caleb leaned back just as Mr. Jarvis returned with their profiteroles. Setting them on the table, he offered a sweet port which he poured into a fresh pair of glasses. "Is everything to your satisfaction?" he asked.

"Yes," Mary said and Caleb concurred.

"It has all been delicious so far," he told Mr. Jarvis. "Our compliments to the chef."

Pleased, Mr. Jarvis excused himself and vanished. Caleb stuck his fork into his profiterole and was just about to cut a bite off when he glanced at Mary and saw she'd beaten him to it. White cream decorated her lips, and as he watched, she licked it away with the tip of her tongue.

Heat flared, deep in his belly. No other woman had ever tempted him as thoroughly as she did. She took another bite of dessert, and his muscles flexed at the sight of her drawing the pastry from her spoon. His body started to thrum with the need to touch her. Instead, he took a bite of his own dessert, savoring the moist vanilla-flavored filling.

"I meant to add something before when I mentioned your consideration and kindness," Mary said as she set her dessert spoon aside on her now-empty plate. Pausing, she seemed to struggle a little with how to phrase her thoughts. Eventually, she met his gaze and told him simply, "You should know that I'm losing my heart to you all over again and that this is—"

Unable to resist any longer, he pressed his mouth to hers.

She tasted delicious with an undercurrent of tartness because of the port. Placing his hands on either side of her face, Caleb held her steady and deepened the kiss. She sighed in response and set her palm tentatively against his chest for added support. The pressure pushed at his beating heart, quickening it until it was racing like a wild stallion across the moors.

Curling one hand around the nape of her neck, he slid the other toward her back and pulled her more firmly against him. She was all soft, pliable curves against his much harder form. Placing a kiss at the edge of her mouth, he continued kissing his way along the side of her jaw. Eyes closed, he inhaled her aroma and brushed her tenderly with his lips. She smelled like jasmine on a warm summer breeze, reminding him of sun-kissed evenings in France where the small white flowers had clung to his garden wall in a fragrant burst of seduction.

Breathing her in, he nuzzled against her and surrendered to the intoxicating effect she wrought on his senses. Her fingers combed through his hair, directing him back to her mouth. He captured it once again, this time with increased urgency and to convey one message above all else: I want you. Right now. In my bed.

They were in a restaurant, for goodness sake, where any number of people could happen upon them at any moment. But Mary did not care. She couldn't explain what had come over her except to say that it wasn't a 'what' but a 'who.' *Caleb.* He was using his mouth in the most provocative way, and she, wanton that she apparently was when in his presence, was enjoying every thrilling moment.

The possessive way he held her with his strong arms cocooning her body completely, one large hand cradling her head while the other supported her back, suggested he meant to conquer her in the most agreeable way imaginable. Welcoming each advance, she adjusted her position and dropped one hand to his thigh. Without even thinking, she tested the hard, well-defined flesh by pressing down into him with her fingertips.

He responded with a rough growl and nipped at her lips with his own until she grew dizzy. "Resisting you is a true act of discipline, Mary." He leaned back a little, allowing her to see that his eyes were gleaming like polished glass lit by moonlight. "But I am determined to court you properly, which means I must resist you a while longer."

Disappointment found a strange companion in gratitude. Even so, she could not stop from asking, "Why?"

"You know the answer to that as well as I do, even if you do not feel like listening." He tucked a loose strand of hair behind her ear, scraping the lobe with his fingers in the process. A shiver went through her, tickling her insides and curling her toes. "Trust me in this," he implored her while withdrawing further. "We have to wait."

"Perhaps I ought to propose to you," she said. Now that she'd made up her mind about what she wanted, she was starting to lose her patience with the whole courtship process. She felt like running with full speed ahead, and he was asking her to walk.

"Please don't." Raising her hand to his lips he pressed a tender kiss against her knuckles. "It would ruin the entire plan."

Sighing, she allowed a faint smile while searching his eyes for the truth she knew could be found there. "Does there have to be one?"

"To secure your heart and regain your trust? Absolutely."

She saw the truth then, flickering like sunshine falling between forest foliage to dance upon a lake. Love, so pure and so simple, it lifted every unhappy moment she'd ever known and swept them away forever.

"Very well," she agreed, "we shall do it your way and follow the plan."

CHAPTER EIGHTEEN

"**H**E STILL HASN'T ASKED YOU?" Cassandra said two days later when Mary returned from another wonderful outing with Caleb. He'd taken her to see a special exhibit on Italian art and architecture at the British Museum and to Gunther's Tea Shop afterward for hot chocolate and strawberry tarts.

"Not yet," Mary said. She'd found her friends in the Clemenses' library with Peter and Penny. The children had to their delight been permitted to explore the impressive collection of books Mary's father had acquired over the years.

Occupying three armchairs while the children studied the shelves, Mary was telling her friends about an interesting reconstruction she'd seen of the Septimius Severus Arch when Cassandra had blurted her question.

"There was no opportunity," Mary explained. "His mother was there with us all the time and never more than a few feet away."

"So he brought a chaperone along with him," Emily remarked. "That's new."

She was right. After their visit to the miniature

museum and The Grotto, Mary had joined Caleb for a walk in the park the following day. Impulsively, he'd suddenly pulled her behind some trees and pressed up against her, whispering things in her ear that no innocent lady ought to hear. And then he'd kissed her again while allowing his hands to roam her body with greater insistence than ever before. He'd touched her most feminine parts, and she'd not only liked it but craved it while begging for more.

"I think it may be a necessary precaution," Mary told her friends.

Cassandra smirked. "I see. All the more reason for him to propose."

"Do you know why he is delaying?" Emily asked.

Mary considered. "He mentioned trying to regain my trust."

"Ah," Cassandra said with a nod as if all was now made clear.

Mary stared at her friend. "Ah?"

"He obviously wants to make a big thing of it," Cassandra explained. "A grand gesture to prove his devotion."

"I don't need a grand gesture," Mary said. What she chose not to mention was how nervous he was making her by acting as if he were mad for her and then failing to act on it. There must have been a dozen opportunities for him to propose by now and yet they remained unbetrothed.

It reminded her too much of her experience with Wrenwick, even if he had never taken her to museums or restaurants. But there had been an understanding. He'd said he would speak with her father.

"Does he know that?" Emily asked, scattering Mary's thoughts. What had they been discussing? Oh yes, grand gestures and how she didn't require any.

"I haven't told him, but he should know me well enough by now to discern as much."

"Men aren't always astute when it comes to such things," Cassandra said. "And since most women would enjoy a big declaration of love from the man they plan to marry, we must not blame Camberly for assuming you would too."

"It does make sense," Emily said.

Mary wasn't so sure, but Caleb had asked her to trust him, and as difficult as it was to do so after everything that had happened, she intended to at least try before suspecting him of leading her along on a path to nowhere.

Because his doing that made the least sense of all. He could have bedded her several times already and been done. Instead, he was making a deliberate effort to entertain her while holding back.

"You're probably right," Mary told her friends. She forced a smile. "No cause for concern."

"He's a good man," Cassandra reminded her. "You must not forget that."

The door opened, halting their conversation. Mary's mother stepped into the room and waved a card vigorously about. "We've been invited to dine at Camberly House tomorrow evening. Goodness, Mary. Can you believe it?" Her enthusiasm poured from every pore. "We are to be admitted into one of the finest homes in London.

Oh, we must consider what to wear." She shifted her gaze to Cassandra and Emily. "You are to come as well. It is all so exciting."

"Would it be terribly wrong to liken your mother to a bee who buzzes in with a flutter and leaves before we've had time to adjust?" Emily asked as soon as the door closed behind Mrs. Clemens.

Mary laughed. "Not at all. I rather think the description suits her."

"She is right to be thrilled on your family's behalf though," Cassandra said. "The duke and his mother have officially accepted you and your parents as social equals." She pursed her lips and shrank back a little in her seat. "Not to sound high in the instep, but for a tradesman and his wife, that is something of a coup."

"I am aware," Mary said. "The gossips will accuse them of being social climbing imposters. They will say the same about me, just as they did five years ago."

"Or," Emily interjected, "they might say nothing. After all, your sister did marry a viscount, so one would think the *ton* has accustomed itself to your family joining its ranks by now."

Mary blinked. She'd been gone so long she forgot how everything had changed during her absence. Sarah had told her how difficult it had been the first weeks after her wedding, but then something else had happened to draw attention, and her marriage to Huntingham had become a footnote in that year's noteworthy events.

"I need something appropriate to wear." For even if she and Caleb intended to live a simple life in a cottage, he was still a duke which meant that if she wished to marry him, she'd best start playing the part of the duchess.

"You must have something here, from before you left," Emily suggested.

"There are a few gowns," Mary said. "Mama had most of them refashioned to fit my sisters, but I'm sure I can find something suitable for all of us to wear tomorrow evening."

"Don't forget," Cassandra said, "it is not just the dinner but also the Christmas ball at your sister's home on Saturday."

Mary gaped at her. She'd been so caught up in Caleb's courtship she'd completely forgotten to think of what to wear to the ball. Living in the country as she had, evening gowns had been the furthest thing from her mind. She had the one she always wore to fancier things like a dance at the assembly room, but she'd left that behind at Clearview.

"I cannot believe my mother neglected to mention that," Mary remarked while going over her gowns in her mind. It did not make for uplifting contemplation. "What are the two of you intending to wear?"

Mary knew neither one had informed their families of their visit to Town. Emily insisted hers would be away until Parliament resumed in the spring, while Cassandra claimed she had no desire to see the people who'd once turned their back on her.

"We were actually planning a last minute excursion to the modiste shop once Peter and Penelope have decided which books they would like to borrow."

"This one looks interesting," Peter said, producing a volume with marvelous pictures of ships, drawn in stunning detail. Penelope, by contrast, picked a book about gardening because she liked the colorful illustrations of flowers.

Carrying their finds with them, they were taken upstairs to join Eliot, Bridget, and Daphne who were playing in the same nursery Mary had used when she was a child. It had since been turned into a private sitting room for her mother, but a few quick changes had made it appropriate for children once more.

"Shall we be off?" Cassandra asked when they'd ensured that the children would all be well looked after by one of the maids during their absence.

"Yes," Emily said. "I have always loved shopping but was never permitted to choose the fabrics I wanted. This will be such a treat!"

Sympathizing, Mary followed her friend down the stairs. Although she'd been chased away from Society after her brief romance with Wrenwick, she'd had a happy life until then. The same could not be said about Emily, whose parents had been incredibly strict and demanding. Since her mother had been of the opinion that men fancied plump figures, she had fed her daughter continuously. Unfortunately, Mrs. Howard had also believed that orange and yellow would make her daughter stand out and had refused to let her wear anything else. The combined result of overeating and wearing unflattering gowns had been disastrous. So it was understandable why she was now eager to decide what she would wear to the Christmas ball.

"This is perfect for you, Mary," Cassandra said when they stood in the shop and had spent a few minutes looking at muslins and silks. She had pulled out a shimmering emerald green satin and was holding it up to Mary's face. "It really brings out your eyes."

"You don't think the color too bright?" Mary asked, allowing her fingers to slide across the slippery fabric.

"Not at all. You are a grown woman, remember? No one can fault you for dressing the part," Cassandra assured her. Moving on to a red color, she asked her friends, "Is this too risqué."

"Maybe," Emily hedged, "although you are the scandalous mother of a girl born out of wedlock, so I am sure no one would be surprised to see you wear it. And it is a pretty color."

"It really is," Mary agreed. "It compliments your complexion immensely."

"Then red it is," Cassandra said with a wicked gleam in her eyes. "I would hate to disappoint the gossips."

"Oh, you mustn't do that," Emily said with a wide smile. She'd selected a turquoise blue silk for herself which went well with her dark brown hair. "Not when I have every intention of making them gape."

Mary believed her friend would succeed very well in that regard. She'd lost so much weight since arriving at Clearview it would be difficult for people to recognize her. And with Emily's new shapely figure dressed in the right kind of gown, Mary could not wait to see the shocked looks on the faces of all the men who'd lost their chance with her.

"I don't think I can continue with this," Caleb told Griffin while the pair enjoyed a brandy in his study. Their mother would be down soon, and then the guests would arrive.

"With what?" Griffin asked. He was lazily sipping his drink in front of the fire while watching Caleb with relaxed interest.

"This courtship. It is likely to make me lose my mind."

"Mama and I have noticed an increased tenseness about you these past few days. You are easily annoyed." Griffin set his glass aside while Caleb drained the last of his drink. "You know the cause, I assume?"

Of course he did. He poured himself another measure of brandy and raked his fingers through his hair, disturbing the neatly combed locks. "The lovely Miss Clemens," he murmured. Hell, his blood stirred just thinking about her. She would be here soon, and then another round of torture would begin as he did his best to behave while she, temptress that she was, lured him with her deep green gaze.

"You need to bed her, Caleb. You're like a pair of lusty cats, circling each other, unsure of who should pounce first." He glanced at Caleb. "With her age and situation taken into consideration, I would think it possible for you to get a head start on your wedding night – release a bit of the tension."

Caleb shook his head. "She's a respectable woman, Griffin. I will not risk ruining that just because I can't keep my needs in check."

"No one has to know," Griffin murmured. "I could make arrangements for you if you like. Under my name."

Caleb stared at his brother, tempted beyond belief to accept his offer. But reason pushed the idea aside. "I would know. And besides, it is not just about the risk of being found out, it is also a matter of gaining her trust and proving to her that my affection is real – that it is not based on sexual desire alone."

"Thus the courtship."

"Precisely." Caleb inhaled deeply and drank his brandy. "I also wanted the chance to show her that things don't have to change between us just because I'm a duke. I want her to fall in love with me without being influenced by lovemaking." Or kisses. Which was why he'd ensured they were no longer left alone.

Griffin barked with laughter. "Are you so adept that you fear she'll lose her heart to you after a night of passion?" He turned instantly serious. "Miss Clemens strikes me as a sensible woman, Caleb. I think it would take more than that to win her heart."

"Precisely. But it is not unheard of for someone to fall into lust with a person, and I worry she's not experienced enough to know the difference." It had, in fact, become something of a concern for him after noticing how eager she was for his touch. The little whimpering sounds she'd made when he'd kissed her in the park had almost resulted in a very indelicate situation.

"You know," Griffin drawled. "I feel for you, Caleb. How agonizing it must be to have a beautiful woman eager for you to make love to her."

"It is rather," Caleb muttered.

The door opened that second, and their mother walked into the room. She still wore black, as she would continue to do until a year had passed since her husband's and son's deaths. "So, what are you discussing?" she asked.

Griffin stood and went to the sideboard, deliberately avoiding her gaze. "Sherry?" he asked.

"Yes, please." She looked at Caleb and instantly chuckled. "Oh, I see. One of *those* conversations was it? If it pertained to Miss Clemens, I think—"

"How was your day, Mama?" Caleb asked, cutting her off before she managed to make him blush.

The duchess started. "Rather pleasant, I suppose."

Griffin handed her the drink he'd prepared for her. "I spent the afternoon at Gentleman Jackson's," he said, directing the conversation further away from Caleb's carnal desires and his constant longing for Mary. "Met a few people I hadn't expected to see, like Gregory Hemstead. Remember him? Apparently he's the Earl of Tyrone now."

Caleb sent his brother a grateful nod and joined the conversation with what little he remembered about Griffin's friend. Their mother followed every word and added the knowledge she had about Gregory's family, his father's death a few years ago, and his current attempts at getting his sister settled.

"Your guests have arrived," Murdoch announced a few minutes later when he entered the room. "Mr. and Mrs. Clemens; their daughter, Miss Mary Clemens; and her friends, Lady Cassandra and Miss Howard." He waited until the group had entered the parlor before hurrying out to answer a knock at the front door.

Griffin, who'd risen upon their guests' arrival, clasped his hands behind his back and smiled. "What a pleasure it is to see you again, Miss Howard." His gaze lingered ever so briefly on the pretty brunette before sliding toward her friends. "Lady Cassansdra Moor, and my brother's favorite, Miss Clemens."

Caleb cleared his throat and tightened his muscles. Apparently, his brother had managed to accomplish what their mother had been prevented from doing, for there was a very distinct bit of warmth creeping into his cheeks. Ignoring it, he stepped forward to greet the small group. Unlike his brother, he began with Mary's parents, whose eyes searched the room with uncanny interest.

Next, he welcomed Lady Cassandra and Miss Howard, and finally Mary. He reached for her hand and raised it to his lips for a brief yet very deliberate kiss. When he straightened, he found her cheeks pink and her eyes slightly glazed. Satisfaction stirred in his belly, prompting him to lean closer to her. "I cannot stop thinking of you," he whispered. "Thank God you're finally here."

"Indeed, Your Grace." She allowed him to lead her further into the room and toward her friends who had both received a glass of sherry, courtesy of Griffin. Mary accepted one as well, and Caleb watched while she set her mouth to the edge of the glass and carefully sipped the fragrant wine.

He flexed his fingers and caught Griffin's gaze, frowning in response to the knowing look in his brother's eyes. The parlor door opened again, and Murdoch returned to announce the Aldridges' arrival. For a second, Caleb wondered if he might have erred by inviting the earl and his wife, Vivien, since he'd not discussed it with Lady Cassandra and wasn't sure if she'd even contacted her brother upon returning to London.

But when she rushed forward and flung her arms around her brother, who laughed with startled surprise while his wife looked on in amusement, Caleb knew he'd done the right thing.

It was a happy reunion, Caleb was pleased to acknowledge, the light in Lady Cassandra's eyes bright and vibrant as she proceeded to quiz Aldridge about his new daughter and his reasons for being in London this time of year when she'd thought he would be away in the country.

"Inviting Aldridge to join us was a lovely surprise," Mary said as they walked in to dinner. "Cassandra is thoroughly pleased."

"I am glad for I feared I might have overstepped by interfering." They reached the table, and Caleb helped her into her chair, which was placed directly next to his own. The meal commenced with a light fish soup followed by roast veal and vegetables, orange slices, and gravy. Conversation ensued, flowing easily around the table as topics ranging from Society news to more private family matters were discussed with friendly ease.

They were just commencing dessert when a loud succession of thumps sounded from the direction of the foyer. "Wait!" Murdoch's voice was more strained than usual and sounded thoroughly startled. "Allow me...I will just...They have guests!"

"No matter," another much louder and firmer voice said.

And then the dining room door swung open, and a man who looked much like Caleb and Griffin walked in. His hair was longer than theirs and swept back in a queue, his brow weightier, and his jaw somehow squarer. His dress coat was cut from midnight blue wool and trimmed with gold braiding on the collar, cuffs, and hem. The buttons were gold too, gleaming like newly minted guineas. White breeches hugged his legs, but rather than the stockings and shoes Caleb would have expected, he wore boots polished to a gleaming shine.

"Devlin!" Their mother was the first to speak. She pushed back from the table and attempted to rise, but her gown caught on one of the chair legs and held her in place.

Rising swiftly, Caleb helped her away from the table so she could go and greet her son, whose eyes swept the length of the table with marked curiosity. "My apologies for disturbing your meal. I believed my mother might be anxious to see me."

"And so I am." The duchess embraced him and pressed her cheek to his chest while Devlin's arms closed around her.

"It is good to see you too," Devlin said. He held her a few seconds more before letting her go. Stepping further into the room, he looked at

Caleb and Griffin in turn. "I set sail for England as soon as the news of Papa and George reached me, but I was off the coast of India, so it took time to get here." Crossing to where Caleb stood, he met his gaze steadily. "It is good to see you again, brother." He turned to Griffin and quirked his lips. "You too, you scoundrel."

Clasping Devlin's hand, Caleb held it firmly while the time wedged between them gradually vanished. "It is good to see you as well," he said. "There is much for us to discuss. But first, allow me to introduce you to some friends of ours."

Devlin bowed to all the women in turn and went to shake Mr. Clemens's hand.

"Would you like some supper to be brought in for you?" the duchess asked.

"No, thank you," Devlin said. "I believe I'll remove myself to a bedchamber. I'll ask Murdoch to have a tray sent up."

"Are you certain?" the duchess asked. She looked very disappointed.

"Yes," he assured her. "I have just stepped off my ship after a month-long voyage. A bath is in order before I sit down to dine, and some rest would not be bad either. I shall see you in the morning."

"I'll walk you out," Caleb said and excused himself before following Devlin into the hallway. "I gather from your attire that you are the captain of your own ship now?"

Devlin nodded. "Worked my way up the ranks these past ten years." He paused by the stairs. "It is strange to think of you as a duke. Never expected it, if you know what I mean."

Caleb nodded. "It doesn't really suit me, which

is why I'm planning a different sort of life for myself."

"Oh?"

"I prefer manual labor, and I think I've found a woman who'll accept that about me – a woman who has no interest in a traditional duke and who won't be disappointed by the simple life I am hoping to lead."

Devlin's eyebrows rose. "Was she in there?" He jutted his chin in the direction of the dining room.

"Miss Clemens is her name," Caleb said. "She's the blonde woman sitting opposite Mama."

A low whistle suggested Devlin's approval. "You'll have to tell me more about her tomorrow."

"And you will have to tell me what you've been up to since I last saw you. I'm sure you've had all manner of adventure. But in the meantime, I think I'll request a bath for you." Caleb made a show of scrunching his nose. "In spite of your fine attire, you reek of seaweed and fish."

Devlin laughed and started up the stairs. "There's no better smell," he told Caleb over his shoulder, "but I'll bow to your sensibilities since I am a guest beneath your roof."

CHAPTER NINETEEN

B Y THE TIME SATURDAY EVENING arrived and it was time to leave for Huntingham House where Sarah now lived, Mary had decided to stop hoping for a speedy engagement because it clearly wasn't going to happen. She wasn't sure what Caleb was waiting for, but apparently he had all the time in the world to make her his wife and build them a cottage. He was not in a hurry, that much was clear.

Also, there was his brother Devlin's return which had, as was to be expected, preoccupied much of his time in the days that followed the dinner he'd hosted at Camberly House. When she had seen him, it had been brief and had invariably ended with him rushing off.

"Do you think Camberly's brothers might be in attendance this evening?" Cassandra casually asked as they rode toward Huntingham House.

Squeezed between her friends on the bench opposite her parents, Mary hoped for a speedy arrival. The voluminous gowns they were wearing weren't helping their comfort.

"I imagine Lord Griffin will be," Mary said. "I

do hope you are right," Emily murmured, so quietly Mary was sure no one else could hear.

"And the captain?" Cassandra pressed with suspicious curiosity.

"I really cannot say," Mary told her. "Considering his recent arrival, it might be unlikely."

"And as long as the duke himself is present, what does it really matter?" Mr. Crawford asked.

"I don't suppose it does," Cassandra said.

Nothing more was said on the subject though it did make Mary wonder if her friends might have developed an interest in Caleb's brothers. Both were handsome, but more importantly, if her friends formed attachments to them and married, they would become her sisters instead of just friends, which truly would be wonderful.

The carriage drew to a halt, and a footman dressed in red and black livery opened the door. Mary's parents climbed out first, followed by Cassandra, Mary, and Emily. They started up the steps while other carriages rolled up behind them. Doors could be heard opening and closing. Excited voices filled the air, mingling with the music spilling from inside Huntingham House.

Entering the foyer, the women removed their cloaks while Mary's father took off his hat. Everything was handed over to footmen who whisked it all away to an upstairs room.

"This way please," said a man dressed in similar livery to the footmen but with extra gold embellishments. He gestured toward a wide doorway at the end of a hallway.

Mary's sister and husband stood just inside it, prepared to greet their guests as they entered the ballroom where pine garlands tied with red ribbons encouraged a Christmastime atmosphere.

"Your home is stunning," Mary told Sarah and Huntingham.

"Thank you," Sarah said, "but I dare say yours will be grander once you and Camberly marry." Lowering her voice, she leaned in and whispered, "Has he asked you yet?"

"No. Not yet," Mary confessed.

"Oh, but he will," Sarah assured her. "According to the daily updates I receive from Mama, it is practically settled."

Mary wasn't sure what surprised her more, the details of Caleb's courtship being aired in correspondence or the notion that anything was settled until he officially asked her to be his wife.

"Lilly is just over there," Sarah added before Mary could comment. "I will join you as soon as I finish with the receiving line."

Mary followed her parents further into the room.

"Do you see Camberly anywhere?" Cassandra asked.

Mary raised her chin in an effort to get a better look. "I don't see him or his brothers, so they must not be here yet." She continued toward Lilly with whom her parents were already speaking.

"Tonight's ball is not as busy as the ones hosted in the spring, but the turnout is still quite impressive," Lilly told Mary when they had finished greeting each other. Excusing themselves, Mr. and Mrs. Clemens moved away to speak with some friends of theirs. "Sarah started the tradition of a Christmas dance the year after marrying

Huntingham," Lilly added. "You know how fond she has always been of this particular holiday, and hosting a ball gives her a chance to celebrate with friends."

"So then I take it she never leaves Town during the winter as so many others tend to do?" Mary was actually quite surprised by how many people there were.

"She and Huntingham usually go away with the children in January, but look at the guests still arriving. I swear there are more this year than last."

"Perhaps they have heard of the ball's success and want to experience it for themselves," Cassandra suggested.

"It does seem that way," Lilly agreed. She stopped a passing footman and looked at Mary and her friends. "How about some champagne?"

Emily, Cassandra, and Mary took a glass each and were preparing to taste it when two handsome gentlemen approached. "Mrs. Gilford. Your husband tells us your sister has returned." The comment was made by the younger-looking man, whose hair was a similar shade to Mary's. He looked at her and her friends with polite curiosity.

"Indeed, Mr. Foster and Mr. Bale. Allow me to introduce my sister, Miss Mary Clemens, and her friends Lady Cassandra Moor and Miss Emily Howard."

"Delighted to make your acquaintances," Mr. Foster, with the blonde hair, said.

"Perhaps you would care to dance," the darker Mr. Bale inquired. He looked at Lilly. "You must forgive us for not inviting you, but we'd rather avoid provoking your husband."

Lilly smiled. "No need for apology, sir. I understand completely."

Mary and her friends produced their dance cards, and the gentlemen scribbled their names.

"A lot must have changed during your absence," Mr. Foster told Mary while Mr. Bale made conversation with Emily and Cassandra. Mr. Gilford, who'd arrived in the meantime, had begged a private word with his wife which, judging from the look in his eye, Mary interpreted as being code for something else entirely.

"A few new shops have appeared on Bond Street and some have disappeared." She gave Mr. Foster her full attention and tried not to think of Caleb and when he might be arriving. "There are also gaslights now, and I have noticed that the Mayfair Chronicle has changed its format."

"Times are changing, Miss Clemens. Before you know it a gentleman shall be able to address a lady without introduction."

Recognizing the innocent flirtation, Mary smiled and gave him a friendly nudge. "Let's not hold our breath, Mr. Foster. Some things will never be different." Chief among them Society's need for rules.

"Perhaps you are right, Miss Clemens. We shall just have to wait and see." He glanced toward the dance floor. "I believe that's our set starting. Shall we proceed?"

Taking his arm, Mary allowed Mr. Foster to lead her onto the dance floor. It wasn't until she stepped forward in time to the music and turned about that her gaze found Caleb's, dark and grave and fixed upon her as if his marching over, picking her up, and carrying her off was a viable option.

It wasn't of course, but the blood in her veins sizzled nonetheless.

Caleb had wanted to arrive before Mary, not after. He'd wanted to welcome her at the door, to offer her a glass of champagne and secure the first dance. This evening was supposed to be perfect. But Devlin, who'd initially claimed to have no interest in a pointless ball as he'd called it, had changed his mind at the very last second and forced everyone to wait the extra half hour it took him to get ready.

Because of him, Caleb's well-thought-out plan for the evening had gone to hell. Mary was now dancing with someone else. Perhaps her dance card had even been filled.

An unpleasant feeling stretched its way through him. "This is your fault," he grumbled.

Devlin, who stood to his right while Griffin stood to his left, took a sip from his recently acquired champagne. "You are too besotted for your own good if Miss Clemens's dancing with other gentlemen bothers you so."

"He does have a point," Griffin said. "And you have no claim to her either until you ask for her hand, which I still think you've been surprisingly sluggish about, considering her popularity."

"You know my reasons," Caleb clipped, but he was starting to wonder if his brothers might have a point.

"Popular, you say?" Devlin murmured. "I suppose I can see why she would be. That hair of hers is absolutely—"

"Not another word." Caleb clenched his jaw and flexed his fingers. *She's mine. No one else's. Don't you dare notice her hair.* Christ, he might be going insane. "Sorry. It is just...difficult seeing her with someone else." She was smiling at the blighter now and grinning in response to something he'd said.

"She received an offer of marriage from a gentleman farmer," Griffin told Devlin. "The man was an ass, so she turned him down, but there was someone else you mentioned, Caleb. A Mr. Porridge or Parridge or—"

"Partridge," Caleb gritted.

Griffin rocked back on his heels. "That's right." He grabbed a couple of champagne glasses and handed one to Caleb. "It is you she's been going to museums and restaurants with though. Must be a reason for that, I suppose."

Griffin was right. As far as he'd been able to tell, he was the only man Mary had shown a deeper interest in. Hell, she'd kissed *him*, not Townsend or Partridge or whomever this too-handsome dance partner of hers might be. She'd shared her dream of an orphanage with Caleb and encouraged him to design a cottage for them to live in. *He* was the man she wanted. He saw that as soon as he pushed his envy aside.

"Let's go and greet Aldridge," he said. "No sense in standing here staring. Not to mention, I intend for both of you to invite Miss Howard and Lady Cassandra to dance."

"I have no intention of dancing with anyone," Devlin said.

"One dance, that is all I ask," Caleb told him sternly. "Miss Howard and Lady Cassandra are both quite lovely. They were extremely hospitable toward me and are good friends of Miss Clemens's. Ensuring they have an enjoyable evening matters."

"Christ, Caleb, I haven't danced in ten years," Devlin complained as they closed in on Aldridge, who was keeping company with his wife, Vivien; Mary's sister, Baroness Huntingham; and her husband, the baron.

"Neither did I until a few weeks ago at an assembly hall," Caleb told him. "You'll figure it out the moment you set foot on the dance floor."

Muttering under his breath, Devlin went to secure the one dance Caleb insisted upon. Griffin excused himself to go do the same, and Caleb joined Aldridge's party. They were discussing infants, however, which was one of those subjects he didn't know much about. So he left them during an appropriate break in the conversation and made his way back to the periphery of the dance floor, remaining there until the dance ended, and Mr. Whoeverhewas escorted Mary off to one side.

Caleb moved toward them, reaching them just in time to catch the last of what Mr. Toohandsomeforhisowngood, was saying. "—call on you tomorrow."

"I fear Miss Clemens will be otherwise engaged from this moment onward," Caleb cut in. His chest was tight, his heart compressed. He glared at Mr. Sinfulintentions until he took a step back.

That's it.

Now be off with you.

"Your Grace," Mary said. Her voice was hard and surprisingly cold. He glanced at her and saw she was glowering. "Mr. Foster has kindly been keeping me company and apparently enjoyed it so much he wishes to do so again, for which I cannot fault him."

She was putting him in his place and reminding him of his manners. Caleb took a deep breath. He did not want Mr. Foster, as he was apparently named, calling on her tomorrow. By then, he intended for her to be completely unavailable, perhaps even married if a special license could be procured at such short notice.

Still, behaving like a jealous lunatic would get him nowhere. "My apologies," he somehow managed to say. "I merely saw the look of hesitation in Miss Clemens's eyes and misinterpreted it as disinterest." Damn, what a cutthroat lie that was. "I'm Camberly." He stuck out his hand, and Mr. Foster shook it with the wariness of a man who believed the act might cause him bodily damage. "Delighted to make your acquaintance."

"Likewise," Mr. Foster said. He drew back his hand and glanced about. "I was hoping to speak with Miss Clemens at greater length, but I see a friend of mine looking for me, so you must excuse me." *Perceptive fellow.* "Thank you for the dance, Miss Clemens. I enjoyed it immensely." Mr. Foster added a hasty parting nod to Caleb and walked away.

"What is the matter with you?" Mary hissed.

"You were uncharacteristically rude to Mr. Foster, who actually happens to be an amicable gentleman."

"All gentlemen are amicable until they get what they want."

She crossed her arms and glared at him. "Ah, well that would explain why you are suddenly so different from the man I knew at Clearview. He was polite. You are playing the high-handed duke, just as your father liked to do." Sparks were practically flying off her incensed person. "I don't know what you were hoping to accomplish with me, but whatever this is," she waved a hand between them, "is insufferable."

Caleb blinked and suddenly realized she was walking away. Hell and damnation. To say this evening was turning into a disaster would now be an understatement. Her words sounded final, and his body shook in response.

"Wait!"

The word was out before he could think, instinctively shouted to keep her from leaving. She turned slowly. Silence ensued and Caleb realized his outburst had caused everyone else to pay attention too.

His lungs strained with the effort to draw a calming breath. Panic had been steadily growing inside him since the moment Devlin had delayed his arrival. It had bloomed and flourished at a steady pace, spiking thorns when he'd seen her dance with another.

Heart thudding as if it wished to escape his chest, Caleb swallowed and took a step forward. "Forgive me, Mary." His voice was louder than he'd intended, but now that he'd started this unplanned spectacle, he might as well see it through. "My only intention was to win your heart." The music, which had still been playing, faded, accentuating the ruffle of gowns and accompanying whispers.

Caleb ignored it all, his focus entirely on the woman before him. Her eyes were wary, but at least she was listening.

"But caution turned me into an ass," he continued. A few muffled snickers followed. "I wanted to be certain that you wanted me for me and that you would be able to look past the title to the man behind it."

"I already did so at Clearview," she said.

"Yes, but how could you know that was really me when everything else was a lie? I had to be sure that you realized the man you got to know there is who I really am. And I had to be certain that you made your choice with a clear mind and not because of the earth-shattering kisses we shared." Gasps vibrated around him, but Caleb ignored those as well. "I wanted to have no doubt in my mind that you love me as much as I have come to love you, as if the world might end if you choose to refuse me." He stepped closer still, so close he could see her eyes shimmer like water catching the moonlight. He reached for her hand and dropped to one knee, deaf to everything save her sharpened breathing. "You are everything to me, Mary: my joy, my heart, my future. I cannot imagine my life without you in it, so please, tell me you will marry me, Mary. Make me the happiest and the most fortunate man there is and be my wife, my duchess, my love."

The gathering tears in her eyes spilled over and streaked down her cheeks. Her bottom lip started to tremble, and the sound she emitted was a broken sob of emotion.

Caleb tightened his hold on her hand and smiled up into her beautiful face. She nodded ever so slightly, and then with increasing vigor. Caleb's heart began to unfurl as the panic receded. He rose and she was suddenly in his arms.

"Yes." The word spilled from her lips and trembled like raindrops clinging to leaves in the wake of a downpour.

Her mouth met his, and a burst of applause accompanied cheers as he hugged her close. Kissing her deeply, he conveyed all the love he felt in his heart and the resounding wish he had to spend every moment of every day with her by his side.

Mary's wedding day dawned to the bright, pristine splendor of new fallen snow. The clouds that had hovered over London since the previous evening had disappeared, receding like waves abandoning shore at low tide.

Rising, Mary went to the window and looked out at the garden below. A robin there hopping from branch to brand with something in its beak made her smile.

As for the day itself...

Her smile widened as she turned to look at the gown she would wear. Freshly pressed, it hung over her wardrobe door, a creamy silk creation trimmed with pale green ribbon to match the accompanying velvet pelisse.

A knock at the door sounded, and Mary granted entry to her mother, who swept into the room with a brilliant smile. "I have brought Fiona to help you prepare," she said as her maid trailed in behind her. "This is all so exciting, and oh, have you seen the weather? It is absolutely glorious."

Her mother and Caleb's had both tried to push for a traditional wedding with three weeks of banns, but Caleb had insisted on marrying sooner, as long as Mary agreed. They'd eventually compromised by waiting a week and a half, allowing the time both mothers had requested to make preparations and order a gown. It had also allowed Mary and Caleb to enjoy a brief engagement. He'd shown her his architectural drawings and the articles praising his skills in France. Although she'd known he was a talented man, she'd been quite impressed and even more determined to support his desire to continue with this profession if he wished.

"Do you know," her mother added, "this will be the first society wedding this year." She clapped her hands and practically bounced up and down.

Fiona helped Mary with her toilette. She completed the task by adding a dab of lilac water to each of her wrists.

"Don't forget the bosom," Mrs. Clemens said. "We want it smelling sweet and—"

"Mama!" Mary clasped her hands over her chemise-covered breasts. "Perhaps you should go and see if Cassandra and Emily need anything."

"But—"

"I will be down when I am ready."

"But, Mary." Her mother's voice was firm. "We have not discussed your wedding night yet." Fiona helped Mary on with her stays, which only distracted her a little. "As your mother it is my duty to explain the mechanics."

"You are making it sound like an engineering project, Mama."

"And in many ways it is," Mrs. Clemens said with a lighter tone. "I can show you the diagram your grandmother gave to me when—"

"Mama," Mary said, stepping into her wedding gown. "I know you mean well, but I think I am well apprised of the subject already. Cassandra explained everything." She left out the part about when she had done so.

Mrs. Clemens expelled a deep breath, and it occurred to Mary that she was relieved to hear this. "Well then," she said while Mary pushed her arms through the sleeves of her gown, "I shall wait downstairs for you, then. Just don't be too long. We must depart within the hour."

Mary's heart fluttered. In another two hours she would be Caleb's wife. The thought caused her to smile while Fiona did up the buttons at the back of her gown. The maid dressed Mary's hair next, styling it in a simple chignon held in place by diamond-tipped pins.

When her parents had gifted them to her, she'd wanted to refuse, but they'd insisted she look the part of a high society bride. Seeing how much it meant to them, Mary had relented. She was now forced to admit that they did flatter her overall appearance.

Standing in front of the cheval glass, Mary thanked Fiona for her assistance, smoothed the skirt of her gown one last time, and exited her bedchamber. With a deep inhale, she turned onto the landing and started down the stairs.

Her mother gasped and her father stared.

"You look incredible," Emily said.

"Like a princess," Cassandra agreed.

"So you think he'll approve?" Mary asked.

"If he doesn't, there's something wrong with him, and I'll protest the nuptials myself when the vicar allows it," her father said.

Mary grinned. "There will be no need for that, Papa. I am confident Camberly will be pleased with Fiona's work."

She was right. Caleb's eyes brightened with deep appreciation when she entered the church half an hour later and made her progress up the aisle. Griffin, who stood at his side, whispered something in his ear, but there was no indication that Caleb heard him. His entire focus was on her.

"A diamond of the first water," he murmured when she reached him. "So stunning I can scarcely believe I get to take you home with me."

Modesty clutched at her heart while the hint of desire clinging to his words swept through her like surging floodwater. "How fitting that I am to marry you then," she whispered right back, "for there is no handsomer gentleman about, and none I would rather go home with."

His chest expanded and when she accepted his arm, she could feel the tightly honed muscles contracting beneath her touch. Starting forward, he kissed her cheek as they went to face the vicar. "I love you, Mary. With all my heart."

"And I love you, my unconventional duke."

CHAPTER TWENTY

IT TOOK AN ETERNITY FOR the ceremony to end, or at least that was how Caleb perceived it. Ever since Mary walked into the church, he'd been entranced, and when she'd said there was no one else she'd rather go home with, his mind had filled with every wonderful detail of what that entailed. But it wasn't just the wedding itself that stopped him from getting on with the part of married life he looked most forward to at the moment. There was also the wedding breakfast hosted by Mary's parents. To announce they would not be attending would be badly done after all the effort, but when the cake still hadn't been cut three hours later, he felt it his right to suggest they did so quickly.

"I think there was a deliberate effort to see how long I would last before simply hauling you off like a marauding pirate," he said to Mary when they were finally alone in his carriage. They were on their way to the Clarendon Hotel where they would spend the next couple of nights before heading off to Montvale Manor, the estate where they planned to open their orphanage and build their cottage.

She laughed. "Yes. This entire day was designed to test our patience, but I am glad of it, you know. At least for the sake of our friends and families, who were all so excited to be in attendance."

"I am sure we'll also look back on it with fondness one day and savor the memory. After we have had a chance to consummate our union in at least a dozen different ways." His arm wound around her waist when she gasped and blushed in response to his words. He was being wicked, he knew, but she was his wife now which meant he could say such things without any apology. But there was one thing he ought to consider... "Are you nervous?"

"A little, I must admit." She dropped her gaze and studied her lap where her hand was holding his. "It would be strange if I weren't, I should think."

"It will be a new experience for you," he told her slowly while stroking the back of her hand in tiny movements intended to soothe. "But I have every intention of making it as pleasurable as possible for you. After all, I don't want to frighten you off after one attempt, or we'll never manage the dozen different ways of making love I just mentioned or produce the five children you have asked me to give you."

Her cheeks turned from pink to scarlet, but she laughed, then smiled with girlish bashfulness in the most endearing way imaginable. "I think you may secretly be a rake," she teased.

"Only when I am with you and we are alone," he assured her.

They arrived at the hotel moments later. A footman lowered the steps and opened the door so Caleb could help his wife down, while another took care of their bags. Caleb was pleased to see that the room in which they would stay had been prepared exactly as he had demanded. Roses stood in full bouquets on every available surface, along with recently lighted candles, a bowl of fruit, a tray of sweetmeats, and a bottle of perfectly chilled champagne.

The footman who'd helped with their bags pointed out the bell pull in one corner and departed. Exhaling slowly, Caleb locked the door and turned to face his wife who was busy untying the green satin ribbon of her bonnet.

"Here," he said, removing his gloves and tossing them aside. "Allow me."

His fingers grasped the slippery fabric and pulled on it gently. The plump bow loosened and sagged as the ribbons slid smoothly apart. Reaching up, Caleb lifted the bonnet from Mary's head and set it aside before turning to her once more. Desperate to touch her, he raised his hand to her cheek and scraped her soft skin with his thumb.

"Enchanting," he murmured and pressed his lips to hers in a brief caress that allowed him to maintain control. "Would you like something to eat or drink?" he asked with every intention of easing her into the intimacies that would follow. This had to be perfect, so he refused to rush her.

"Honestly, I feel as though I've been eating and drinking all day," she said, surprising him with her answer. "I don't want anything else right now. Except you, Caleb. I have wanted you since the moment I saw you, so please—"

He kissed her again, with greater insistence and far less restraint. If this was what she wanted, then by God, so did he, with a desperation unlike any he'd ever known before. Hell, he was beyond ready. So he wound his arms tightly around her and crushed her to him. The sweetness of rich vanilla and chocolate still lingered on her tongue from their cake.

She moaned and he took advantage, deepening the kiss. Her hands were on his back, around his neck, in his hair, exploring and caressing with frenzied movements that made him mad for more.

"We have to slow down," he heard himself say with a detached voice even as his fingers unfastened the long row of buttons along her spine.

"Not now," she gasped while arching in to him, offering herself as her gown fell away. "I need you too much."

He needed her too, her throaty murmurs and eager touch, her mouth kissing its way along his jaw. Helping him, she shoved her gown down in a flurry of movement so he could undo her stays. His cravat seemed to loosen; he felt her fingertips on his skin and then the long length of fine cotton slipping away. Her mouth sought his neck, and a ripping sound cut through the air. Christ, he'd torn her chemise. His hands clutched the translucent fabric, and for one split second he froze, unsure if this elemental behavior was the proper way to attend to his innocent wife.

But then her hands crept under his jacket to work on the fastenings of his waistcoat, and all such concern fled. After all, she seemed to be enjoying herself with equal fervor, so who was he to deny her? He drew the remnants of her chemise away from her body and spread his palm wide at the small of her back. Returning to her mouth, he kissed her again, this time with explicit imitation of what he craved. Matching his efforts, she pushed back his jacket and waistcoat in one swift movement and pulled his shirt out of his trousers.

When her hand snuck beneath to explore his skin, Caleb almost forgot himself completely. A fierce need to possess her hardened his body to the brink of pure agony, forcing him to step back for a moment and catch his breath.

"Christ, Mary." He looked at her for the first time since taking her clothes off and shuddered with pleasure. "You are my every dream come true." He gazed at her with abandon, deliberately lingering on the parts of her body he knew she'd soon beg him to touch.

"So are you," she said, her voice a little rougher than usual.

He smiled with wicked intent and took off his shoes. "I'm pleased to hear that." Straightening, he unfastened the placket of his trousers and slid the garment down over his hips as if he had all the time in the world to undress. His hose followed while Mary watched with unfeigned interest. His smalls came off last, revealing the part that seemed to have her enthralled, for she stared at it as if it possessed the power to make her the happiest woman in the world.

Satisfied with her wide-eyed response, Caleb closed the distance between them and pulled her back into his arms. It was different now. Better. Skin against skin. Her soft rounded curves against his firm contours.

"Yes," she breathed as she arched against him, connecting with him in a way that had him lifting her onto the bad and settling her gently against the pillows. He climbed beside her, kissing and stroking until she writhed and clasped the sheets and begged for something she could not name.

Meeting her need, he gave her the pleasure she sought, savoring her body's response to each touch. She was beautiful in every way, and Caleb told her this as he settled between her thighs and joined his body with hers, distracting her from the small discomfort with loving kisses and tender caresses.

Straining against his own instinct, he waited for her to adjust to his presence, the effort forcing a hiss of relief between his clenched teeth when she finally said she was ready to move.

Showing her what to do, he taught her the timeless rhythm that would carry them both up toward the stars. His eyes met hers in the heat of their passion, and his heart beat fast against his chest.

"You're mine," he said as he reached for the peak, climbing toward it with her by his side. They arrived there together in a burst of pleasure that reminded them both of the love they shared.

Cradled in Caleb's embrace, Mary stared at the ornately painted ceiling and savored the languor. Who knew a man and a woman could come together in such perfect harmony? A smile tugged at her lips. It made her wonder why anyone would be reluctant to marry when the benefit was so undeniably good.

"I am so glad I married you," she said. Turning her head, she pressed a kiss to his chest while smoothing her hand across his stomach. A muscle flexed beneath her fingers, and his arm tightened around her shoulders.

"Me too." He rolled onto his side and pulled his arm from under her so he could shift his weight onto his forearm and elbow. A large hand smoothed over her hip. It trailed down her thigh and to the back of her knee. "We can now do this as much as we like. Without the risk of scandal." He raised her leg and hooked it over his waist before pulling her in for more deliberate contact.

"Which is just as well since there are eleven more positions to go."

His eyes darkened. "I see you are keeping count."

"How can I not when there is so much to look forward to?" She pulled his mouth to hers and allowed him to sweep her away on the second of a dozen earth-shattering experiences that night and toward countless others to come.

EPILOGUE

MARY SAT ON THE BENCH in front of her cottage and inhaled deeply. Her sight wasn't what it had once been, and unfortunately, the spectacles Caleb had bought her a few years ago no longer seemed to help. But she could still enjoy the vibrant scents from her garden: the climbing roses flanking the front door, peonies bordering the path toward the gate, a hint of honeysuckle carried on the breeze along with lavender, mint, and thyme.

She heard the cottage door open and close, then the slow, careful tread of Caleb's feet as he came toward her. "I brought your shawl," he said and placed the soft cashmere around her shoulders. Lowering himself to the bench beside her, he took her hand in his and leaned in to kiss her wrinkled cheek.

"Can you believe it has been forty years since you knocked on the door at Clearview?" She settled her head against his shoulder and drew in his scent. It was still the same after all this time. Bergamot, sandalwood, and pine.

"Feels like yesterday, my darling." He smoothed his callused thumb across her hand.

"Like the blink of an eye," she whispered as the afternoon sun cast a ray of warmth upon her face.

"We did well though, I think. My life could not have been better, Mary."

"Nor mine, Caleb."

They'd had their five children just as they'd planned. Amanda, Richard, William, Susan and Wendy. And they had provided Caleb and Mary with eighteen lovely grandchildren.

Amanda, who'd taken over the running of the orphanage ten years earlier with her husband, loved the children she cared for as much as Mary loved Peter, Eliot, Penelope, Daphne and Beatrice.

Richard, who had no more desire to inherit a title than his father once did, had been encouraged by Caleb and Mary to find a balance between responsibility toward the title and whatever made him happy. So he'd studied medicine and opened a clinic, which was how he'd met his wife, who'd applied to be his assistant.

William had followed in his father's footsteps and to everyone's surprise, so had Wendy. Of course there were many who disapproved when a woman showed up to fix their roof, but her attention to detail and her masonry capabilities rarely went unnoticed and usually resulted in earning respect.

And then there was Susan, the only one of their children who'd married a nobleman, because as she'd once said, someone had to take after Mary.

As for Peter and Eliot, they'd opened a fish shop together and visited Caleb and Mary weekly with supplies. Penelope, who'd married a French sea captain, was often away traveling the world, while

Daphne became a governess and ended up marrying her employer, whose brother fell in love with Beatrice the moment he met her. Beatrice and her husband, Geoffrey, spent most of their time in London where he was a rather successful barrister.

"You are still as beautiful as the day I met you," Caleb said. He squeezed Mary's hand for added assurance.

"And you still make my knees go weak."

He chuckled lightly. "You always did like a man with capable hands."

She snorted. "I liked you. There is a difference."

"Quite so," he murmured with contentment. He no longer climbed onto roofs, but he hadn't stopped making other less strenuous repairs, both at the cottage and at the manor.

"I love you," she said as daylight dimmed to a softer evening hue.

"As I love you," he told her sincerely. Shifting, he tipped up her chin and pressed a tender kiss to her lips.

Who knew how many years they had left, but at least they had lived the lives of their choosing. Heedless of gossip and censure, they'd both been thoroughly happy, not only because they'd had each other, but because they knew there was more to life than amassing a fortune. There was sitting on a bench in the evening sun with the person they loved, and nothing in the world would ever make more sense to either than that.

ACKNOWLEDGMENTS

I would like to thank the Killion Group for their incredible help with the editing and formatting of this book. My thanks also go to Chris Cocozza for providing the stunning artwork. And to my friends and family, thank you for your constant support. I would be lost without you!

ABOUT THE AUTHOR

Born in Denmark, Sophie has spent her youth traveling with her parents to wonderful places around the world. She's lived in five different countries, on three different continents, has studied design in Paris and New York, and has a bachelor's degree from Parson's School of design. But most impressive of all – she's been married to the same man three times, in three different countries and in three different dresses.

While living in Africa, Sophie turned to her lifelong passion – writing. When she's not busy, dreaming up her next romance novel, Sophie enjoys spending time with her family, swimming, cooking, gardening, watching romantic comedies and, of course, reading. She currently lives on the East Coast.

You can contact her through her website at *www.sophiebarnes.com*

And Please consider leaving a review for this book.

Every review is greatly appreciated!